Forever Family in a Small Town

Melinda Curtis

D1739103

Franny Beth Books

Copyright

Chapter One

When Kathy Harris was a teenager, she'd dreamed of being a fashion designer, a professional basketball player and an airline pilot—anything to get out of her small hometown.

So much for dreams.

She shoveled another pile of manure into the wheelbarrow.

She was back in Harmony Valley, the smallest of small towns in the remotest of remote corners of Sonoma County, California.

She made a clucking noise with her tongue and gave Sugar Lips a gentle shove in her chestnut haunches. The former racehorse turned brood mare nickered softly and ambled to the other corner of the paddock. Kathy scooped her manure-filled shovel again, beginning to feel warm in her jacket despite the brisk breeze that had the last reddish-gold leaves of fall swirling around her feet.

"You must be Kathy." An unfamiliar, masculine voice.

Kathy looked toward the veterinary clinic where she worked, trying to identify the source of the voice, but the afternoon sun was in her eyes and all she could see was a silhouette of a man—tall, broad-shouldered, a baseball cap on his head.

"I'm Dylan." His voice was smooth as molasses, sweet as honey to a fly. It drew her closer. "I'm here to help with the horses. Dr. Jamero said you'd be back here."

Dr. Gage Jamero was Kathy's boss. He ran a small-animal clinic for the locals and a horse obstetrics unit at the rear of the property. Kathy hadn't seen Gage in action yet, but she imagined him to be an equestrian midwife, high-strung mares being his specialty, although his tales of Sugar Lips hadn't lived up to her reputation. The mare may have been a hellcat during her first pregnancy, but most of the time she was more like a tired kitten.

Gage had hired Kathy despite her just getting out of rehab. She kept the animals, big and small, fed and watered, and cleaned the clinic, inside and out. Out being her preference. That was where the horses were and where she felt she could breathe.

The fifteen-hundred-pound kitten nudged Kathy forward, causing her to drop the shovel. "Knock it off, Sugar."

Dylan, whose face she still couldn't make out with the sun in her eyes, laughed. It was a friendly laugh. An I-don't-know-you're-an-alcoholic laugh. Whoever Dylan was, Kathy dreaded telling him the truth, as she did with any- one. And she was blunt about the truth nowadays. She'd hid her addiction too long. She hid very little lately, only her most painful of secrets.

Kathy hefted the shovel and walked toward Dylan. The mare trailed behind her. They both stopped in the shadow of a sixty-foot-tall eucalyptus tree near the paddock gate. Its silver-green leaves rustled like tissue paper in a gift box on Christmas morning.

Dylan's appearance didn't match his voice or his laugh. His silhouette was deceptive, too. Who'd seen those cowboy boots coming? Broad shoulders, yeah, but he was linebacker-solid beneath that navy vest jacket and those blue flannel sleeves. His laugh might have been friendly, but his scrutiny of her was not. A fringe of soft brown hair beneath his red ball cap contrasted with sharp gray eyes, a strong nose that looked as if it'd been broken at least once and a firm slash of a mouth.

Someone had already told him who she was—*what* she was.

Kathy swallowed back the sudden bitterness in her throat, tugged off a work glove and extended her hand. "Hi, I'm Kathy, and I'm an alcoholic. Four months sober."

She expected his mouth to turn down. She expected his eyes to drift away from hers. Instead, he smiled. The smile transformed his face from intimidating to accepting to handsome. "Good to meet you, Kathy." His grip was warm and firm, almost too firm.

She retrieved her hand, resisting the urge to shake the bones back into place. "Are you delivering another mare to us? Gage didn't tell me we were expecting a new guest." The veterinary clinic made most of its money from their high-end racehorse breeding clientele.

Dylan hooked his arms over the metal paddock rail, still smiling at her. "No, I didn't bring any horses. I came to assess the ones here and work with them a few days a week. If things work out."

Suddenly, she remembered Gage mentioning him. "Oh, shoot. You're the miracle worker."

"Horse trainer," he corrected, gaze dropping to his scuffed and stained cowboy boots.

Sugar rubbed her long, elegant chin back and forth over Kathy's shoulder. Kathy resisted the urge to check for slobber streaks on her pink jacket. "Go on, have your fun, Sugar. Your spa days are over. This man's going to save Chance and put you through your paces."

Sugar blew a raspberry at Dylan.

"Never mind her." Kathy patted Sugar's cheek. "She's a tease."

Dylan blew a raspberry of his own, smiling not at Kathy but at the horse. The mare sniffed the brisk air, then stretched her head toward Dylan, bumping Kathy out of the way.

"Careful," Kathy warned Dylan as Sugar gummed the navy flannel sleeve of his shirt. "Sugar prides herself on being unpredictable." She'd already chewed the finger off one of Kathy's gloves. Good thing Kathy's finger hadn't been in it at the time. "Her papers say she's a Thoroughbred, but I think she's part mule."

"It's okay. She and I understand each other." Dylan scratched beneath the crown of Sugar's halter. "Dr. Jamero is busy with a patient. He said you could show me around."

"Of course. You'll be wanting to see Chance." Kathy put the shovel into the wheelbarrow and pushed it outside the paddock, thanking Dylan for opening and closing the gate. "We've got two pregnant mares stabled, plus Sugar and her colt, Chance. We have room for eight horses back here, pregnant or otherwise, and expect to be booked up come spring."

Dylan walked with a slight limp, but with a gracefulness that reminded her of Sugar when she trotted around the paddock. Another contradiction in a man so big and muscular.

The stables were up a gentle incline from the clinic. The walk was quiet except for their cowboy boots on pavement. Dylan stopped in the stable's entry and breathed in deeply, as if reveling in the smells of home. It smelled of hay and manure. Kathy was growing used to those aromas, but she still spritzed herself with perfume every morning.

"I thought Dr. Jamero only took in mares ready to deliver," he said in that honeyed voice.

"Chance is Sugar's." When Dylan didn't say anything, Kathy's suspicion sensor went off—like a finger tap-tap-tapping her temple. She cast a quick glance his way. "Didn't Gage tell you about Chance?"

Dylan quirked one eyebrow, as if to say, *What? You doubt me?* "I'm here to evaluate. I like to see for myself."

Two equine heads poked over stall doors.

"This is Trixie." Kathy pointed to the tall gray mare who nickered a welcome. "And that's Isabo." A tired-looking bay who seemed too long in the tooth to be having babies. The mare stretched her nose toward Kathy.

"They like you." Dylan sounded surprised.

His reaction pressed her pause button. Was it surprising because she was an alcoholic? A woman? Or...

There was a loud thud in one of the rear stalls.

"That would be Chance." Kathy hurried to the stall. "I hear you, baby." She slipped inside, moving slowly, surveying the stitches and bandages on the chestnut colt's lower neck and chest. He pranced nervously through the straw, eyeing Kathy as if he'd never seen her before. The stitches beneath his round cheek were oozing and needed attention. "What's up with you, baby? Are you lonely?"

Despite the long gashes, Chance was beautiful. He was only a few months old, his head barely reached Kathy's, and yet he held himself with the proud dignity of a long line of racing Thoroughbreds.

Chance froze, staring at the stall door. A moment later, he began kicking, striking out at anything within range—imaginary foes, walls, Kathy.

A large hand gripped Kathy's shoulder and yanked her out of the stall.

"Let me go. I can calm him down." Kathy struggled to free herself as Dylan dragged her back several feet.

In the paddock outside, Sugar whinnied.

"You're not going back in there." Dylan's voice became clipped and seemed to harden until his words hit her like gravel spitting from beneath a semi's tires. "That. Colt's. A. Killer."

Kathy twisted free of his hold. "That colt is why you're here." She was shaking. Shaking with anger and fear and adrenaline. She was shaking and it wasn't because she needed a drink. She and Chance had a lot in common—social handicaps. He by his appearance and outbursts. She by her reputation as a drinker and parental failure.

She tugged Dylan out of Chance's line of sight. Sugar trotted back and forth along the paddock fence.

"I heard about this colt, but not from Gage." Dylan raised his voice to be heard above the huffing and hoof strikes Chance was making. "Mountain-lion attack."

Kathy nodded. "Since the drought, they've been coming closer to civilization looking for food. Chance and Sugar were in a remote pasture at Far Turn Farms. They moved them here a few weeks ago." She pitched her voice high, as if she was talking to a baby, taking a few steps back until Chance could see her again. "He's just a scared lamb."

At the sight of her and the sound of her voice, Chance's outburst seemed to lose some steam, just like when her son, Truman, would throw a tantrum as a toddler. A bit of gentle reassurance and everything would be okay.

"He's not a lamb. He's nearly as large as you are." Dylan's face was set in hard, disapproving planes, a cookie cutter of most people's reaction to her past mistakes. She didn't want to admit how disappointing it was to see that familiar expression on his face, especially since she'd just met the man. "I've seen that look before. Don't go in there. He's a lost cause."

The stall latch was cold beneath her fingers as she prepared to rejoin Chance. "That's what some people say about me."

The colt was a deal-breaker.

"Your sister's not what I expected based on what you told me," Dylan O'Brien said an hour later to his prospective employer, Flynn Harris. "Kathy's grounded and honest. You don't need me." The words knotted Dylan's insides. Flynn's paycheck would help get him back on track. He'd met recovering alcoholics in much worse shape than Kathy. Sure, she might benefit from a session or two with him. But the colt...

"I disagree." The resemblance between Kathy and her brother was strong. The same straight nose. The same fair skin and keen blue eyes. Although where Kathy's hair was a fiery red, Flynn's was a burnished red-brown. "My sister's good at hiding stress. She has a lot on her plate right now—a new job, reestablishing a relationship with her son, plans to take college courses online—and she wants to move into a place of her own." Flynn's voice was wound tighter than a fresh spool of kite string. "Dr. O'Brien..."

"I'm not a psychiatrist." Best get that out in the open straightaway. "And I'm not a licensed therapist, either. I'm just a guy who's good with horses and people." *Or he used to be.* "Besides, my clients usually come to me." To Redemption Ranch, where a combination of straight talk and working with horses helped give them confidence to face life's challenges without alcohol.

Am I really talking Flynn out of a paycheck?

With hefty child-support payments, a large mortgage and a near-empty bank account, Dylan couldn't afford to turn down work. But the colt made it necessary.

Those eyes.

They doubled the knots in his already knotted insides.

Dylan and Flynn stood on a winding road on Parish Hill. Harmony Valley stretched beneath them with grid-like streets, slanted roofs and tall mature evergreens, interspersed with trees that were losing their leaves for the winter and neat rows of grapevines. The early-November breeze had more force and nip to it up on this hill.

Dylan shoved his hands into his vest-jacket pockets.

An older model white truck with a dented fender pulled up behind Flynn's.

"That's Gage," Flynn said.

Dr. Gage Jamero got out. He was taller than Dylan, but just as direct. "Well, what did you think of the colt?"

"The colt neither of you told me about?" A sour taste bubbled from Dylan's knotted stomach into his throat. Flynn had mentioned using the horses at the clinic only as a way to disguise Dylan's visits with Kathy. "I didn't like the look of him."

Gage took Dylan's measure. His lip curled. "Bandaged and stitched up, you'd look like Frankenstein, too. But he's not a monster."

"He lashes out like one." Even as he said the words, Dylan realized that wasn't fair. The colt could've easily hurt Kathy. It hadn't. He'd waited outside the stall until she'd come out safely the second time. But all he could think of was how the feral look in the colt's eyes was similar to that of one hulking, raging black stallion. He shifted his stance, taking most of the weight off his injured right leg. "First impression only," he allowed.

"Sorry, Gage, but first and foremost, Dylan's here for Kathy." Flynn's fortune might be new, made in the dot-com world, but his work boots showed serious wear and he seemed to sincerely care about his sister. "She's been in and out of rehab twice since June. My wife, Becca, and I have been helping, but it's not enough." Flynn's words slowed. "Kathy used to laugh. I never hear her laugh anymore. She needs a sober companion, and we hear you're doing great things with alcoholics at your ranch."

"Sober companions are usually with their client 24/7." Dylan bit back a definitive turndown. He always had trouble walking away from those in need—horse or human. He'd admired Kathy's honesty and her guts. But the colt... "I can only get up for an hour or two each day. I won't be much help if I'm not with Kathy when she's hit with her biggest stress-inducers. And as for the colt..."

"You're afraid," Gage said in a soothing voice, as if being careful not to strike a nerve. "Let me assure you that he's not like—"

"If you've heard about Phantom—" and what horse person in Sonoma County hadn't, since he'd almost killed a vet technician under Dylan's watch? "—you know I have reason to be cautious." *And afraid.* Dylan's hands fisted in his jacket pockets. "I still believe that most horses are redeemable. It's just that I..." *Don't go there.* "That you..." *Don't go there either.* "I was only briefed on Kathy, not Chance."

"You were blindsided." The vet rubbed a hand through the tuft of black hair already askew on his forehead. "I apologize for that, as should Flynn." Dr. Jamero gave Kathy's brother a significant look, which elicited a quickly muttered apology. "But the fact remains that I'm excited that you're here, no matter what the pretense that brought you to Harmony Valley. I strongly believe that Chance is still young enough to save."

The unspoken part of that speech being Phantom wasn't.

Dylan's fisted hands pressed deeper into his pockets.

Both men scrutinized him, asking without verbalizing: *Are you the one? The one who can make things right?*

Dylan had once believed his own hype—that he was a miracle worker when it came to horses.

Oh, Dylan's father was having a good laugh in whatever part of the afterlife he'd been sent to.

Flynn sighed, gazing back over the valley. "So, Kathy showed no warning signs? Not even a hint of weakness that she's in danger of relapsing?"

Dylan didn't immediately respond. A red-tailed hawk flew overhead, its mournful cry an echo of Kathy's shocking sentiment—some people considered her a lost cause. Why?

Flynn pounced on Dylan's hesitation. "You did sense something." He went into older-brother protective mode. His chest thrust out and his voice railed at the clouds. "Don't toy with me. Name your terms."

"You can't keep her from backsliding." Dylan was far too experienced with trying exactly that to pretend different. "Only Kathy can do that."

Flynn took a step toward him, eyes narrowing. "But you can make sure she gets the support she needs."

"Under what pretext? A horse trainer? She doesn't own any of the horses at the clinic. There's no legitimate reason for me to spend time with her." Dylan resettled his baseball cap and his standards. "I don't deceive my clients. That's why they trust me. I give it to them straight up."

"You can't tell Kathy who you are. She hates it when I meddle in her personal life." Flynn ran his fingers through his short hair. "That's why having Gage hire you to work with the colt is a perfect alibi for you to interact with her."

"For the record," Gage said, "I'd prefer Kathy knew what you do, Dylan, and why you're here."

"For the record, I appreciate that."

Flynn fisted his key fob. "I'll double your normal fee in exchange for your silence." His offer was so unexpected, so overwhelming, so blatantly ensnaring, that it sucked the air from the mountain.

Take the money.

Dylan's mouth hung open, his principles leaking like drool from a Saint Bernard's jowls. Flynn's offer would go a long way toward making his current situation better. And yet, Kathy's clear blue eyes came to mind, along with her gut-wrenching honesty. A shaft of guilt, barbed and sharp, lodged itself in his chest. She'd hate Dylan for being a man who could be bought.

Take the money.

"A simple search online and she'll know the truth," Dylan said, mouth dry.

"I'm betting she won't look you up." Flynn's eyes reflected the guilt Dylan was feeling. "She asked about a sober companion, but then talked herself out of it. Addiction runs in our family. Our mom." His voice didn't trail off; it shut off. And it took Flynn a moment to get it working again. "That's why I don't want Kathy to do this on her own."

The sour taste was back in Dylan's mouth, along with the crimping knots in his gut. Children of alcoholics had a higher probability of having emotional problems. Add in an addiction of their own, and their risk of relapsing was higher than average.

Poor Kathy.

"Do we have a deal, O'Brien?" Flynn extended his hand. "If not for me, then for her young son. If Kathy relapses, Truman may never open up to her again."

The money. Kathy's low opinion of herself. The risks she took with the colt. An image of his own young son's face, hopeful and trusting, came to mind.

"Please help me help her," Flynn urged. "In secret. At least through Thanksgiving." A handful of weeks away.

Take the money.

Dylan knew he'd regret this. The lies. The deception. The unanswered questions.

He accepted the assignment anyway with a handshake and a promise he wasn't sure he could keep.

Chapter Two

"I'm home." Kathy entered the front door, shedding her pink, slobber-streaked jacket.

No one greeted her. The house smelled of savory pot roast steeped in bittersweet memories.

Her grandfather had passed away four months ago, but memorabilia from his military career still hung on the living room wall—medals, pictures, certificates of service—along with black-and-white wedding photos and baby pictures. Add in the 1970s furniture and color scheme, and everything looked the same as when he'd been alive, except there was no dust, no newspaper piles, no faint smell of hair tonic. Flynn said he'd update the place once he was done grieving. Until then, the house looked the same as it had twenty years ago.

It'd been almost two decades since their mother left them here, since Kathy had sat in Grandpa Ed's lap while he braided her hair (a skill he'd learned in the military for making horses presentable). He'd told her she was going to be just like all the other girls in Harmony Valley. But she was different.

Back then, she'd been surprised every time she opened the pantry and discovered it was full. She'd been wary of strangers, even smiling ones in town. And her heart stuttered every time she saw a woman with red hair or heard a female with a smoker's throaty laugh.

She'd stayed close to home in those early years, under the watchful eye of her grandfather. Eventually, when her mother didn't come back and Kathy reached her teens, she felt confident enough to push the small-town limits that had kept her safe for so long.

Kathy missed Grandpa Ed's booming voice as he chastised her teenage self for wearing skirts that were too short. She missed his barked rules and pieces of advice, however unwanted they'd been at the time. She could still feel his strong arms around her when she had come home after only a few months at college, alone, an emotional wreck and pregnant. He'd talked her into keeping Truman. It'd been the best decision of her life.

Until the text messages started...

The screen door banged behind her. Abby, her son's small, mostly black Australian shepherd, trotted over to greet Kathy.

"Hi, Mama," Truman said flatly, standing in the foyer. He was eight, but he might just as well have been eighteen for all his sullenness. Everything about him was dirt smudged and disheveled—from his unzipped blue jacket, slightly askew on his thin shoulders, to his sneakers, laces dangling, the color of spent earthworms. "I thought you were Uncle Flynn."

Her chest felt cavernous, as if somewhere along her alcohol-blazed trail the heart she'd given to her little boy had been lost. "I brought you a chocolate bar."

When he was younger and she'd disappointed him, she'd bring him gifts and sweets, and he'd fling his arms around her as if she had never failed him. Kathy pulled it from her jacket pocket, distressed to find the dark chocolate soft beneath her fingers.

Without looking at her, Truman turned up his nose. "I don't eat treats before dinner. Aunt Becca says I can only have one treat a day, and I already had cookies."

Kathy remembered baking cookies with Truman last Christmas in this kitchen. He'd stood on a stool, mixing the dough, chattering a mile a minute. When they slid the cookies in the oven, Truman had hugged her tight and then run to play checkers with Grandpa Ed. If only she'd known how fragile their bond was, she wouldn't ever have let him go. Except...then she'd never have gone to rehab and gotten sober.

"How about a hug?" Kathy dropped the candy onto the low wooden coffee table and extended her arms, knowing they'd remain empty, but still stubbornly hopeful. So very hopeful. "Your mom's had a long day."

"I hug you every night at bedtime, like I'm supposed to."

So young to be able to wound her so deeply. Kathy couldn't seem to draw a breath.

Abby sat quietly in front of Kathy, soft eyes patient for affection. She'd been Becca's dog until last summer, when Kathy went into rehab and Truman moved in here. Kathy reached in her pocket for a doggy treat. Presents worked great with animals. With her son? Not so much. Not anymore.

Truman walked past Kathy to the kitchen. "Where's Aunt Becca and Uncle Flynn?"

"I don't know," Kathy said, trying to sound cheerful. "I smell dinner, though. We should check to make sure it doesn't burn."

He shook his ginger-haired head. "Becca never burns anything." Another accusation. Another oxygen-robbed moment.

Unlike her sister-in-law, Kathy was a horrible cook. Granted, in the past two years she'd been operating the stove under the influence, but she was convinced you either had the cooking gene or you didn't. The more Becca's perfection contrasted against Kathy's flaws, the stronger the desire to get a place of her own. All she needed was rent money—and Truman by her side.

Becca hurried down the hall toward them, looking put-together-cute in yoga pants and a thin green sweater. For sure, she didn't smell of manure and disinfectant. "I didn't hear you two come in. I was on the phone checking on a client." She hugged Kathy and then kissed the top of Truman's head.

Kathy's ears filled with a rushing noise, much like the time she'd got caught by a submerged branch at the bend in the Harmony Valley River and nearly drowned. She turned away.

"Did you meet Felix's new litter of kittens, Tru?" Becca asked Truman.

Kathy couldn't resist turning back.

Truman beamed. He used to smile at Kathy like that. "I also saw Bea's baby goats. She calls them kids." He giggled.

"I'm going to wash up." Kathy fled down the hallway. She locked herself in the bathroom and stared at her reflection in the mirror. What an afternoon. A confrontation with a handsome stranger and then to be met with the same brick wall Truman had made around his heart. Not that she could blame him but...

She needed...something. She didn't want a drink. Alcohol didn't solve anything. But she wanted her son to look up to her and love her, like he used to. Like he did to Becca. She wanted them to be a family again, to have a bond with her son that no one could break. If only he would agree to spend time with her. Alone time. Together time. Precious time. He'd see she was the mother he'd once loved wholeheartedly.

The shower beckoned. She knew the family wouldn't hold dinner for her. She could eat alone. But that was the coward's way out. And her grandfather hadn't raised any cowards. He'd passed on words of wisdom to her and Flynn after their mother left them here for good—pep talks he'd most likely used on the military men who'd reported to him during his career.

She met her gaze in the mirror. "Don't let life push you around. You can win back Truman's love and trust."

She could.

The more often she said it, the better chance she had of believing it.

Tragedy did awful things to a man.

It drained Dylan of energy and hope.

His old man would have said Dylan had let Phantom best him. And then he'd have followed that up with a besting of his own.

Dylan shut away the bad memories. It was getting late workday-wise, being a little after five. But it was already dark.

He'd agreed to help both the colt, Chance, and Kathy. The latter under false pretenses, a fact that chipped away at the crack to his self-image that Phantom's accident had caused. It helped only a little that his fee was helping him climb out of the financial hole he was in. But unless he solved things with Phantom, it would only be a temporary leg up, not a permanent one.

Dylan drove down Redemption Ranch's thinly graveled, potholed driveway, illuminated only by his headlights. A small car turned in behind him.

He parked in front of his paint-peeling, two-story clapboard house. Motion-activated lights flipped on—one from the front porch, one over the separate garage and one near the corner of the double row of stables. They illuminated his crabgrass and scraggly shrubbery. Despite needing work, it was home and Dylan felt a measure of relief.

He got out of the truck and shut the door. Phantom let out a shrill whinny. No other horse in his stable sounded like that. A warning? Or a welcome? Uncertainty ate at him. He wasn't used to the feeling when it came to a horse.

Dylan leaned against the dented tailgate, pushing all his concerns—for the black stallion, Kathy and the wounded colt—to the side.

"Daddy!" His son, a brown-haired, stubby-legged five-year-old boy, tumbled out of the backseat as soon as his mother unbuckled him. Zach wrapped his wiry arms around Dylan's legs. "I want a pony ride."

Eileen stood at the expensive sedan, arms crossed, a look of concern on her face. His ex-wife was caring and beautiful—short wavy brown hair, whiskey-colored eyes and a button nose. She'd loved him once, the horse miracle worker whom everyone wanted to hire. But his drive had pushed her away. "You're just getting home, Dylan? Everything okay?"

"I had a meeting run over." He'd stayed too long in Harmony Valley, stopped at the bank to deposit Flynn's check, and then run into the feed store for a bag of oats. "New business." Much needed since he was behind on child support.

"You're lucky." Eileen closed the rear car door. "We're running late."

"I'll have him home on time." After a few brief hours of father-son bonding, traffic permitting. The highway between Redemption Ranch in Cloverdale and Eileen's home in Santa Rosa was often crowded and slow-moving, no matter the time of day.

"See you later." Eileen left, heading back to Santa Rosa, her second husband, and the so-called normal life she'd always dreamed of in suburbia.

"Dad." Zach squeezed Dylan's legs, a ray of sunshine in the world of gray. "I had early dinner. I'm ready to race." Horserace, he meant.

"Come on, sport. Let's saddle Peaches." Dylan took his son's small hand and led him toward the tack room, ignoring the end-of-the-day ache in his knee.

Barry, the former jockey turned caretaker, waved at them from his apartment window above the garage.

Zach leapfrogged forward. "Was Peaches a racehorse?"

If only Dylan had a dollar for each time Zach asked him this. "Peaches? She prefers to walk regally in the arena." Plod along happily was more like it.

An owl hooted in an oak tree. A white barn cat with a crooked tail followed them into the barn where Dylan collected the pony's tack. And then it was a long walk through the barn's breezeway to her stall. Horses stretched their graceful necks between stall bars, sniffing, nickering and stomping in greeting—Sam, a former jumper who balked at fences; Rickshaw, a half-blind bay; Marty, a headstrong trail horse; and so on down the line. Horses that were untrainable or unlovable—at least in their last owners' eyes, until they'd come here.

"Peaches is a good racehorse." Zach defended his faithful steed, running ahead as if he'd been born wearing cowboy boots. "I could race her."

Little Zach couldn't kick that pony into a trot if he wore spurs and shot off fireworks, but Dylan wasn't telling his son that.

Zach fumbled with the latch and then entered the pony's stall, leaving the door ajar. Peaches greeted him with a thorough inspection of pockets, looking for treats. Giggling, Zach pulled out some baby carrots from one pocket and held them in the flat of his hand for her to eat. "She knows I always bring food."

Dylan followed Zach into her stall. Peaches was an ancient palomino Shetland pony, formerly a mascot at Far Turn Farms.

Peaches ate carrots while Dylan quickly saddled her. When he was done, Dylan hoisted Zach into the saddle and handed his son the reins. He walked next to the pony toward the barn door nearest the arena.

"Where was Peaches when Phantom kicked you?" Zach glanced toward the farthest stall on the end. The last stall had red and white signs posted: *Danger! Stay Back!*

A shrill whinny pierced the air. The other horses drew back into their stalls.

Startled, Zach searched the gathering gloom as if expecting the black stallion to charge out of the shadows.

"Peaches was in her stall." The stallion's vocalization reminded Dylan of Chance and the courageous way Kathy had entered the colt's stall earlier. She had a confidence he used to have, a determination he envied.

"Phantom is mean," Zach said in a hushed voice.

"He's just a horse." A large brute of a horse with incredible speed and the bloodlines of Thoroughbred royalty in his veins. He was worth a lot as a breeder...if he could be safely handled. "You know, even if you try to be careful, accidents happen."

"He's mean," Zach repeated. His brown hair was crisply cut and gelled into place, just the way Eileen liked it.

Dylan ruffled his son's hair, eliciting a giggle.

Zach, with his ready smile and buoyant attitude, was the balm to Dylan's spirits. With his son in his life, Dylan could bear any burden and ride out any storm. Financial worries would be weathered. Physical setbacks overcome. Shattered dreams rebuilt. Maybe even his faith in a horse could be restored, given time.

It was full-on dark now. Dylan flipped the arena lights on. Then he opened the gate and set Zach and Peaches free.

Needing no cuing, the pony walked directly toward the fence and began her slow circuit. Small puffs of dirt rose from each footfall.

"Dad. Dad. Daddy." Zach twisted in the saddle. His grin was so bright it sparked a feeling of joy in Dylan's chest that chased away the day's concerns. "Say it, Daddy. Say it."

Dylan grinned. "Place your bets, ladies and gentlemen. The Cloverdale Derby is about to begin." Dylan latched the gate. "Peaches and her jockey, Zach O'Brien, are the odds-on favorite tonight. *And*—" he drew out the word as he

---

climbed atop the highest rung on the arena fence "—they're off. It's Peaches in the lead."

With a whoop, Zach leaned over the pony's golden neck and jiggled the reins as if they were galloping. "Come on, Peaches. You can do it."

The pony continued plodding along.

"Keep going, Dad."

Grinning, Dylan didn't need much prompting. He could go on like this forever. "They're heading into the first turn with Peaches ahead."

Later that night, as Dylan pulled into the driveway of Eileen's prestigious home in her prestigious neighborhood in Santa Rosa, Zach was fast asleep in his car seat in the rear of the truck.

Eileen's outdoor lighting cast a glow over the perfectly manicured yard, highlighting verdant shrubs and small tufts of autumn color.

Eileen and her husband, Bob, came outside to meet them. They wore matching red plaid flannel pajama pants, green T-shirts (his: Santa; hers: Mrs. Claus) and red suede slippers. Cute, but not exactly Dylan's thing. Not to mention, Thanksgiving was still weeks away—never mind Christmas.

"I was getting worried." Eileen's voice was taut with concern. So much for her ho-ho-ho. "You didn't answer my texts or my calls."

"Sorry. I left my phone at the barn. There was traffic." That last part was a little white lie. He'd taken Zach for ice cream. Dylan unbuckled his son from his seat and transferred him to Eileen. He dug out his wallet. "I brought you a check." His income wasn't what it had been before the accident, but it was fairly steady. Big paychecks loomed on the horizon—if he could help Kathy, if he could help the colt, if he could harvest Phantom's sperm. *If.* If he could rediscover the heart to work with severely untrainable horses, then he could make the dream of a steady income a reality. "This gets me caught up."

Bob took Zach from Eileen and tucked the little man to his shoulder as if he'd had years of practice. Something cold solidified in Dylan's stomach. And it wasn't rocky-road ice cream.

Eileen took the check Dylan held, her tone regretful. "You can't be late anymore. We rely on that money."

Dylan's gaze drifted to the fancy house, thought about Bob's job as an attorney.

"Not now, honey," Bob said steadily. "Let's get Zach to bed. He's got school tomorrow."

Dylan hadn't forgotten it was a school night, but... "It's only eight thirty."

"His bedtime is seven-thirty." Bob sighed, as if he knew better what Zach needed than Dylan did. He disappeared inside the house.

Eileen's mouth worked in that way it did when she was having trouble getting out words that needed to be said. "You need to pay on time, Dylan. Or things are going to change. Bob says... Well, you know how he is about the law."

Bob was a stickler for it. Dylan knew that much. But how much more could things change? Dylan only saw Zach Saturdays and Wednesday nights.

Still holding Zach, Bob opened the living room curtains, watching them. Zach murmured something. Bob murmured back, stroking Zach's little shoulders.

The cold fist in Dylan's gut expanded.

The other man met Dylan's gaze.

The cold fist sucker-punched Dylan from the inside out.

He knew how things could get worse.

They could take Zach from him. Not for Saturdays. Not for Wednesday nights.

Forever.

Chapter Three

"Do you know how hard it is to see the screen and type with you in my lap?" Kathy's arms bent as she tried to navigate the online university's website around Abby's sleek body.

They sat at a desk in her bedroom. Growing up, it had been Flynn's room—geek command central and off-limits to Kathy. The posters of Batman, World of Warcraft, and a young Steve Jobs may have come down, but it still felt like her brother's room. Navy plaid wallpaper and tired green shag contrasted against her teal leopard-print comforter and pink slippers.

When she'd gone into rehab, Grandpa Ed was still alive. Flynn had been staying in this room, and so Truman had been put across the hall in Kathy's childhood space. After Grandpa's death, Flynn and Becca had married and then moved into the master bedroom. And so, Kathy took this room—not wanting to upset Truman by asking him to switch.

The dog turned and licked Kathy's cheek, as if to say get on with it. While outside her window, birds sang a happy good morning. She was convinced there was one bird that had designated itself as her alarm clock. Regular as a rooster, that little guy. Tweet-tweet-tweet as the sun approached the horizon.

"I'm just not excited about a business degree," she whispered to Abby. Accounting, economics, business law. Ugh. But Flynn insisted that she needed a college diploma to rebuild her life, and he said she could do anything with a business degree. Lacking a clear idea of what she wanted to do, Kathy had bent to her brother's will. She'd get a business degree to prove to him she was serious about creating a solid future for Truman. If only she could make herself complete the college application form.

The dog faced the screen again, her black fur soft against Kathy's arms. She smelled of freshly dug dirt, green grass...and freedom.

More than happy to postpone signing up for college courses, Kathy gave the dog a kibble from a teacup on her desk, then scratched Abby behind her pointy ears. "You're just here for the food." She didn't much care why Abby kept her company. She enjoyed the affection, even if the conversation was one-sided.

Her bedroom door swung open. Truman's gaze swept the carpet and corners of the room. "Abby?"

Truman never came in here. He barely acknowledged Kathy's existence. She couldn't have moved if someone had shouted, *"Fire!"*

Her son finally noticed where his dog was. "Abby." Disappointment. Betrayal. Truman's cheeks flushed. He patted his jeans-clad thigh urgently. "Abby, come."

Neither Kathy nor Abby moved. In fact, the dog gazed back at Kathy, as if encouraging her to speak. And what would she say?

Abby heaved a doggy sigh and stared at the computer screen again. Or, more accurately, at the teacup below the computer screen.

"Tru." His name came out as deep and hoarse as the bullfrogs' songs down by the Harmony River. Kathy stared in the vicinity of her son, cleared her throat and tried again. "I like your T-shirt."

It was a green-and-purple tie-dyed shirt with a black running-horse weathervane screen-printed on his chest.

He gazed up and down the hall, either looking for support or making sure no one caught him talking to her. "The mayor gave this to me. It's Uncle Flynn's winery logo."

Of course, it was. Everyone in Harmony Valley was embracing the winery and its attempts to revitalize the town. But hello, people, should her son be wearing a shirt advertising alcohol?

It doesn't say Harmony Valley Vineyards, said the voice of reason.

It promotes underage drinking, said the fearful side of her, the one that had been riding shotgun on her shoulder since rehab.

"It's just a shirt," Kathy said defensively, bringing her internal argument into the open.

Truman gave her the my-mom-has-lost-it look. He lost his patience and raised his voice. "Abby. Come here. Now."

Abby jumped from Kathy's lap and trotted to Truman, circling him and nudging him inside the bedroom. Her herding instincts were to unite, not divide.

"I don't have time for games," Truman grumbled, making his escape. "It's time for lessons."

Kathy listened to their footsteps move into the kitchen, made immobile by the fact that that was the most successful interaction she'd had with Truman since she'd come home a few weeks ago.

Grandpa Ed used to say, "First the battle, then the war."

Kathy stood and did a battle victory dance.

"Smooth moves." Flynn stood in the doorway with that older-brother grin that little sisters hated. "A bit *'Put a Ring on It'* and a bit *'Harlem Shake.'* What are we celebrating?"

"Shh." Kathy yanked him inside and closed the door. "Truman talked to me." They high-fived.

"How're you feeling, Kathy?" His grin faded. His gaze took inventory.

"Stop. You aren't my sponsor." She widened her eyes and breathed on him. "I'm sober." No bloodshot eyes. No fire-starting breath.

"You'd tell me if you were tempted, right?" He asked her that every morning, but there was an urgency to his question today that hadn't been there in the weeks since she'd come home.

"Of course, I'd tell you if I was tempted." That was a lie. If Kathy was tempted, she wouldn't tell him. Not in a thousand years. Her brother would try to lock her up in rehab quicker than you could say, *"Reboot my computer,"* and she'd lose what little ground she'd gained with Truman.

"I was thinking of hiring someone to find Mom," Flynn said out of the blue.

There must have been a bomb blast, because Kathy couldn't feel her limbs and it was quiet. Deathly quiet. Not even the bird alarm clock made a sound.

"I made peace with my dad." Flynn's voice cut through the aftershock. "Maybe it's time we made peace with Mom. I could get her into rehab. Truman needs you to have a strong support system and..."

"Don't you dare bring her around me or Truman." Kathy's lips felt numb. The words she had to say formed too slowly until she was nearly robbed of what little power she had left. "I mean it, Flynn."

Flynn spoke in his brother-knows-best voice. "It's been nearly two years since I've heard from her. I just thought..."

"She doesn't deserve your compassion."

And that's all she felt comfortable telling him.

The trouble with selling your soul to the devil was that there was a debt to be repaid.

Or, in Dylan's case, several.

He had thirty days. Thirty days to deliver the semen orders he'd sold for Phantom. Thirty days until his next mortgage and child-support payments were due. Thirty days to make progress with Kathy and the injured colt.

Dylan leaned on the porch railing at Redemption Ranch, trying not to let the pressure get to him.

Wisps of mist clung to the brown grass in his pastures as the first rays of daylight crested the Sonoma Mountains. Steam rose from the cup of coffee cradled in his hands. In the distance, tall, sturdy eucalyptus trees created a natural border to his property. Whoever had planted those trees had wanted a visual marker, a boundary, that said, *This is mine.* If Dylan couldn't keep up

with the payments, he'd have to sell off a parcel of the land to a developer. The
trees would go. Cookie-cutter houses would fill the pasture. Noise would invade
his borders.

As a kid, he'd longed for peace. He'd longed for silence. He'd longed for a
place where his father's belligerence and words and fists couldn't touch or hurt
him. At his mother's church, they'd talked about forgiveness and redemption.
Those concepts were as unreachable back then as the stars. But today?

Does Phantom deserve redemption?

Put him down. His father's command, chilling and frozen in his memory.

"What's wrong, Dylan? Knee bothering you?" Barry came down the outdoor
steps from his garage apartment. With his shoulder-length, snowy hair and
diminutive height, the former jockey could pass himself off as one of Santa's
elves.

Dylan let his gaze drift back to the tree-lined horizon. "My knee's fine."
Aching in the brisk morning, but that was his new normal.

"Then let's work Phantom."

Dylan's grip on the coffee mug tightened. He gazed out over the pasture, but
he saw a different scene now, one from long ago. A boy wearing pajamas shut in
a stall with a crippled horse and a gun.

"We need to make a withdrawal." Barry gestured toward an outdoor paddock,
the one with the door to Phantom's stall. "We can't keep taking orders if there's
no product to sell. Lots of breeders are anxious for Phantom's genes."

Because they expected Dylan to destroy the champion. "Maybe tomorrow.
Or next week." Dylan set the coffee cup down. "Maggie Mae should be in heat
soon. We can't collect the goods from Phantom without a mare in her cycle."

"Excuses." Barry's hands swung Dylan's reasoning aside. He probably waved
off flies with less vigor. "It's been six months, son. It's time to get back in the
saddle."

Dylan flinched inside. "I've lost my touch."

"The only thing you've lost is your nerve." Barry propped a foot on the front
porch step, gazing up at Dylan. "If I had quit riding races after one fall, I would

have never won the Kentucky Derby. I had a gift for the ride. I'm too old now to compete, but if my body was able, I'd still be out there every week."

"You'd have to give up beer and chili-cheese fries." Dylan tried to make light of it.

"After twenty years of racing, I earned every extra pound." Barry patted his still-svelte gut. He was only fifteen pounds over his racing weight, normal by most people's standards. "But don't go changing the subject. You've let that horse get into your head."

Dylan didn't argue that point. Everyone thought he'd lost his nerve after the accident, that he was afraid of Phantom and others like him. Because he didn't hire out as a horse behavior specialist anymore. At first, he'd used the excuse that he was healing. But now...

Barry tsked. "If you think he's so dangerous, why did you buy him?"

"Because they were going to put him down." Because Dylan felt partly to blame for Phantom's attack, seeing as how he'd held the lead rope. "Because they were practically giving him away and his stud fees can save us." On its own, his idea to run a ranch where unwanted horses could be rehabilitated and re-covering alcoholics could build confidence wasn't a profit-making proposition. "We barely make ends meet but Phantom can support everything." All the good work Dylan wanted to do.

"There you go again. Money," Barry grumbled, pausing to face Dylan. "Money doesn't make you a good man. Or a good father."

"The bank and the family-court judge don't agree." Nor did Bob, Zach's stepfather. Dylan had to be a good provider, a better one than his own drunken, volatile father had been.

Barry made a noise that Dylan took for disapproval. The older man glanced back at Phantom's paddock. "When I served overseas, they sent me into places larger men couldn't access. I acted like a man and said I'd do it, but the truth was, I was scared. All you need to do is take a step forward."

"All right. All right." Message received. Dylan and the horse were both prob-ably anxious about things. "I'll pay Phantom a visit." And yet Dylan didn't move.

Barry headed for the stables. "I'm going to open up his paddock door and muck out his stall. The Dylan O'Brien who used to live here would take advantage of that time. And if that Dylan O'Brien still lives here, he needs to make an appearance."

A white cat wended its way between Dylan's legs, then moved slowly down the porch steps, pausing at the bottom to look back at him and flick her crooked tail.

Even Ghost knows it's time to do this.

Dylan left his coffee on a porch rail and made his way to the barn.

One by one, horses extended their heads as Dylan passed their stalls. He paused to greet Peaches, leaning in to look at the little palomino. She extended her nose to reach his hand, as if to say she had complete faith in Dylan. She'd been Phantom's stablemate through his racing career and his retirement to stud.

"He'd like to see you, I bet." Dylan put on her halter and led her out of the barn just as Barry tripped the lever that opened Phantom's stall to the paddock.

Phantom charged into the gray light of morning as if he was the last vestige of darkness racing toward the horizon. Or perhaps he just missed the starting gates of his youth. He skidded to a stop at the far end of the paddock, nearly sitting on his haunches, then began his patrol of the perimeter. He made a circuit, rearing in front of Dylan, ready to strike him as he'd done months ago. His eyes rolled, until the whites showed, and Dylan's gut twisted, but he stood his ground.

And so did Peaches. She barely batted an eye.

Phantom's front hooves landed in the dirt. He let out a shrill whinny, prancing in front of them. The stallion bared his teeth and made as if he was going to lunge, but he never extended his nose between the paddock rails. And his tail was raised proudly, not swishing with anger.

What a faker.

That's what Dylan would have thought before the accident. He almost smiled.

Peaches, bless her, snorted. She was accustomed to the stallion's theatrics. The pony knew Phantom used to have more bark than bite.

Maybe he still was a big faker. *Mostly.*

Maybe he was just a more dramatic faker. *Mostly.*

Dylan began to hum *Itsy Bitsy Spider,* noticing that the stallion's hooves needed trimming, along with the rest of him needing a good grooming.

Barry slid the gate to his stall closed, calling out from inside, "That horse needs a different tune. That spider song is getting old."

"I like it." Dylan led Peaches around the paddock.

Phantom followed, rearing, kicking and announcing to the world that he was one upset dude. One in a line of many.

Dylan blew out a breath.

A lifetime of living with horses, years of horsemanship training, and after one tremendous failure, Dylan had grown too cautious.

"You almost had me, Dad," he whispered to the mist. His father had excelled at breaking things—bottles, bones, boys. Some of the past had been wrapped up with the injury Phantom had given him. "You almost had me."

Phantom's hoof struck the metal rail.

Dylan flinched.

But other than that, he didn't let on he was rattled. He resumed humming his tune and gave Peaches a few pats to let Phantom know what he was missing.

Love.

"Far Turn Farms is only giving us a few more weeks with Chance." Gage's words echoed ominously in the near-empty clinic.

Behind the partition separating the animal cages from the hallway to the office and exam rooms, Kathy stopped refilling a cat's water dish to eavesdrop. Gage wasn't an ominous-announcement type of guy. And Chance... That colt had won a place in her heart.

"You got that horse-whispering fella," Doc replied to Gage in his rumbly voice. Officially, the Harmony Valley Veterinary Clinic was owned and run by Gage. Unofficially, it was run by his wife's grandfather, Dr. Warren Wentworth. Doc had founded the place in the fifties, closed it after his wife died, then reopened it when Gage came back this year and married his granddaughter. "What's his name? Dylan? He used to be good. That should be enough."

Kathy stepped into the hallway. "Are they taking Chance back?" He'd been bred to win the Triple Crown. With no permanent physical damage, in a little more than a year the colt could be a contender.

Gage and Doc exchanged glances that seemed to say, *How much should we tell her?*

It was Gage who finally spoke. "Chance... Well, he only has a few more weeks to show he's salvageable."

"Salvageable?" Kathy's voice escalated. "Don't talk about him as if he's disposable." As if no one would care if he went away forever. "We've been nursing him back to health. He's so much better. He has...he has...a right to live!" A right to a home and security. And people who loved him.

That was what Grandpa Ed had provided Kathy. He'd washed his hands of her mother and stepfather, paying them to stay away from Harmony Valley. He'd given Kathy the stability and safety a child should have. No more sneaking bills from her mother's wallet after she passed out and then slipping away to the convenience store to buy milk and snack cakes for dinner. No more being locked in an apartment for days at a time while her mother disappeared on drunken binges, all the while wondering if she'd ever return. No more nights spent huddled beneath a thin blanket when there was no heat.

"Nothing's been decided yet, girl." Doc's shaggy white hair brushed the upper rim of his thick eyeglasses. He was a man fully grounded in the why-worry-about-tomorrow philosophy.

"That's right, Kathy. Nothing's been decided. And you can help Dylan with Chance." Gage spoke as if Kathy was their ace in the hole. He nodded at Doc in a way that said there was something they weren't telling her.

Well, there was something Kathy wasn't telling them, too. And it sickened her. Dylan thought Chance's fate was inevitable. He'd said as much the first day he came.

Kathy hoped that Dylan was wrong.

Because if it was, her odds at being salvageable were no better.

Chapter Four

"I can't walk." Wilson Hammacker gripped the arms of his tan recliner as if that would keep him anchored in his living room in Harmony Valley. "I have no toes." His toes. His toes! He still dreamed that they were attached to his feet.

"You have special inserts for your shoes." Becca Harris held up what were essentially plastic socks with marble-size plastic toes attached. Becca was young and pretty, and for some reason she wasn't squeamish about needles, surgery scars, or false toes. "You were released from rehab. So now it's time to get back out in the world."

"I'm not going to walk anywhere outside this house." Wilson knew he sounded like a child. But in the past year, he'd lost his wife, been diagnosed with diabetes and had his toes amputated. "I'm a recluse and happy with that status."

"Dolly needs her shots." Becca pointed to his wife's rotund dachshund, who, upon hearing her name, rolled onto her back on the brown carpet for a tummy rub.

Wilson couldn't reach that low to rub her tummy without losing his balance. "I paid you to take care of me for a month. Take her to the vet."

"You said it. I'm paid to take care of you." Becca's smile was as resilient as the woman herself. "I'm also paid to help the Mionettis. I'm due there in fifteen minutes." Becca was the only caregiver in a town where the majority of residents needed caregivers. "If you don't feel up to driving, I can drop you two off." She knelt at the base of the recliner and took his hand. "Don't be afraid. You walk around here just fine."

"Without shoes." And only because he'd insisted Becca move his living room furniture so that he could stagger on his heels, feet pointed out like a duck, reaching from one chair-back to another. "What if I fall?" His old bones were as fragile as his wife's teacup collection.

"You'll get up." She slipped a prosthetic set of toes on his right foot. It was cold against his skin, but soft, and smelled of new plastic. "Comfortable?"

Wilson arched his foot as he'd been taught. Five fake toes moved as one. "As comfortable as I could be without my own toes."

Becca slid on the other prosthetic.

His petulance lingered. "If Helen were alive, she wouldn't make me go."

"I'm sorry your wife's not here." Becca put his shoes on next. Her touch was firm, yet gentle. It reminded him of his mother, gone thirty years. "But you have to take better care of yourself. You've seen what can happen when you let diabetes get out of control. And who knows what's wrong with Dolly."

He let the conversation about control drop. "Nothing's wrong with that dog but old age."

"Besides needing her shots, she's a bit round." Becca stood, tossing her brown braid over her shoulder. She held out her hand. "Come on."

The thing about Becca was she didn't put up with nonsense. You paid her in advance and then you were stuck with her. She showed up, listened to your complaints and did what the doctor ordered, even if that wasn't what you wanted. He'd hired her to help him transition to this new reality. Shots? She didn't sweat a bit. Finger pokes? Performed efficiently. Whining? She ignored it. Helen would have loved her.

He gripped the armrests again. "Once you get to a certain age, the rules shouldn't apply to you anymore."

Becca captured his hand and helped him to his feet. He took a step and then another, relearning the gently rolling feeling of something extending beyond the balls of his feet.

She hurried about, gathering her purse and Dolly. "Just because you're old doesn't mean you can cut corners on diabetes. We've got to get your blood sugar down, especially in the afternoon."

"Poke-poke-poke. That's what diabetes is. I hate it." He much preferred drinking.

"Was all that skipped poking worth losing toes over?"

He'd like to say no, but that would be admitting that his current predicament was all his fault.

Chapter Five

"I need a minute with you alone." Gage met Dylan in the Harmony Valley clinic's parking lot. There was a stubborn tilt to the vet's chin. "I know this is awkward. You're here primarily for Kathy. But the colt, Chance, he needs your help."

Dylan's training had already failed one horse. He hesitated to make any promises. "I'll do what I can, but that colt..."

"Is a fighter." Gage grinned, but it was a fighter's grin, an I'm-gonna-get-you-to-my-side-eventually grin. "I delivered him. I know what he was like before—happy-go-lucky, trusting, curious. And sometimes, he remembers, too."

"You can rationalize the situation all you like," Dylan told him evenly. "But the fact remains that Chance is a danger to himself and others. He'll probably always be unpredictable." Like Phantom. "I'll only be here a few weeks, but he'll need special care and a caring owner for the rest of his life."

"Please." Gage glanced away, as if he felt uncomfortable asking Dylan for anything. "Far Turn Farms called today and said if he isn't suitably socialized in three weeks, they're putting him down. They'll destroy him for no other reason than the fact that he's operating on survival instinct."

"I don't like to hear that any more than you do, but odds are that even if I can transition the colt to a place where he's willing to let people close, there's always the risk that someone will do something stupid and get hurt." Or worse.

Defeat tumbled in his gut. Dylan didn't like it. Or the realization that he'd stopped believing in redemption—not just in himself, but in horses, as well.

Gage frowned. "I just… I've always been a believer in second chances."

"Me, too." Dylan admitted. And because he wanted to reclaim that belief, he said, "It'll take more than me working with him a few hours a day."

The world is run by profit-and-loss statements, not heart and hope. That was what his old man used to say. And for years, Dylan had reveled in the fact that he could prove his father wrong.

The vet's attitude shifted subtly, like a horse who'd just realized what you wanted was what he wanted. "Whatever you need. Just tell me."

"If Chance doesn't send me to the emergency room in an hour, I'll make you a list of activities that might help."

"If things don't work out…" Gage's jaw hardened. "Is there room at Redemption Ranch?"

"If I still own the Double R in thirty days, we can talk." Dylan hadn't meant to say that. But facts were facts. "This is a make or break month for me." In more ways than one.

"I'm sorry. I hadn't realized." Gage's gaze turned understanding. "You let me know if you need anything. Not just here. But with your ranch."

It was kind of him to say. "Thanks," Dylan said gruffly.

The vet went back inside.

Dylan opened the back door of his truck and rooted around the variety of items covering seats and floorboards for the thin, four-foot plastic pole with a red flag on one end.

"It's no big deal," he told himself as he headed toward the stable. And it shouldn't have been. He had plenty of experience gentling and training horses.

When he was a boy, his family had lived in a small ramshackle place, the land not large enough to call a ranch. His mother waitressed, and his father worked odd jobs, but mostly people brought Dad horses to break. The money was good, but it was the chance to make another living thing suffer that appealed to Dad most. His old man was old-school. Tie the horse. Beat the horse. Defeat the horse.

It got to the point where Dylan heard a horse trailer coming down the drive and ran for his bedroom. He couldn't stand the sound of a horse's shrill protests.

They sounded too much like his and his brother Billy's when there were no horses around to train.

It wasn't until Child Protective Services took him and his brother away and placed them on a legitimate ranch with ten other foster boys that Dylan learned there was a gentler way to work with horses. To follow the more natural path, a horse trainer had to think like a horse, see the world like a horse, be the horse. Recognize every nuanced flicker of movement for what it was—confidence, trust, anxiety, fear, defense, rebellion.

But it wasn't Dylan's recent injury and hiatus from horse training that gave Dylan a glass half-empty attitude toward the colt's chances of racing.

Despite the Chance's incredibly clean lines and heritage, he'd probably never make it on the track. There were too many noises, too much visual stimuli. A racehorse was a trained athlete, one who could channel his focus down to one thing—outrunning the competition. Fears, phobias, quirks. They distracted. And distractions slowed a horse down.

Dylan came through the back gate, and Sugar ambled toward him, ears perked forward, a marked contradiction to the colt's quick steps and threatening posture. The colt probably assumed anything over one hundred pounds had the potential to pounce on him. Which might explain why Kathy, who was short and lacked meat on her bones, was the least threatening person at the clinic.

He paused to greet the mare and stroke her sleek neck. "You probably want to tell me how important it is to save Chance, too."

She blew air through her nose onto his chest, a sign of relaxed affection that might just as easily have translated to: *I love him, you dummy.*

"Yeah, I thought so."

Kathy came out the back door of the clinic as Dylan limped up the path to the stables. "Hey, wait up."

Dylan mentally shifted from horse-mode to people-mode.

Kathy approached him eagerly. As thin as she was, as hidden as her form was beneath jeans that were too loose and that pink jacket, she shouldn't have been mesmerizing. But there was an energy and confidence to her walk that said: *Look at me. Ain't I something?*

Much like a seasoned racehorse passing the stands on the way to the starting gate.

For a moment, Dylan forgot his purpose and his apprehension, both being edged aside by the unexpected power of Kathy's presence.

She stopped within touching distance and crossed her arms over her chest. "We need to talk about Chance."

Dylan held up a hand. "Gage told me about the urgency with the colt. And..."

"Good." She nodded briskly, long red hair glinting in the sun. "What can I do to help?"

More than anything, Dylan wanted to tell her to go back to the kennel, where it was safe. The last thing anyone needed was an injury on-premises. But the determination in her blue eyes registered. He knew she wouldn't listen. "You can observe."

"But..."

"No buts. You took risks yesterday. You can stay if you follow my lead. Agreed?"

It took her too long to nod. And there was a flash to her blue eyes that matched the fire of her hair. She might just as well have said: *Agreed. For now.*

As happened yesterday, they entered the stable to greetings from the two pregnant mares and a kick to the wall from the colt.

Dylan's steps slowed. "Does he know what grain is?"

"Yes." Kathy flashed him a small, proud smile. Dylan felt a corresponding grin try to slip past his guard. And then she added, "Because of the accident, he was weaned early."

And that wiped out any cause for Dylan to grin.

Early weaning was a strike against the foal's odds to recover his confidence, just as certainly as one of Kathy's parents being an alcoholic was a strike against her odds to stay sober.

I defied the odds.

Dylan wasn't a drunk or an abusive father. But since the accident, he felt as if someone had narrowed the rails bordering his life. His options and possibilities were fewer than before because he was more likely to see danger at every turn, the way he'd been as a boy.

I need to rebuild myself from the inside out, just like before.

If only he wasn't a jaded adult with responsibilities.

The grain bin was stored near the colt's stall. Dylan indicated Kathy stay back and walked past the stall without acknowledging the colt. He hummed a few jazzy bars of *Itsy Bitsy Spider,* scooped out some grain into a feed bucket and shook it.

The colt didn't kick. He was probably salivating for some oats.

Dylan turned his back on Chance and kept up the song.

Kathy moved closer. Her footsteps were clunky, those of the recently boot-converted. She clomped like a Clydesdale and waved a hand to catch his attention. "Uh, Chance is in the stall behind you." Skepticism colored her voice.

Had Gage told her about Dylan's failure with Phantom? "I know that." Dylan kept his voice smooth and easy. "He doesn't like to be looked at, though, does he?"

"No." There was a little grudging respect. "Or touched." Kathy came to stand next to him, bringing the scent of flowery perfume and the aura of raw courage.

Her tenacity pulsed between them, as noticeable as the notes of the song he hummed.

The colt blew an impatient breath, signaling his desire for oats.

Dylan lowered his voice. "Whenever we're in here together, Kathy, we need to keep our voices as soft as a baby's blanket." He resumed his spiderly song.

"I'm not going to whisper sweet nothings to you." But she was. Whispering, that is.

So prickly.

Despite himself, Dylan smiled, enjoying their banter. In between verses, he asked, "Have you noticed anything about Chance?"

"He hasn't thrown a tantrum." There was wonder in her voice, the sweetness of a newly converted believer in the man who'd once been the equine miracle worker. "What do we do now?"

"We stay here and whisper where he can see us."

She glanced over her shoulder.

The colt huffed.

"Don't look him in the eye." Dylan rattled the bucket of grain. He hummed louder. "Do you know this song?"

"What mother doesn't?" Her humming blended with his, filling the stable. Not surprisingly, after a while, Kathy fidgeted. He'd suspected she wasn't the type to stand still for long. Her boots scraped loudly across the concrete floor.

"Remind me not to take you dancing."

Her gaze dropped to her tan leather cowboy boots, so new the soles still shined on the sides. "Nobody can walk quietly or gracefully in these things."

"There are millions who'd argue that point."

She huffed.

The colt copied her.

"Red," he said, assigning Kathy a nickname. "You need to use your happy indoor voice."

She huffed again.

Dylan shook the grain, giving himself a mental headshake, as well. He was here primarily to support Kathy's foundation of sobriety. He couldn't do that without getting to know her better. "Tell me a story about yourself, Red."

She didn't blow smoke at the hair-color-related nickname. "My life isn't the stuff of fairy tales."

The colt shuffled about the stall, pushing straw with each step. Whoosh-whoosh-whoosh.

"Red," he scolded gently. "Nobody's life is rainbows and pots of gold." His certainly hadn't been.

"You should meet my brother, Flynn." Oh, there was sarcasm there, but it was almost hidden in the most saccharine of whispery tones. "He and his friends have the Midas touch. They created a popular farm app, sold it for millions. Came home to decompress and fell in love. Tra-la-la."

He smiled. "So, you're the ugly stepsister? Never to find Prince Charming? Blaming Cinderella for your lot in life?"

"My mistakes are my own, Rumpelstiltskin."

"Ah, you're assigning me a tragedy," he said, referring to Rumpelstiltskin's fate. Behind him, the colt's steps slowed. "But what was the cause of your downfall? Spindle prick? Poisoned apple? Evil stepmother?"

At his last joking guess, she seemed to shrink.

Finally, a clue, a path he could follow to help her overcome the triggers of addiction. He felt energized, like a hunting dog getting a burst of adrenaline as he picked up a scent.

Dylan would have played out the conversation, probing further, except misery pinched Kathy's forehead, flattened her lips and color drained from her cheeks. The breadcrumbs leading to the answer he sought would have to be picked up with care.

Otherwise, instead of helping Kathy stay sober, he might send her right back to the bottle's embrace.

Kathy didn't know what to say to Dylan. Or how much to say.

Her story? It wasn't a fairy tale.

When word first broke of Flynn's success nearly two years ago, the texted threats had begun.

I know what happened to you in college.

Nobody knew, except the man or men responsible.

There's a price for silence.

A price to pay for protecting Kathy's secrets, for protecting her son. She didn't want people to know she'd been a victim. But more importantly, she didn't want Truman to know he was a product of a brutal crime.

And so, she'd sold off things to pay the piper. And yet those payments were never enough. As the threats and demands continued, Kathy found it increasingly hard to sleep, hard to concentrate at work. The drinking started out innocently enough. A nightcap to ease her fears. A shot in her morning orange juice to smooth the jumpiness.

All because he was watching. Whoever he was.

And then the blackmailer made a mistake...

"Can you spare a minute, Kathy?" Standing in the stable door, Doc's mop of white hair ruffled in the breeze.

"Sure. Be there in a minute." Kathy glanced at Dylan, then over her shoulder, not quite meeting Chance's gaze.

The colt stood calmly, staring at Dylan's back, the man holding the oats.

"I'll be right here waiting for more of that story." Dylan's deep, smooth voice held her rooted in place. Since his last question, Dylan was treating her just like Chance. He didn't look at her directly. He didn't make any sudden moves. He was just there, a shoulder ready to lean on.

Kathy couldn't read Dylan. Yesterday he'd been coldhearted toward Chance. She'd written him off as the type of man who'd consider her a waste of time, too. Today he was humming children's songs and joking with her about fairy tales. If she was the type of woman to lean on a man, she might have considered his broad shoulders to be leanable.

"There's no story to tell." Kathy forced her feet to move away from Dylan, trying not to register his handsome face, his silky brown hair or compassionate gray eyes. "And you don't need me for this."

"Aren't you curious to see if you're his security blanket?" Dylan shook the oat bucket. "I am."

She was, too. But she hurried off anyway.

Doc was ahead of her on the path. He had a rolling gait that implied hip pain, moving the way Kathy imagined she had when she'd been drunk. He led her into an exam room where another old man sat holding a leash to an overweight dachshund, which was lying on the brick-patterned linoleum doing its best Superman impression—front paws extended forward, short back legs barely stretching beyond its little tail. "This is Wilson Hammacker. He needs help every day walking his dog, Dolly."

Mr. Hammacker had an age-spotted, shaved head and the pale skin of a shut-in. Kathy vaguely remembered him from growing up in town, but she couldn't remember what he'd done. Not the butcher. Not the ice-cream-shop owner. Not the barber.

"I'm willing to pay." Mr. Hammacker interrupted her thoughts with a hard-as-nails voice.

Kathy turned to Doc expectantly, waiting for him to name the clinic's price.

"Dogs, all mighty, girl." Doc spouted his favorite exclamation. "Take charge of your life and quote him a price. I thought you could use some extra money."

Pride warmed her and made her smile. She hadn't expected a referral. Not from Doc. Not from anyone.

Kathy met Mr. Hammacker's gaze. "I wouldn't know what to charge." Or, on second thought, if she even wanted the work. She put in thirty hours a week at the clinic, and Flynn had to drive her sixty miles round-trip to her support group once a week in Cloverdale. That was a full schedule. She knew that walking one dog shouldn't be such a big deal, but commitments were important to Kathy. She wanted to be certain she could honor each and every one she made these days since she'd already blown so many.

"This generation has no business savvy, Wilson," Doc said, not without a tinge of humor. "Charge him ten dollars, girl."

Kathy waited for Mr. Hammacker to protest. When he didn't, she said, "Before you accept, did Doc tell you I'm a recovering alcoholic?"

Doc rolled his eyes.

Mr. Hammacker didn't bat a gray eyelash. "As long as you come on time—three thirty—and you drop Dolly off by four, you'll do." His wrinkled lines smoothed into a more somber demeanor. "Dr. Jamero told me Dolly is overweight, which contributes to her back problems. And if her back hurts, then she just lies around all day. My diabetes prevents me from walking her." He stared down at his feet glumly.

"What he won't tell you is he's lost his toes to the disease, and he just sits around all day," Doc said gruffly.

"No toes?" Kathy had lost a lot of things, but at least she had all her toes.

"No toes," Mr. Hammacker confirmed, staring at his black orthopedic sneakers.

That must make it hard to walk. His situation made it impossible for Kathy to refuse. "I'd love to help."

"Give the girl your address, Wilson, and take her cell phone number. She'll be by later this afternoon for the first walk."

"I don't have a cell phone," Kathy said quickly. "Can he call here if he needs me?"

"I suppose he'll have to." Doc studied her over the top of his thick and grimy glasses but didn't question her about not having a phone.

The first time Dylan had helped a "ruined" horse return to productivity, he'd been twelve and in a foster home.

No one was sure why the gelding began bucking when someone put a foot in his stirrup, but no amount of whipping and intimidation had worked on the animal. The horse grew to hate everyone.

His foster father Nick Webb had taken in the horse just as optimistically as he'd taken in Dylan and Billy months before. But the horses had turned Dylan's stomach. He couldn't look at them without thinking of guns and his father. And unlike Billy, who'd thrived from day one with the Webbs, Dylan had kept to himself. He'd stayed away from the horses and hidden every time a truck pulled into the driveway, expecting his father to show up and take them back.

"That horse needs to trust someone," his foster father had said to Dylan in a kind way. The man had put an old ladder-back chair near a paddock post. "Sit here until he trusts you."

For days, Dylan had sat in that chair doing his homework and watching the other foster kids go about their chores. Bored out of his mind, he'd begun humming to himself. But he never turned around. He never looked that gelding in the eye. He couldn't.

And then one day while humming *Itsy Bitsy Spider*, the gelding nuzzled Dylan's head.

A sense of peace descended. Dylan reached up to touch the bay's velvety muzzle. A sense of forgiveness filled him. He stood, turning slowly. The gelding pressed his forehead against Dylan's skinny chest. It seemed natural to hug, to scratch the base of the animal's ears, to stroke his long neck, to rediscover the joy of a bond with a soul who only wanted to be accepted on his terms and be given unconditional love.

Without building a firmer foundation of trust, Kathy wouldn't give up anything more to Dylan. And neither would the colt.

Dylan had backed up slowly, small steps, and as soon as he was within a foot of the stall door, the colt went into survival mode—bucking and whinnying a warning. *Stay away. Don't come any closer. I'll hurt you.*

"What are you doing?" Kathy charged into the stable, shouting and upsetting the colt even further. "Sugar's racing around the paddock."

Dylan snagged Kathy's arm and led her back to the point where he'd started. "Red. I've been testing your little friend."

"He didn't fail. You did." Kathy sounded so certain.

A chill wind blew through the stable, sweeping in a few brown-gold leaves.

"Remember your tone, Red. I didn't say *he* failed." Her arm beneath her pink jacket was bone thin and trembling. "We have to start all over. Ready?" He began the spidery tune, pausing when she didn't join in. "If you don't feel up to a song, how about a game?"

"Shouldn't you be paying attention to Chance, not me?" Gossamer spiderwebs weren't as thin as Kathy's voice. Her fingers knotted and twisted at her waist. "I'm no one."

That nonsense had to stop. "Red... *Kathy...*" He set down the bucket of oats and turned her to face him, taking both her cold hands in his. He didn't usually hold his clients' hands, but her small ones felt right in his. "Is Chance no one?"

She wouldn't look at him. "No."

"Am I no one?"

She shuffled her feet. "No."

He gave her hands a gentle shake. "Then you are not no one." When she didn't react, he said, "I'm waiting for a head nod, something to acknowledge that you matter in this world."

The movement of her chin was infinitesimal.

It was a start. He'd take it.

"Now." Dylan was reluctant to let her hands go, but he did, once more presenting his back to the colt. "Chance needs to pay attention to us, not the other way around. Horses are social animals, like dogs. By saving his life and isolating him, you've taken away his herd. Also, his wounds hurt, and when you come in to clean them, you hurt him more. To him, the way he's learned to survive and avoid pain is by moving and kicking."

"Now I feel like the bad guy," Kathy whispered mournfully.

Me, too. With Phantom.

"It's a trade-off necessary to save his life. Now we need to swing things around, let him come to us. Let's play a game." Get her talking again. "This one is called 'tell me something about your name, something that no one else knows.'" He often used icebreakers to learn more about a client and how they viewed their problems. "I'll start. My middle name is Jerraway, which is my mother's maiden name. So, if I were to use my initials, I'd be..."

"D.J." She rolled her eyes. "You are so not a D.J. I mean, you play pool with D.J. He's your drinking buddy and..." Kathy stiffened.

"Yeah, I don't drink," he rushed on to say. "My dad was a drinker." Violent, too. Both topics he seldom shared. Time to hear about her. "Your turn. Tell me about your name."

"Kathy is usually short for Katharine. But my mom just named me Kathy." She paused, and when she spoke again, it was with forced optimism. "Short and sweet, no middle name."

Mom. Definitely a hot button, possibly a trigger to drink. "Makes it easier to fill out paperwork though. So, Cinderella, were you blessed with a wicked stepmother, too?"

"No." He could swear that one syllable also meant: *Thank heavens for that.* "Do you have any horses of your own, Mr. Horse Whisperer?"

"Many. The Double R is a place for misfits." In his mind's eye, Phantom reared in front of him again. Dylan's gaze sought reality and landed on Kathy's face. It was a pretty face, if too thin and sharp. "Some horses respond well to training and go to new homes."

"And the others?" Her voice cracked with urgency. "Are they lost causes? Do you...get rid of them?"

For a moment, Dylan couldn't breathe. Phantom's territorial paddock dance this morning came to mind, his future unclear. "I haven't given up on one yet," he managed to say.

His father's voice seemed to whisper in his ear: *liar.*

Since, Dylan qualified. *I haven't given up on one since...*

Somewhere in his head a door to a long-suppressed memory opened. His father's slurred voice, shouting commands, making threats, moonlight glinting off the barrel of a gun.

Dylan's stomach tumbled over and over in a sickeningly familiar corkscrew. His vision began to funnel. Sweat broke out at the base of his spine. He needed something to hold on to.

His gaze caught on a bent nail sticking out of a post a few feet away. He told himself he was like that piece of steel. Bent, but not broken. Strong despite his wounds. His stomach kept tumbling and the nail seemed to be moving farther and farther away, out of reach, almost out of sight.

The opening bars of *Itsy Bitsy Spider* drifted into his ears, bringing with it memories of velvety muzzles and forgiveness.

It was Kathy.

But she wasn't just humming. She was singing. She was singing as she slid her small hand into his. She was singing as she gave his hand a gentle squeeze.

Behind them, the colt chuffed, oddly at peace.

Dylan's stomach tumbled back into place. The nail still had a foothold in the beam an arm's length away. The door to his memories slammed shut.

And for a moment, hope flowed through his veins.

Chapter Six

K athy couldn't stop thinking about Dylan, the horse savior, and his ranch full of misfit horses.

He may look like a cowboy, but he acted like a four-legged rehab counselor. Both she and Chance had been put at ease during their "session."

"Mama, what are you doing?" Truman stood on the far side of the town square, his feet buried in reddish-brown leaves. He tugged on Abby's leash, while she strained toward Kathy.

"I'm walking Mr. Hammacker's dog." Perhaps walking was the wrong word. For every few steps she encouraged Dolly forward, the dog sat down, or tried to. Kathy had to be quick with the leash, while doing her best not to choke the little dear.

But forget about Dolly. Truman was here. Talking to her. And thoughts of dogs and extra money in her pocket evaporated as she tried to think of what she had to offer Truman. All her pockets contained were a Band-Aid, some kibbles and lip balm—nothing to entice a young boy.

Dolly flopped to the ground in defeat, the flopping not worrying Kathy since the dog's legs were extremely short and her belly extremely large.

Truman's eyes narrowed suspiciously. "Aren't you supposed to be at the clinic?"

Of course, her bright, young son would know where Kathy was supposed to be. "I got a second job as a dog walker." He should be proud of her.

"You're not very good at it." He pointed at Dolly, who'd closed her eyes, rolled onto her back and extended her paws heavenward.

If the dog hadn't blinked at Kathy, she might have thought she'd killed her. "It's my first day." Kathy glanced at Truman hopefully. She'd walked Grandpa Ed's elderly Labrador a time or two as a kid, but that dog had been trained to military standards—Kathy hadn't needed any skills of her own to do a good job of it. And since Abby had been given to Truman while Kathy was in rehab—and presumably been trained during that time, as well—she had little knowledge of how to convince a dog to walk. "Can you help me?"

It was the wrong thing to say.

Truman's face turned as pale as spoiled milk. He spun around and ran in the direction of home, Abby at his side.

Kathy waited until her son was out of sight to sink to the cold curb next to Dolly. Memories assailed her in a swarm of guilt and remorse.

"Mama, it's time to go to work."

"Can you help me get dressed, Truman? Mama feels sick."

She'd vomited more than once on her precious son during her dark days.

"Mama, what are you doing on the kitchen floor?"

"I fell, baby. Can you help me get to bed? I don't think I'm going to work today."

She'd missed so much work they'd fired her.

"Mama, it's time to leave for school."

"Can you help me by staying home today, Tru?"

Becca homeschooled him now and was committed to doing it until the school re-opened.

"I'm such a loser, Dolly." She'd stolen her little boy's childhood. Kathy couldn't blame Tru for trying to defend it now that Becca and Flynn had given it back to him. "I've never told anyone what I did to him. How I took away his innocence by being a drunk."

The small brown dog climbed into Kathy's lap and licked her chin.

Kathy stroked Dolly's short, silky fur. "That won't make up for the fact that you've only walked a block, you know."

It didn't make up for it, but it was a start. And that was what Kathy needed. A start.

A late-model, faded green Buick pulled up in front of her. It was the ladies of the town council—Agnes drove (although she could barely see above the dashboard), Mildred rode shotgun (although her eyes behind her thick lenses were vaguely unfocused) and Rose sat in back (ballerina prim as ever with her white hair in a tight bun at the base of her neck).

"Do you need a ride, dear?" Agnes asked, which may or may not have been code for: *We stopped to make sure you weren't sneaking a drink.*

"No, I was just sitting here..." Feeling sorry for myself. An answer that would earn her more questions from the councilwomen than less. The peaked green gable of the empty Reedley home was visible above the Buick. "I'm admiring the Reedley place."

Agnes and Rose looked at the unkempt craftsman-style home on the other side of the street.

And then Agnes turned back and said the darnedest thing. "I have a key to that one. Let's take a look, shall we?"

"Oh, no. I'm not in the market for a place." Kathy didn't want a look-see at this house. When she moved out on her own, she wanted to go someplace where no one would report back to Flynn. But what could she say except yes? They were already pulling away, assuming she was interested.

Agnes parked the car in the Reedleys' driveway. They'd moved away not long after the grain mill exploded. That catastrophe had started a mass exodus since the mill had been the town's primary employer. Harmony Valley had less than a hundred residents now, most of whom were elderly, too set in their ways, or financially unable, to leave. Flynn's winery was slowly bringing people and services back to the geriatric town.

Walking at a speed Dolly appreciated and one that fit Mildred's walker pace, Kathy followed Agnes along the front yard's gently curving path to the steps. The bushes were overgrown, and the paint was peeling. It needed some TLC. A man like Dylan would know how to fix things.

Where did that thought come from?

From the fact that Dylan took her guff and gave back some of his own. From the way he stood by a colt he thought the odds were stacked against. That was why she'd held his hand earlier in the stable, because he didn't give up on horses the way others did. A man like that would know how to take a neglected house and make it a home. He'd see things that others didn't. And the things he did notice wouldn't make him run away.

And okay, she had to admit, he was attractive in a rough-around-the-edges type of way. All of which meant... It meant...

That he's the type of man I'd be proud to call a friend, she told herself firmly.

With Truman and her sobriety her priorities, love was the furthest thing from her mind.

There was a small lockbox hanging from the front doorknob and Agnes had a key. "The town council reached out to several homeowners who've left town to determine which properties are for sale or rent. This one's available either way."

"One of many we're finding." Rose had stopped to examine a rosebush by the steps. "This bush really should be cut back. Cynthia used to get beautiful blooms. Yellow tinged with pink."

While Rose and Kathy helped Mildred up the steps, Agnes opened the door and said, "We've been inundated with house keys. It got too confusing, so Flynn bought us a set of lockboxes."

"That boy is brilliant," Rose said.

Someday, Kathy hoped people would describe her in such glowing terms. Maybe not brilliant. But kind and reliable.

She and Dolly followed the trio inside the house. Their footsteps disturbed the layer of dust on the hardwood floor. Rose tap-danced toward the kitchen. Dolly sneezed.

Kathy hadn't wanted to enter, but the house was charming. Sunlight slanted through the windows, catching the dust motes. Built-in bookshelves flanked either side of the brick fireplace. Kathy could almost see Truman playing with Abby in front of the fire. The other corner would be perfect for a Christmas tree.

"If you like it, we can show you the rest," Agnes said.

Kathy had no money to speak of, certainly not enough for a down payment on a house or even first and last months' rent.

So, it made no sense when she said yes.

Chapter Seven

S ince his wife's death, Wilson liked things just so.

He had a routine with the television—morning talk shows, afternoon movies, evening crime shows.

The kitchen was organized for ease of use and by the time of day. The first cupboard over the dishwasher held the utensils he needed to make breakfast—spatula, frying pan, a small plate and fork. The cupboard in the corner held his lunch supplies—napkins, peanut butter, bread and a knife. The cupboard next to the stove held his dinner needs—a small saucepan, a bowl, a soup spoon. The spice cupboard held his stash of alcohol, hidden behind a tin of cinnamon and a bottle of vanilla. In the corner, near the door that led to the backyard, was a red braided rug with Dolly's food and water feeders. He let her out at three-hour intervals—six, nine, twelve, three, six, nine. And took a nip of alcohol each time.

Then his carefully organized life had been thrown a curve. Diabetes required a different diet—vegetables were in his fridge for the first time since Helen had died. It also required lots of pokes—fingers for blood-sugar readings and his abdomen for shots. Becca stopped by twice a day to help him with the pokes and blood-sugar readings. And now, on top of everything else, Dolly needed walking.

Kathy had shown up promptly at three thirty during a commercial break. The change in schedule required a second nip of rum. Now it was after four.

Wilson rocked in the living room, waiting for her to return. He couldn't watch the late-afternoon movie if he was interrupted, so he watched nothing at all.

One thousand twenty-three rocks of the chair later, there was a knock on the door. He shouted for whoever was there to come in. Kathy brought Dolly inside and removed her leash.

When she'd arrived, Kathy had looked as worn-out as Wilson's brown carpet. Now her expression seemed bright and cheerful.

"You're late," Wilson said, holding out a ten-dollar bill.

"I know we agreed on twenty minutes. I didn't think you'd complain if it took me longer." She produced a treat from her pocket and fed it to Dolly.

"Should you be doing that? She's supposed to be losing weight."

"It's okay. Dolly needs protein after all that exercise. And..." Before he knew what was happening, she'd crossed the room and hugged him. "Thank you for believing in me."

What began as a loose, comfortable gesture ended with her jerking away from him. She stared at his face as intently as a traffic cop studied a driver caught weaving. She stared into his eyes, his dry-as-a-wheat-field-after-harvest eyes.

She smelled the rum.

"My wife was an alcoholic," Wilson blurted. What was he doing telling her this? No one in town knew. No one had to know. "Recovering, that is."

Kathy, the recovering alcoholic, stood frozen, the joy stolen from her face. Her bright red hair made her skin look as white as a sheet.

Wilson almost felt guilty. Almost. But he wasn't hurting anybody. And he wasn't drinking to excess.

But she knows, she knows, she knows.

He wavered from nonchalance to near panic. No one knew his secret, because no one needed to know.

What if Kathy tells someone?

He swallowed thickly. "I don't *need* to drink but I like it. Living with Helen and pretending I wasn't drinking *occasionally* was the hardest thing I ever did." Did Kathy believe him? If only he could hold a shot glass in his hand. Even an empty one made him feel more in control. Less guilty. "But I loved her."

Kathy's gaze cataloged the family pictures around the room. Helen in her Sunday best and pearls. Their kids—two of his, three of hers. Grandkids. Kathy didn't speak. She was waiting for him to admit that he had a problem. That was what recovering alcoholics did.

That was what Helen had done.

Kathy could wait as long as Helen had.

Anger stomped through his veins. Wilson didn't have a problem. He didn't overindulge and drive drunk. He'd never flown into a drunken rage and beat his wife. He wanted a little nip now and then. That didn't mean he had a problem. Not like Helen. Not like Kathy. They couldn't control their urges. They'd quit it completely.

Finally, with stiff features, Kathy asked, "How long was she sober?"

"Our entire marriage. Twenty years." His voice had turned into an unrecognizable thing, twisting and twining like a lying snake. "If you need to talk to anybody about...you know. You can come here. Anytime. But..." He had to stop talking. "Come back tomorrow at three thirty to walk Dolly. Don't be late."

Her murmured thanks were so soft he almost thought he imagined it.

And then she was gone.

His routine hopelessly disrupted, Wilson rocked a thousand times more, waiting for Becca.

And wondering if Kathy would tell his secret.

Chapter Eight

"What's he still doing out?" Dylan demanded, pointing toward the black stallion trotting around the paddock. "We've got clients coming soon. You know how he gets."

In a word: *scary*.

"Yeah, well, I thought he should get over it. Kind of like you need to get over it." When Dylan started to protest, Barry cut him off. "Ah-ah-ah. This is my home, too. I don't want to lose it." He dragged an old wooden chair from outside Peaches' stall and put it near the paddock. "A wise man once told me that music soothes the savage beast. You also told me that establishing trust is a process. Start processing."

Dylan hesitated. It was true that he'd had some success with both Chance and Kathy earlier today. But this...

Phantom reared up on the other side of the fence from Barry, but the old jockey ignored him and returned to the tack room, where the ranch phone was ringing. In his absence, Dylan and the black beast had a stare-down.

Phantom used to be ornery, but he'd loved to race. Back when Dylan had worked at Far Turn Farms, on race day Phantom had been as well-behaved as a police dog, a bundle of controlled energy. Now he was just plain out of control.

Or putting on a darn good act.

"That was your attorney's secretary," Barry said. "You have another family-court date."

"What? I'm all paid up." Eileen had warned him change was coming if he didn't pay on time next month. Bob, her attorney, must have already set this in motion. Dylan gritted his teeth and plopped into the chair, his back to Phantom. His knee throbbed and the trees at the edge of the property seemed closer than ever.

"I wrote the court date and time on the calendar." Barry's handwriting was about as legible as a doctor's on a prescription pad.

Dylan would need to confirm things with Eileen on Saturday. Best case, he'd get her to cancel.

He began to hum *Itsy Bitsy Spider,* which reminded him of Kathy's soft, clear voice.

Those sad eyes of hers contradicted her dry humor. He needed to discover the stress points that made her drink—her mother was a good start. But it wasn't enough for him to fully understand what had caused Kathy to fall into addiction and what might make her fall again.

Phantom pawed the ground, unshod hooves pounding packed dirt, reminding Dylan who his priority was in this moment.

Dylan hummed louder and closed his eyes, the better to pick up on what the stallion was doing.

Behind him, Phantom's tantrum mellowed. He still pranced around, but the shrill whinny had stopped.

Dylan should get in the paddock with him next. But the stallion hadn't been handled since they'd delivered him here months ago, rearing and kicking as if coming to Redemption Ranch was a fate worse than death.

Death. There was no fate worse than that.

With a weary sigh, Dylan acknowledged what Barry had been saying all along. He had to get the doubts and second-guesses out of his head. And the only way to do that was to get into Phantom's personal space and prove everyone wrong.

Fat chance of that, boy. His father's negativity was also in his head too much lately.

"What's Big and Bad doing outside?" A young male voice.

Dylan opened his eyes.

Carter stood before him, an awestruck expression on his face. The slim teenage boy wore jeans and a navy T-shirt beneath a blue plaid button-down.

His styled brown hair had enough product in it to defy the breeze. "He's huge. I mean, you could kind of see that in his stall. But he's..."

Phantom let out a shrill whistle. His hooves pounded the dirt as if he was rearing up and landing hard.

"Don't look him in the eye. It's a dominance thing." Back still to the stallion, Dylan stood and walked to the tack room. "Pick your poison today. Do you want to work with Maggie Mae on the lunge line or give Brownie a bath?"

Some people responded to talking to a therapist, some sought group support, a few others found solace in art therapy. And a handful of people in Sonoma County found working with Dylan and his horses helpful to their sobriety.

"I want to work with Big and Bad." Carter sported the enthused grin of the young and naive. His youth and clean-cut appearance made it hard to believe he was a recovering alcoholic.

"No, you don't. You'll bathe Brownie." The swayback gelding wouldn't excite Phantom like the mare would.

"Someday, I'm gonna work Big and Bad."

"That day's a long way off." But Dylan grinned. It was good to have a goal.

"Let the boy have his dream." Barry sat on a bench in the meager afternoon sun, leaning a bridle. His white hair was a stark contrast to his black jacket. "I admire Carter's guts."

"His guts'll be on the ground if he goes in there before Phantom is ready. Just sayin'." Dylan handed Brownie's halter and lead line to Carter. "Instead of bathing him near the arena, why don't you do it outside the door here?"

"Where Big and Bad can see?" Carter brightened. "Awesome."

It wasn't awesome. It would keep Dylan on edge. But he mustered a pleasant smile for Carter. "Tell me how your weekend went. No drinking, right?"

"*Moi*?" Carter quirked his brow. "Three months sober, dude."

"The homecoming dance is a week away. What's your sobriety plan?"

"Same as always. Refusal. I got a couple of after-party invitations, but I'm not going to cave." Carter's smile was worthy of a political career.

In fact, he was senior class president at his high school. That smile was one of his best defenses and his biggest obstacle to sobriety. Charming, popular, good-looking. Everyone wanted Carter around. The boy couldn't seem to resist the limelight. Odds were he'd be bargaining with Dylan about attending a party before next weekend. He was more open with Dylan than he was with his parents.

"We'll practice turning down drinks," Dylan said. Peer pressure had already knocked Carter off the wagon over the summer.

Carter opened Brownie's stall. "Hello, old guy. Someone thinks you stink and need a bath."

Dylan leaned against the stall door, hearing Phantom snort and prance around the paddock outside. He'd picked up a training flag in the tack room just in case the stallion needed a little correction. His grip on it tightened. "Did you talk to that girl? The one who..."

"Despises drunks? Yep." The carefree note in Carter's voice became forced. "The good news is, she seemed open to believing my claims of sobriety." He led Brownie out of the stall. The horse was all saggy angles and soft musculature—a direct contrast to Phantom.

"Carter, don't sound so sarcastic. If you like this girl, keep trying."

"I'm... It's..." The veneer dropped, and with it Carter's smile. "She's different. She's the kind of girl who looks you in the eyes and doesn't sugarcoat anything. She told me we could be *friends*."

A pair of bright blue eyes beneath a fringe of fiery red hair came to mind. "A keeper." Dylan had only said that for the boy's sake. Clearly, Carter had a crush on the girl. Dylan didn't have a crush on Kathy.

"Not a keeper." Carter tied Brownie's lead to a ring near the hose. His smile wavered like a flag in a spring breeze. "I'm not the kind of guy who stays with one woman. And she knows it."

"You're seventeen!" For the sake of the horses, Dylan kept his voice at a civil volume when he wanted to shout. "You drank your way through your junior year. What do you know about relationships? What do you know about the man you're going to be?"

"I know I'm a waste of her time. Sometimes you just know when things are a dead end, don't you?"

Dylan glanced at Phantom, who was walking a circuit around the paddock instead of running. "No, I don't think I do."

Kathy's day had been a roller-coaster ride.

Up-up-up. Truman had talked to her before breakfast.

And then a downward plunge when she learned Chance might be destroyed.

Up-up. Dylan's hypnotic voice had given her hope the colt might be saved.

A corkscrew spiral when she said the wrong thing to Truman, reminding them both how low she'd once sunk.

Up. The Reedley place had spoken to her, of fresh starts and clean breaks.

An unexpected drop when she'd caught the scent of alcohol on Mr. Hammacker's breath and no glass next to him on the table. She recognized his double-talk for what it was—denial. He was an alcoholic. And she knew diabetics shouldn't drink. Grandpa Ed had developed type 2 diabetes a decade earlier and stopped indulging in his nightly glass of wine.

Kathy left Mr. Hammacker's house and started walking, but her walk was a near-run.

Identifying his problem didn't mean she could help him. In fact, it was demoralizing to her.

She knew how a few drinks could take the edge off. Her worries would melt away. It would be easy to find his bottle and take a drink while Mr. Hammacker sat in his chair. It was easy to fool others. She'd bamboozled Flynn the entire time she'd been drinking. And Mr. Hammacker had apparently pulled the wool over the town's eyes for years, quite a feat since there were few secrets in this burg. If Doc knew Mr. Hammacker was drinking, he wouldn't have recommended Kathy walk Dolly. Everyone knew that alcoholics had to distance themselves from temptation. Which was why Flynn and Becca didn't keep alcohol in the house.

But Mr. Hammacker...

Her heart pounded out an alcohol-engraved invitation.

If Kathy went back to the bottle, she could let Flynn take care of everything, including Truman. There'd be no more battles for Truman's affection, no more questioning looks from Flynn. Under an alcoholic haze, she could disappear, just like her mother. She could be no one, nothing, invisible.

That was what her early childhood had been like. She'd been no one, nothing, invisible, and disposable. Flynn had been the first child her mother had jetti-soned. And without her older brother to protect her, Kathy had lost some of her fight. She no longer argued when her mother told her to crouch outside the apartment bushes until her company left. She didn't put up a stink when her mother shut her in the dark hall closet. She didn't cry or whine or rebel as Flynn had done.

"Pretend you're a ghost," Mom would say, locking Kathy in the dark. "A quiet ghost."

No one, nothing, invisible.

The memory of Dylan's steadying grip on her hands returned. He didn't think she was no one.

But the college disaster. The texts. The betrayal. The fight for Truman and the fight to stay clean. It was hard to be an adult. What harm would there be in finding Mr. Hammacker's stash tomorrow and taking a sip?

She'd hate herself for it. And Truman would hate her more.

I can't go back to Mr. Hammacker's.

But if she didn't, Doc would question her about it.

She found herself walking the switchbacks up Parish Hill, pace finally slow-ing. This time of year, the sun set early. It would be dark soon, but Kathy kept going. Walking away from the easy way out that Mr. Hammacker was taking. Stepping away from Becca's sweet understanding and Flynn's edge of the cliff disappointment. Marching away from the temptation hidden in Mr. Hammacker's house.

I can't go back.

She didn't stop until she reached the top.

A full moon rose over the mountain. Kathy wanted to be as calm and dependable as the moon. But she couldn't escape the fact that no matter how diligently she guarded her life from alcohol and its seductive call, it could blindside her at any time, leaving her shattered and broken once more.

No one, nothing, invisible.

Tomorrow, she'd show up at Mr. Hammacker's at precisely three thirty, hoping not to be blindsided.

Chapter Nine

"You missed dinner." Flynn sat on the front steps in the autumn darkness. Light spilled from the big window in the living room onto his shoulders. "Everything okay?"

"I went for a walk up Parish Hill." Hoping to clear her head. Hoping to exhaust herself so she could sleep. She clutched a Hot Wheels fire truck in her hand. She'd found it on her walk alongside the road near the closed school and wondered if Truman would like it. Now she realized he'd probably like her to stay sober more than he'd like any toy or chocolate bar.

Flynn stood and held out his arms.

Kathy hesitated on the step. Above her, the eucalyptus trees rustled in the brisk evening breeze, their light minty scent filling the air. "Is this your human Breathalyzer test?"

"No." Flynn didn't sound convincing. He'd never been a good liar, especially when he'd tried cheating at checkers when they were kids.

She closed the distance between them and hugged her brother, pressing a kiss to his cheek for good measure.

When they'd lived with their mother, he'd always watched out for Kathy. After his father went to prison the second time and Kathy's dad was AWOL, Flynn had become more vocal with Mom about her drinking. His words had the wrong effect. Instead of quitting alcohol, Mom discarded Flynn. Kathy had been devastated when Mom left him with Grandpa Ed. Alone and only six, she'd had to learn to fend for herself for another two years until she, too, was abandoned in Harmony Valley.

"You need to eat more." Flynn kept an arm around her and drew her up the stairs. "You're skin and bones."

"I don't have much of an appetite these days."

"Humor me." Flynn released her and opened the door to outdated linoleum and green shag carpet. "Truman said he saw you walking someone's dog today."

"Doc started a side business for me. You can add dog walker to my list of time-killing activities." She supposed she should appreciate anything that filled her day. The living room was empty. The television off. "Did Truman go to bed already?" It wasn't even eight.

Flynn nodded. "Come on. Becca made lasagna."

Kathy sighed. "I should thank her." She was a better mom than Kathy had been. But oh, how it hurt.

"Don't go there." Flynn moved to the kitchen. "We're trying to help you, not stand in your way."

"I know." Kathy removed her boots and padded into the kitchen. "Becca's just so perfect. I know she means well. It's just..." Kathy wanted to turn and run back into the darkness. She wanted to erase the last two years.

I need a drink.

No. She didn't want to lose control like that. She wanted the placebo of a drink. Something to calm her down and make her feel as if everything was going to be fine.

Dylan's smile came to mind. The feel of her hand in his. The tone of his humming.

Flynn placed a portion of lasagna into the microwave. "We're lucky to have Becca around. She was there for Truman tonight and all through your time away."

"Don't talk about it as if I went on vacation. I was in rehab. I'm an alcoholic." Kathy's voice scrambled up toward the ceiling, scratching her throat as it did so. "You need to remind me every day, don't you? Isn't that why you talked me into staying here? So, you could be my jailer? So, you and Becca could keep Truman for yourselves?" That was her worst fear.

"That's enough." Becca appeared behind Kathy, calm and composed. "Let's take this conversation outside so we don't wake Truman."

"Even when you're right, I hate it." Kathy regretted the words as soon as they escaped her chapped lips.

Becca paled.

Flynn's face mottled with anger. "Careful, Kath."

"I'm sorry, but... I'm tired of being careful." Kathy was horrified by the panicky tenor of her tone. It was as if she was trapped inside, watching her own meltdown without any way of stopping herself. "I'm tired of everyone tiptoeing around me, waiting for me to fail. I'm tired of being treated as if I have an infectious disease."

Becca put her arm over Kathy's shoulders. "Honey, we're not waiting for you to fall off the wagon."

"Aren't you?" Kathy shrugged her off. She should stop. She should shut up and be grateful for their help and support. But the fear... The fear consumed her. "That would mean you could turn Truman against me forever."

"You're doing a good job of that yourself." Flynn's voice was as hard as granite, and ugly. So ugly.

"That's because I didn't think it would be this difficult." Kathy sobbed. She dodged around Becca and headed down the hall.

"What about dinner?" Even when Flynn was mad, he still tried to watch out for her. "You need to eat something."

"I'm sorry but no. Just...no." Kathy needed to look in the mirror. She needed a pep talk. She needed Grandpa Ed, who'd always been the loud voice of reason whenever Kathy was unreasonable.

She shut herself in the bathroom.

But when she looked in the mirror, she couldn't remember a single encouraging word Grandpa Ed used to say.

No one, nothing, invisible.

And not even thoughts of Dylan or the memory of his supportive words could make her feel better.

After a restless night spent wondering if everyone would be better off if she gave in to temptation, Kathy woke before dawn—before her alarm-clocking songbird—made coffee and sat out on the back porch overlooking the Harmony Valley River.

She huddled in her jacket, hoping the cold would provide the answer she sought: *How will I know that I'll never drink again?*

"I thought you could use this." Dressed in baggy gray sweats that looked as if they belonged to Flynn, Becca carried her grandmother's red-and-blue wedding-ring quilt. She laid it over Kathy. "Would you like some company?"

"It's o'dark thirty." As in early. Too early for company and coherent words. Especially when Kathy felt so low for the unkind words of the night before. "I can barely apologize to you at this hour."

And with that out in the open, Kathy knew she needed to call her sponsor and get to an AA meeting. But since she'd surrendered her car keys to Flynn, that meant she'd have to ask him either for her keys or to drive her as he usually did. And if she went to an unscheduled AA meeting, he'd know she'd been tempted.

Despite Kathy's grumpiness, Becca sat in a white plastic chair next to her and drew part of the quilt over her legs. "I love dark chocolate."

Kathy's life and happiness were hanging in the balance and Becca wanted to make inconsequential small talk? Tears welled in her eyes.

"Milk chocolate is good." Her sister-in-law made a small, frustrated noise. "But dark chocolate gives me... I don't know...an emotional high?" Becca smiled sheepishly. "I know it's not the same as..."

Drinking alcohol. Becca didn't need to say the words. Kathy knew where she was going.

Becca plucked at the quilt. "When I lived with my grandmother, I used to hoard dark chocolate. I'd wait, knowing where I'd hidden it. I'd torture myself until I couldn't stand it any longer, until I told myself I deserved it because I'd waited so long. And then I'd eat it. All in one sitting." She rubbed a hand up and down her forearm. "I'd feel great for about thirty minutes. And then I'd break out in hives because I'm allergic to dark chocolate."

"Oh." Kathy knew her sister-in-law was trying to reach out, but she was still tied up in indecision over attending an AA meeting.

"I, um, ate that dark-chocolate bar you left on the coffee table the other night." Becca drew up the sleeve of her sweatshirt, revealing a set of pus-crested hives that covered her arm from elbow to wrist. "I know saying I'm addicted to one kind of chocolate is nothing at all like you saying you're addicted to alcohol. But I just want you to know that I'm not perfect."

Kathy slumped in her chair. "I appreciate you saying that."

"I'm not trying to replace you." There was an earnestness in Becca's voice that hooked Kathy's heartstrings and reeled her in. "I'm just trying to be a good person and do what's right for me and my family. I understand what it's like to give in to something you know isn't good for you."

"I hear you. Thank you," Kathy whispered. "I'm sorry about the hives. I'm just... I've never been...perfect."

"You don't have to be." Becca stood, leaning over to give Kathy a hug. "You just keep moving forward and know that we've got your back." She returned to the house.

Kathy sat with her coffee, watching the sun sift through the fog and dapple the green river with yellow. Then she left for the clinic and went directly to Chance's stall, whistling to provide warning that she was coming. She was really hoping he showed some improvement. After all, she and Dylan had talked for an hour yesterday outside the stall, and Chance hadn't kicked once.

If the colt could improve, she could stay sober. Not that her sobriety hinged on a horse, but she'd take it as a sign.

She got a sign, all right. A loud bang filled the stables. Chance's hooves against wood.

Kathy's hopes sprang a leak that made her shoulders sag.

"Hey, boy. How are you this morning?" She made the mistake of looking Chance in the eye.

He bucked. Out in the paddock, Sugar whinnied. Kathy's hopes sank to her toes.

He has to make it. He has to.

"Now, Chance, the clock is ticking. You need to settle down." She slipped inside his stall. His stitches looked good. His bandages were clean. This time she kept her gaze away from his as she began humming *Itsy Bitsy Spider.*"

Chance trotted around, kicking out and making noises expressing his displeasure.

Except for the humming, Kathy kept very still. He wasn't hurting her.

Chance slowed. His chestnut coat gleamed.

Without realizing what she was doing, her hand came out to stroke his silky back.

He whirled and kicked out. Kicking her.

She saw it happen in slow motion. His unshod hoof cut through the air and struck the inside of her right wrist. Her forearm was flung back against the wall, abrading her knuckles. If there was sound,, if she screamed, she couldn't hear it above the rush of adrenaline in her ears.

She stumbled out of his stall, tugging up her jacket sleeve to see her wrist. A round, red circle was already beginning to swell. And there was pain. Doubled-over, air-robbing, silent-screaming pain.

She was reminded of Grandpa Ed's story of being shot during a spy campaign in Russia amid the Cold War. Or rather, his most frequently repeated quote about the episode: *You don't just roll over and die when you get hit.*

Fantastic. It took pain to bring his words back to her.

Nothing is gained without sacrifice. He'd told her these words of wisdom when she'd had trouble passing algebra. And then he'd told her she couldn't get up from the kitchen table until she'd finished all the word problems.

What was the point of those word problems? They'd never solved anything real. It would have been more practical if the math book had presented something like: *If a colt kicked out with an extension of four feet and struck a woman's fifteen-inch limb, how much force would be needed to break a bone? Solve for x.*

Despite the pain, Kathy twisted her wrist. She'd heard Grandpa Ed tell Flynn once that if a bone was broken, the pain would be excruciating with movement. Hers wasn't. It was just fiercely breath-stealing.

Giving-birth hurt. Getting-sober hurt. Saving-Chance hurt. But she wouldn't complain. And she wouldn't give up.

She sat huddled on the bench, cradling her wrist.

Clearly, Chance needed more work than the hour Dylan could provide five days a week. Just as clearly, she wasn't a horse whisperer. If talking helped, Kathy would talk up a storm. It was just that she couldn't talk all day to Chance and get her work done, too. She wasn't the wife of a wealthy man or retired.

But many people in Harmony Valley were. Retired, that was.

"Hello, boy." Dylan looked through the stall bars from inside Phantom's paddock. "Ready to rejoin the happy and productive horse population?"

Inside his stall, Phantom released a shrill whinny. Straw rustled as he moved around in the shadows.

"I'll take that for a yes."

The sun was just rising over the mountains. Mist clung to the ground, but the sky promised to be a clear, crisp and blue. A great day for second chances.

"You ready?" On the other side of the stall, Barry had his hand on the gate lever.

Time to step up and act like a man. Dylan's father's voice.

Dylan stepped to one side, gripping a training flag in one hand and a halter with a lead rope in the other. "Yep."

The gate mechanism squeaked and clunked open. Phantom lunged forward as if coming out of a starting gate. Ears up, tail high. He was in a good mood. And then he rounded the far side and bore down on Dylan, ears back.

"Easy, boy." Dylan waved the flag high, adrenaline rushing through his veins, minimizing his limp.

"I've got my cell in case we need to call 9-1-1," Barry said in a calm voice.

"Thanks for the vote of confidence."

Phantom dashed forward, weaving a bit like a running back on a crowded football field, looking for an opponent's weakness.

"Whoa!" Both Dylan's arms went up. "Easy, easy."

Phantom slid to a halt in front of him.

"He's gonna let you put a halter on him." Barry sounded amazed.

Dylan studied the stallion. Phantom didn't do anything he didn't want to do. Head high. Ears rotating. Nostrils flared. His tail was still at attention. He looked the same as he had the day he'd nearly killed the vet tech.

Dylan swallowed. "That's a good show you've been putting on, boy." He hoped to heck it had been a show.

Phantom pawed the ground with his too-long hooves.

"If we get this halter on you and you behave," Dylan said, "we'll call the blacksmith out." He moved forward, holding out the halter.

Could it be this easy?

Phantom lunged at Dylan, teeth bared. Dylan barely turned him away with a quick swipe of the training flag. The stallion leaped two feet sideways and then trotted around the paddock, happy with himself, if his jaunty stride was any indication.

The birds were quiet. The horses were quiet. Even Barry was quiet. It was so quiet Dylan could hear his heart pounding in his ears.

A horse like that is only good for one thing. Dog food. His father's drunken, raspy voice cut through the quiet, propelling Dylan forward again, flag up and ready.

I'll prove you wrong.

"He's got that murderous look in his eye," Barry said unhelpfully.

"Come on, boy," Dylan crooned, trying to take in all of Phantom's body language, not just his steely-eyed gaze. "You remember what it's like to be brushed down, don't you? A good ear rub?"

The black stallion trotted past him, kicking up his heels.

Dylan lowered the flag and the halter, letting them drag in the dirt. It was too much to hope for that it was only Dylan's fear that was holding Phantom back. It was Phantom's fault, too. They both needed an attitude adjustment. And a miracle.

A gentle breeze swirled past. Kathy's version of *Itsy Bitsy Spider* seemed to drift in with it. She had faith in Chance. She had faith in Dylan. If only Dylan had faith in Phantom.

The white barn cat walked confidently into the paddock, rubbing against a post before heading straight for Phantom. The stallion stopped prancing at the sight of the cat. He sniffed the air, ears twitching back and forth.

Ghost kept walking toward him, crooked tail swishing casually.

"That cat always did have a death wish," Barry murmured.

But instead of trampling the feline, Phantom lowered his head and nuzzled the cat, blowing into its fur. And then Ghost walked away, easy as you please.

"You are such a faker." Dylan chuckled as he lifted the training flag and halter. And then he began to sing *Itsy Bitsy Spider*.

Phantom lowered his head, shooting a glance toward the cat and then toward Dylan, who was waving the flag slowly back and forth as he approached. The stallion raised his head and blew out a breath that reached Dylan's hands.

A truce? Dylan was willing to risk it.

Tucking the flag beneath his armpit, Dylan stepped to Phantom's left shoulder, looped his arms about the stallion's neck and slipped on the bridle. Then he stepped back, gripping the flag and lead rope.

Phantom blew out another breath and didn't take his gaze off Dylan, who was starting to get a bad feeling in the pit of his coffee-lined stomach.

"He likes you," Barry said, just as the horse lunged at Dylan.

The flag and a tug on the lead deterred the stallion from trampling him.

And that was pretty much how the next hour went. One step forward, two steps back. Dylan wasn't always sure who was moving forward and who was losing ground.

But one thing was certain. Dylan wasn't ready to give up on the stallion. Not by a long shot.

Recruiting some retirees was easier than Kathy had expected.

The hardest part was hiding the pain in her wrist. It was still morning and Kathy felt as wrung out as an old sponge.

Rose wiped the stable bench with a handkerchief. She was dressed in fashionable slacks and a thick fisherman's sweater that hung off her ballerina frame. "Remind me what we're doing here again."

"We're bartering." Agnes had already taken a seat on the bench. She fluffed her short gray hair. "Kathy is going to help us with the Christmas pageant, and we're going to... What is it we're doing again?"

"You're singing." Kathy led Mildred to the bench, guiding the old woman's hand to the sturdy wood planks. She couldn't believe she'd been trapped into helping with the pageant. She only hoped she wouldn't be asked to dress up in Victorian garb and sing Christmas carols up and down Main Street.

"Is there a horse behind me?" Mildred pointed to the empty stall in front of her. "I hear something."

Chance was restless, pacing in the straw, but he hadn't worked himself into a tizzy yet because Kathy had coached them into keeping their backs turned.

"There's a colt behind you," Kathy reminded them. When all three elderly ladies began turning around, Kathy added quickly and sweetly, "Please, don't look. Remember what I told you. He's still in the early stages of socialization. Eye-to-eye contact or touching…sets him off."

"So, we're singing to an equine?" Rose sniffed. "I'm used to seeing and interacting with my audience." In addition to her stint as a ballerina, Rose had performed minor roles in Broadway musicals and if rumors were true, as a high flyer in the circus. "What is it we're getting out of this?"

"In addition to assistance with the pageant, we're helping Kathy. Look at her. She looks as if Gage is running her ragged."

Kathy forced herself to smile, hoping it didn't look like a grimace. Despite taking Tylenol, her wrist throbbed and had swollen to the point where her jacket sleeve was tight. She really needed to tell someone, like Doc or Gage about her injury. It was just that she felt so foolish for it happening, and she worried they wouldn't let her help with Chance anymore if they knew.

"Oh, Rose, you know you'll take any excuse to sing." Agnes rolled her eyes.

Rose thrust her nose in the air. "I have nothing selected for cattle."

"Don't tell me you've forgotten *Oklahoma!*" Mildred deadpanned. "Classic cowboy material."

"Oh, Mildred, how could I forget?" Rose brightened. "I've been practicing a solo from *Mamma Mia* for Will and Emma's wedding for so long, that cowboys have been the furthest thing from my mind." She raised her voice to sing about a surrey with fringe on top.

The other women followed her lead.

Kathy leaned against the wall, cradling her wrist against her stomach. Chance put his nose on top of the stall door, sniffing and taking a peek. Satisfied that things were working, Kathy went about cleaning Trixie's stall, trying very hard not to use her wrist. Too bad she was right-handed.

"What's with the choir?" Dylan showed up a few minutes later in his usual uniform of jeans, flannel shirt, navy vest jacket and cowboy boots. He held that slender, white plastic pole in his hand, topped with a red flag, and stared at the singers from beneath the brim of a dusty black baseball cap. "You couldn't sit and sing a few bars for him yourself?"

Everything seemed to hum as if brought to life by Dylan's presence. The heating unit for the clinic, the bug light, her.

Kathy frowned. He certainly did not make her hum. "I'm a working, single mom. You can't expect me to sing to Chance all day."

"Well, I..." He turned to face her, eyes widening.

Did he notice she was in pain? Kathy set her shovel on top of her wheelbarrow load, keeping her head down. "There are still things that need to be done. Manure waits for no one. Why don't you introduce yourself to the ladies?"

The song came to a close, and the choir glanced toward Kathy and Dylan, even Mildred, who was legally blind but still saw shapes.

"Are you okay?" Dylan asked.

"Yes." Kathy gave Dylan a gentle push forward with her good hand. "This is Dylan, the miracle worker who's going to help us save the colt you're singing to."

"Horse trainer," he grumbled, still looking at Kathy.

"Handsome, talented, and humble." Agnes sported a Cheshire-cat smile. "Kathy loves animals, too."

"Matchmaking wasn't part of our deal," Kathy said through gritted teeth as she positioned one wheelbarrow handle against her abdomen and pushed it out of Trixie's stall. She set it down with a thump and a grimace, placing both hands on the wooden handles as she caught her breath.

Dylan hurried to her side, removing her hands from the wheelbarrow.

His touch unexpectedly sent Kathy's heart racing. Their gazes collided. *Yawzer.*

Kathy tried to hide her attraction, wondering where it had come from. Wondering what it would feel like to be taken in his strong arms and receive his kiss.

Oh, no.

This was a disaster waiting to happen. She wasn't stable enough in her sobriety to pursue a relationship.

While she argued with herself about her heart's silly intentions, Dylan absconded with the wheelbarrow to the compost heap.

Chivalry wasn't dead, but she wouldn't let him do her job. She needed him to focus on Chance.

Tromping after him, Kathy crossed her arms gingerly, wrinkling her nose against the smell of manure. "If you'd like to muck Isabo's stall next, let me know. I have plenty of cleanup to do inside the clinic." A demoralizing amount given the pain in her wrist.

"I just want to help you finish your chores so you can spend time with Chance and me," Dylan said, adding a smile that Kathy felt from head to toe. "You look like you need a break."

She cleared her throat, trying to also clear out attraction. "You're not the one being paid to clean up after horses. I'll help you with Chance after I've satisfied my other duties." That sounded like legalese. Maybe she should study law, not business.

Kathy did a sashay turn a model would have been proud of and left him at the manure pile.

Chapter Ten

"Hold up," Dylan said, following her from the compost heap because he was concerned. He took hold of her arm and gingerly turned her around to face him.

Something had happened since he'd seen her last. The change in her appearance from yesterday was drastic. Sure, her slight frame still barely filled out her jeans and gray T-shirt beneath her pink jacket, but now her face was pinched with exhaustion, and her blue eyes were dull and listless. He might have suspected a vampire invasion, if not for her standing in broad daylight.

"Are you okay? How's your back?" Dylan gave her a quick once-over. She'd been struggling with the wheelbarrow when he'd stepped in to help.

"Fine. I'm fine." Avoiding meeting his gaze, Kathy thrust her lip out, as if she'd already been told at least once today that she looked worse than something the cat had dragged in and would deny it if told again.

"I'll let the ladies serenade the colt awhile longer." Dylan waved the horsemanship flag back and forth slowly, like a hypnotist's pendulum.

Calm down, Red.

Her eyes became ensnared by the movement. "I need to spray down the kennels," she said slowly. Her fiery red hair was limp across her shoulders.

Sugar wandered to the upper corner of the corral, nickering softly, as if she, too, was worried about Kathy.

Dylan kept the flag moving and his voice gentle, hoping to relax Kathy enough to let her guard down. "That can wait."

"He's good," one of the old ladies said, making the others nod and giggle.

Kathy blinked. "Are you trying to get me in trouble? I'm supposed to be working for Gage, not you."

Dylan made sure the flag kept marking time. "Gage said you could help me if I needed it."

Instead of watching the flag, Kathy's gaze shifted to Dylan. "Yeah. He told me. Why would he do that?"

Dylan sighed and planted the flag pole in the dirt. "Because he realizes you have a rapport with these horses, and it would benefit his business if you learned more."

"Oh." That was a very small oh, a no-one-ever-says-nice-things-about-me oh. "Before you say anything, I didn't get much sleep last night. And..." She shifted awkwardly.

"And?"

She wouldn't look at him. "That's all."

That wasn't all. Questions threatened to collide in his head like cars edging out of a crowded parking lot after a big horse race. *Why didn't you sleep? Were you drinking? Were you tempted to drink?*

"I know I look...bad." Her arms were crossed loosely in front of her.

Something was wrong here. But until he figured it out, levity was called for. "I don't usually talk to a woman about her appearance. There are too many pitfalls. What is the proper answer to *'Do these pants make my butt look big?'* I'm an honest guy. If you ask, I'll answer the way I see it."

Kathy chuckled softly as her hands fell slowly to her sides.

He handed her the horsemanship flag. "Hold this for me."

"What's it for?"

"It's a distraction, like batting at a gorilla with a bandanna to keep him from pondering other things." Like how to trample the man holding his lead rope. "Gage told me Trixie rears up when startled." Dylan took Trixie's lead rope and attached a second lead to her halter. The mare seemed to be almost as wide as her torso was long. Her thin, gray-dappled, graceful legs were a contradiction to her bulk.

"Shouldn't we work with Chance?" Kathy asked.

"We will. As soon as the choir's done."

The old ladies were singing something about a beautiful morning. Their voices blended thinly, like small almost-harmonizing birds.

Dylan led the gray out, half his attention on the pregnant mare and half on his human charge. "We're going to take Trixie for a walk around the neighborhood and get her used to the sounds and smells of the place."

Kathy had taken off her gloves and held the flag very still. "You don't need me for that."

Smart girl. "Training, remember? Although I don't want you to do any of this alone until you have my blessing." Dylan stopped a few feet away from her, checking the pallor of her skin. She looked pale. There was a sheen to her skin, almost a sweatiness, the kind that he associated with a bad hangover or withdrawals. "Are you sure you're okay?"

"I'm fine." Her chin came up and he almost believed her.

Still, Dylan wasn't going anywhere until he was certain he knew what was bothering her. "Walk on the other side of Trixie and take this lead in your left hand."

"You know, up until a few weeks ago, I'd never been around horses other than the occasional trail ride." Kathy glanced up at the tall mare. "If she rears, I'm so short she's likely to pull me in the air."

"If she startles, step back and give her room on the rope, like this." Dylan took Kathy's small left hand. Her skin was soft, her fingers pliant beneath his. He leaned in closer, but she didn't smell of alcohol. The mystery remained. He positioned her hand at the end of the lead. "The backing-off part is important. I don't want you getting struck by a hoof."

She stepped back, eyeing Trixie warily.

He reclaimed the flag. Trixie had seen one before. She barely twitched an ear as it passed by her nose.

They set off at a brisk pace. He on the mare's left, Kathy on her right. Soon they were strolling down the middle of Main, between brick sidewalks and gas lamps. Traffic on the streets was sparse. Trixie's hooves and their boots echoed between the old brick buildings.

"You don't talk much, do you?" Kathy broke the silence between them.

"I'm a listener." He'd learned young that speaking often came with some form of retribution. And so, he'd watched and listened, measuring people by the sincerity of their words and their body language, just as he did with horses. He waited, but Kathy didn't take him up on his subtle invitation to listen to whatever was bothering her.

Loud bangs echoed in the distance. Trixie pranced, her baby bulge bumping against Dylan's shoulder.

"Easy, girl," Dylan soothed. He tightened his grip on the end of the rope, but didn't pull her head, and was pleased to note Kathy did the same. "That's good. Give her slack. Let her know we're not worried about those noises."

"My brother and his partners are building a wine cellar on the other side of the block." Kathy sounded odd, like she was being left out of things as a way of punishment. "The store they're building it in used to have all the pretty dresses for proms and weddings."

"I heard this was becoming a winery town. Are you involved in it at all?"

"No." There was definitely some resentment there, but it was mild, not seemingly the cause of Kathy's upset.

They approached the square, which was a big patch of grass with a large oak tree in the center and a wrought-iron bench beneath it. Leaves from bordering trees covered the grass like a brown carpet of snow. On one corner was a colorful Mexican restaurant, El Rosal, with sidewalk seating.

"Is that restaurant open?" The air was filled with spicy scents that enticed.

"Yes. If you're hungry, we just passed the small pizza place. It's practically all take-out. But El Rosal is where most people go to eat out. It's also the one grocery and the one bar in town." Kathy sighed. "I don't go in there."

Dylan wanted to see her expression but couldn't.

At the distant whir of a power saw, Trixie sidled sideways, crowding Dylan toward the curb with her baby bump.

Without yanking on the lead, Dylan waved the flag gently against her flank until the mare straightened her pace. "Why don't you go in El Rosal?"

"Remember me? The alcoholic?" There was a goodly amount of self-loathing in her voice.

Her pessimism bothered Dylan. Did she deserve the self-loathing? Or was she harder on herself than anyone else?

"It's too soon for me to risk it," Kathy was saying. "The other night I asked someone to go in and buy my son a candy bar." Her boots landed with a heavy cadence that contrasted against Trixie's graceful clip-clop.

Some people might have called that smart, but Kathy couldn't live her life hiding from every challenge. "Are you struggling to stay sober?"

"I'm struggling with life." Kathy spoke without humor or panic, without doubt or hope. She was in the disbelieving zone, an emotional stasis where she felt safe, like a rabbit hiding in a hole, too scared to emerge into the sunshine to eat fresh grass. "I had a great job before I screwed things up. I had a great relationship with my kid. And then..."

"You're scared." Dylan was so surprised he didn't phrase it as a question. How could she present herself so plainly, lay herself so bare to the world by telling everyone the mistakes she'd made, and still see traps around every corner?

"Wouldn't you be?" Her voice rasped with raw emotion and then dropped to a shaky, tenuous thread.

That fragility. That question. It was the exact opposite of Dylan's father's attitude. His father had been proud to call the demons in the bottle friends. "Yes, I'd be wary."

"When I lost control of the drinking, I didn't just let myself down. I let my son down." Kathy's words came without pretense, without packaging for public consumption. "Mothers are supposed to be...perfect."

"No one is perfect."

"Truman deserves a perfect mom!" Kathy yanked on the lead rope, causing Trixie to stop and toss her head. And because Kathy didn't stop pulling, the mare kept tossing her head.

Dylan crossed to Kathy's side of the horse and took her lead. "It's okay. It's okay." He wasn't sure whom he was comforting—the mare, Kathy or himself. "It's okay."

Kathy shook her head, sending shoulder-length red hair fluttering in the breeze. "I blew my life before I turned thirty. I blew it and now I feel as if the rest of my life is a dead end. Here. In Harmony Valley."

"Don't think that." Dylan shook his head. "Look at all you have going for you. A place to regroup, brains, beauty." He touched her forearm.

She cringed, as if his touch pained her physically. "I'm sorry, Dylan. I dumped all my problems on the ground at your feet. Anyway, I'm headed in the right direction. There are no more texts and…"

A baby blue, bubble-fendered Cadillac turned onto the far side of the town square, sped up and honked.

Trixie did a little dance, raising her front legs a foot off the ground.

Dylan stepped back and spoke meaningless, reassuring words, even as he led her over to the broad sidewalk out of the oncoming car's path.

"Have you ever been addicted to anything?" Kathy peered at him once he'd calmed the mare, blue eyes hopeful that he'd say yes. "You seem to know a lot about addiction and recovery."

Here was where Dylan should tell her who he was and what he did for a living. He should never have made that promise to Flynn. His deception was shaming in the face of her candor. It made him admit, "I learned some hard lessons from my dad." Like the nights when his dad came home drunk, kicked out of the bar for fighting, but with the fight still in him.

She turned away. "Then I shouldn't whine about my problems to you. I'm not saying you don't have your own perspective, but you can't understand what I'm going through."

Oh, he understood. He understood too well.

The trio of councilwomen was exiting the stables when Kathy and Dylan returned.

Kathy's wrist throbbed as regularly as the clop of Trixie's hooves. The day and its challenges stretched overwhelmingly ahead of her. She still had things to do around the clinic, plus Mr. Hammacker's dog to walk.

Mildred paused with her walker and patted Kathy's shoulder. "We had a good time singing to your horse."

"*Performing* for your horse," Rose muttered under her breath.

"It was like singing lullabies." Agnes had a cheerful delivery and an innocuous smile as she ribbed her friend. "Mildred very nearly fell asleep."

Mildred harrumphed and set her walker in motion again. "Race car drivers are like soldiers. We can catnap anywhere."

Agnes kissed Kathy's cheek. "We'd like to come back tomorrow. That is, if you and the horse whisperer agree."

"Can't hurt." Dylan led Trixie up the path toward the stable.

"I'll find the sheet music to *Annie Get Your Gun*." Rose did a series of kick-ball-changes toward the Buick and opened the door for Mildred.

"You could ask Mayor Larry to come by," Mildred told Kathy. "He loves listening to himself talk."

Kathy blew out a breath, feeling hopeful. How could Chance not improve with so much attention?

"The mayor is often busy." Agnes nodded at Dylan's retreating back. "Now, there's a man you can rely on."

"How can you tell?" Kathy hadn't had much experience with men, or with people she could trust, yet she couldn't disagree with Agnes' statement. There was something about Dylan that called to her like dark chocolate did to Becca.

"It's the way he stands." Agnes tilted her head. "Almost as if he's had to carry heavy burdens, but he could keep on carrying them. And his smile. Well, it's a bit wicked, isn't it? It tells you all you need to know."

Kathy hadn't noticed any wicked expression. She just noticed Dylan. She noticed him the same way she was aware of the sunshine warming her face or gentle rain landing on the roof or a monarch butterfly as it fluttered in the garden. He was there, and she appreciated his presence. There was nothing wicked or enticing about him.

And if she told herself that five more times until sundown, it would be true.

"We are going to be friends," Kathy said firmly, because Agnes was watching with dreams of romance sparkling in her eyes.

"Has he asked you out?" Agnes raised a silver brow. "The way he looks at you..."

"No." The thought sent a kaleidoscope of butterflies fluttering through her.

"Give it time," Agnes said sagely, heading toward her car.

After the ladies left, Kathy slowly completed her duties indoors. Cleaning cages and feeding and watering animals was challenging with a bum wrist, but not impossible. Nearly an hour later she headed toward the paddock, intending to shovel it clean.

Dylan had Sugar on a lunge line and was trotting her in a big circle in the paddock. He'd taken off his flannel shirt, revealing a forest green T-shirt and muscles. Plenty of intriguing muscles.

Not that she felt anything but a mild sense of appreciation, like a museum visitor enjoying her study of a bronze sculpture.

"Hey, Kathy." Dylan flashed that smile, the one she couldn't look away from. It wasn't wicked at all. "Want to take a turn?"

"No, thanks." Kathy slid her hands into her jacket pockets, providing support for her wrist. She'd barely held on to Trixie's lead. A lunge line? "Sugar would recognize an amateur. It took me a week to get her to trust me at all. She doesn't like change."

Dylan took his attention off the moving mare and met Kathy's gaze. There was an intensity in his gray eyes she hadn't experienced with anyone in a long time, as if he could see inside her soul, as if he wanted to know her secrets, as if he wanted...her.

An alarm rang through her veins.

"Sugar is misunderstood. Same as you." That grin. It spun a thread that spanned between them. One that beckoned: *trust me*.

Kathy stepped back, breaking the connection, denying the call. She didn't let people get close, especially men. Besides, what decent man would want to get close to a woman like her? "I don't date." The words came out with a shake and a tremor.

Dylan brought Sugar to a halt with a minimal flip of the lead and gave Kathy his full attention. If she'd thought his gaze was intent before, she'd been wrong. His gray-eyed stare held her in place. "What do you mean?"

The world was suddenly too silent, too still, too anticipatory. Sugar pawed the ground.

Kathy didn't feel as sure of her internal alarm as she had a moment before, but she defended herself anyway. "I told you how vulnerable I am. I'm not at a point in my life where I want to date." She glanced down at her cowboy boots, rumpled jeans and T-shirt, seeing instead leather boots, a black slinky miniskirt and a revealing tank top. The uniform of her youth. The red flag signifying trouble.

Dylan reeled in the lunge line and led Sugar over to her. "I can't remember making a pass at you or asking you out. Did we get our wires crossed?"

Her cheeks heated. A crow cackled in the eucalyptus.

"I'm a friendly guy. And animals..." Dylan rubbed the curve of Sugar's round cheekbone. "Animals can't hold up their end of the conversation. I'm a listener, remember? My apologies if you misread me."

Sugar huffed.

"Oops?" Kathy wanted to melt into a puddle and dribble away to the curb. "My bad?" Were her guy-reading skills that rusty? "How long did you say you'll be working here?" Suddenly, she desperately needed to know. Hopefully, he was only temporary.

"A long time." Dylan's smile softened all the hard, strong edges of his face. If Kathy hadn't been so embarrassed, she'd have told him to smile more often. "And you?"

"Longer." A life's sentence worth. "Harmony Valley is my safety net."

His smile disappeared. Such a shame. "You think you'll always need a safety net?"

"My brother, Flynn, thinks so." If Flynn didn't believe in her ability to stay away from the booze, why would Kathy believe she could? Even Becca couldn't resist her addiction. Kathy's first big test would be this afternoon at Mr. Hammacker's.

"Half the challenge of managing sobriety is being honest about it. You can't go wrong with honesty. And you, Red, have honesty in spades." Dylan reached across the paddock railing to tuck a lock of hair behind her ear. He paused, as if realizing what he'd done.

But his touch... His touch was electric. The air around them buzzed with tension. How had she felt no masculine vibes from him before today? He was... That smile...

And why was she feeling them now?

Because I have the worst luck.

But that didn't mean she'd let luck dictate her actions.

Kathy swallowed twice and stepped back, needing space and more than the paddock railing between them. "I feel the same way."

Dylan smile returned. This time there was a wicked slant to his lips. And just like Agnes said, it made Kathy think about kisses. His kisses.

Really? Who knew the man could have so many sides to a smile? Or that they'd send her thoughts in all the wrong directions?

"I feel the same way about honesty, I mean," she hastened to add before he got the wrong idea about what his touch did to her.

That wicked smile again. It arced between them like a ray beam intent upon destroying the hinge-lock on her knees. "You're gonna be all right, Red."

Not unless she kept her distance from this man.

She backed away and fled into the stable.

Chapter Eleven

K athy was a client.

Attractive, but a client nonetheless.

He'd touched her. And not just a handshake or a supportive squeeze of her hands. He'd touched her hair. He could still feel the silky texture of her red tresses between his fingers. Her bright blue eyes pierced his professionalism. Her hesitant smile made him want to draw her reassuringly close. And the dark circles under her eyes made him want to lie down with her in the tall grass, fold her in the shelter of his arms and encourage her to trust him with all her cares so she could rest.

None of which he'd act on. Because she was a client—an alcoholic still in the fragile state of recovery. But...he'd forgotten all that and touched her when he saw the uncertainty in her eyes.

Dylan wiped the sweat from Sugar's flanks with a towel and then brushed her down until her chestnut coat was dry and gleaming. All the while he couldn't stop thinking about Kathy.

He knew what his clients needed—the unvarnished truth and a patient ear. And he knew how to deliver it—with the same steady approach that he used on horses. Boundaries of respect. A kind word. Clear motives. Consistent behavior. He was adhering to all that with Kathy, except his truths were varnished. His motives unclear. A lie stood between them. He wasn't just here for the colt. He was here for her. And not because she needed kissing. Though heaven help him, he wanted to kiss her.

But he'd promised Flynn he'd carry out this charade and convince Kathy he was here for Chance. Speaking of the colt, he'd been avoiding working with him. He headed toward the stables with a weary limp, trying to hamstring his feelings toward Kathy.

She'd tied Isabo to a ring in the stable hall while she mucked the mare's stall.

"Need any help, Kathy?"

She startled and dropped her shovel, bending over and cradling her wrist.

"What's wrong?" Dylan was at her side almost immediately, taking her wrist gingerly in his hands and sliding back her coat sleeve. The bruise was hideous. Purple and red...and the size of a colt's hoof.

She'd put herself in danger. Something cold and hard stiffened his voice. "When did this happen?"

"This morning." She eased her wrist free.

Her sickly pallor had nothing to do with alcohol. Dylan should have felt relief. There was only frustration, tension because she'd endangered herself. "You went in *his* stall alone?"

I need to get her to a doctor.

Her pointed chin thrust out. "I clean his stall. I help change the bandages on his wounds. I..."

"You went in his stall alone?" Dylan went cold. The kick could just as easily have landed on her skull.

"Yes! Yes! I went in his stall alone this morning." Kathy's voice had that frantic, hollow note to it that admitted guilt while simultaneously conveying that she wouldn't do anything different next time.

"I told you he was dangerous." There was no mercy in Dylan's voice. No kindness. He'd seen a woman nearly die beneath a horse's hooves. He would not allow that to happen to her.

Kathy's features pinched. "It wasn't his fault. I...I tried to touch him."

"I told you..." Dylan held up a hand when she would have interrupted. "I'm trying to be helpful here. Let me finish."

She didn't. "Help the horse. Help Chance." There was a panicked note to her voice.

"Don't change the subject," he said, admiring her attempt to lift blame from the colt. "You should have said something to me or Gage right away."

"I didn't want to lose my job." Defensiveness morphed into misery. Everything about her drooped. "Or to abandon Chance."

The colt kicked the stall wall. They both glanced his way.

Done deal, that one. His father's sarcasm.

Dylan lowered his voice, for Chance's sake, for Kathy's sake, for his own sake. "I get a feeling sometimes about horses. If they don't respond, if they don't interact, I know I can't help them." He should have stopped there but he couldn't. "Do you have any idea what it's like to invest your time and emotion into a horse only to have him betray you on every level?"

"Yes." She held up her wrist.

She knows.

A part of Dylan that had felt separate and alone for years suddenly yearned to tell her things—about Phantom and betrayal and guilt. About risks he wasn't ready to take with his private life.

He pressed his lips together.

"This was my fault, not his," Kathy said. So certain. So determined not to be the reason Dylan didn't believe in Chance's rehabilitation.

He'd said those exact same words to Barry the day of Phantom's accident.

Dylan and Kathy were in an elite club together, bound by compassion and injury. He felt a bond form, one that she—as his client—could never be aware he felt.

Kathy poked his shoulder with her good hand. "You do *not* have a bad feeling about Chance. He's...he's..." Her gaze drifted around the stable. "How can you be nice to me and not him? He's a baby. A victim. I made bad choices with alcohol. But you seem able to overlook that. Why can't you see past Chance's scars?" Her desperate gaze landed on him. "You haven't really tried. What good is humming when he only has twenty days left?"

The clock was ticking for everyone.

Kathy slid her sleeve back in place and pushed the wheelbarrow out of Isabo's stall by balancing one handle against her stomach, dropping the wheelbarrow and swatting at him with her good hand when he would have taken the handles from her. Her load nearly tumbled to the ground. "I've got this."

"You don't have to do everything alone."

"Clearly, you don't know my brother. Flynn doesn't ever let me do anything for myself, except shovel poop." She set the wheelbarrow outside Isabo's stall and studied Dylan with the kind of detachment a wounded animal at rest used. "If he hears about this..."

Dylan brushed off her complaint, continuing to dig into her past. "Are you afraid of going to the doctor?"

"You want me to seek medical treatment?" Kathy nodded, showing him some of her determination. "All right. First you show me you deserve that miracle-working reputation Gage spoke so highly of. Prove it to me by working with Chance."

Dylan was afraid his miraculous touch was too rusty to make a difference in the colt's attitude. Fool that he was, he accepted Kathy's challenge anyway. With conditions, of course.

A few minutes later, Kathy had an ice pack on her wrist as she sat on the bench previously occupied by the trio of elderly singers. The veterinarians had been told of her injury and Gage had promised to look at her wrist soon.

"I want to go inside the stall with you, Dylan." Of course, Kathy did. Stubborn. She was so stubborn. She made mules look cooperative by comparison.

"You've lost your stall privileges until this colt minds his manners or you show some common sense." He took her injured hand, gently lifted it up and curled her fingers around her jacket collar. Then he took her hand holding the bag of ice and propped it just as gently on top of her swollen wrist. Their gazes met and bounced apart. There were pitfalls here, and not just in the colt's stall. He couldn't afford these feelings she created in him. "You need elevation and ice to reduce the swelling."

She made a huffing noise.

The colt kicked the wall.

Yeah, Kathy and Chance were unhappy. Deal with it.

Dylan took his training flag, a halter, lead rope and his resolve into the stall. The chestnut colt defended his turf, first with a high head, then by trying to get Dylan in his rear sights.

"Dude, that is so not happening." Dylan used the flag on the colt's flank, just a gentle wave, but one that herded the animal to the back of the stall.

Cornered, the colt's eyes rolled, eerily similar to Phantom's devil-like eye roll. His breath came and went in deep blows. His ears swiveled every which way.

"Easy, fella." Dylan tipped the flag slowly back and forth, the same way he'd done with Kathy. "It's just me."

Kathy started singing *Itsy Bitsy Spider* softly.

The colt's ears pricked.

"That's it. You like that song, don't you?" Dylan took the halter and rubbed it against the colt's withers, high above the stitches and claw marks on the front of his chest and lower neck where the mountain lion had attacked.

Chestnut legs went into action, propelling the colt past Dylan and in a circuit of the stall. Baseball-size hooves kicked up straw, then kicked the air where Dylan had been standing when he'd touched him. But Dylan had moved with the colt, following as if they were in a dance that the colt was leading.

Again, the colt stopped in a corner.

Again, Dylan brushed the halter against the colt, imprinting it strongly with his scent in case it hadn't been before.

Again, the kicking dance commenced. Straw motes filled the air, floating on the song Kathy kept singing.

"How've you been changing his bandages?" he asked in a whisper when Chance stopped.

"I offer him oats in a bucket. Gage puts the halter on. We hold him while Doc does the work."

Dylan gave the flag a pendulum swing. "So, he may not have ever had a halter put on him without trauma." Some of Far Turn's colts weren't halter broken until they were several months old.

"He's smart," Kathy told him, back still facing the stall. "He'll get this."

It might have been Kathy's hopes influencing what Dylan saw, but the colt's eyes didn't seem to roll quite as fearfully this time when he approached. "That's right, fella. You're ready for me to put this on, aren't you?"

He wasn't, of course. As soon as Dylan tried to circle his neck with his arms, Chance bucked and darted around the stall again.

Oats rustled in the hallway. The stall door slid open and closed behind Kathy. The colt raised his nose and sniffed.

Dylan kept his eyes on one hundred pounds of chestnut-covered energy. "Kathy, put the bucket down and get out."

"Not yet." Kathy's footsteps stopped in the straw behind him.

"I mean it." It was hard to whisper commands without sounding threatening. "Chance has to learn to be haltered without food."

"Put the halter on him now, while he's thinking about it." Kathy's voice was soft and hopeful. She believed in miracles. "I'll leave as soon as you have it on him."

What choice did he have? Dylan stepped forward and slid the halter on, easy as pie.

As promised, Kathy left.

The colt whinnied.

Outside, Sugar whinnied back.

And then the fun began again, but this time Dylan had the colt tethered. With the leverage of the lead and the distraction of the training flag, it took only a few minutes for the colt to calm.

"You are a miracle worker," Kathy whispered.

The colt startled at her words, but Dylan was ready.

"Don't be fooled, Kathy." Dylan reeled him in closer, soothing him by murmuring nonsensical words. "He's learning. He's not rehabilitated." They walked the perimeter of the stall until Chance's trembling stopped. Never taking his gaze off the colt, Dylan rubbed him behind his ears and along the unscarred curve of his neck and stroked him down his back. "He wouldn't let me do this if he wasn't spent." He walked him a little more. "You're about done for the day, aren't you, fella?"

The colt blew a raspberry. He truly was Sugar's baby. She was a character, too. "Kathy, now you can hand me the bucket of oats." He fed the colt and then removed the halter. The colt ambled to the center of the stall and looked at him. And in that look, a fire was reignited. Dylan raised the flag, just as the latch behind him opened. "Watch out!" he yelled as he moved between the colt and Kathy.

Her squeak. His sharp intake of breath as he waved the flag. The colt veering off, away from the door.

Dylan swung Kathy out like a sack of potatoes, quickly and without finesse. His heart beat like crazy.

His arms were still around her. His feet planted outside of hers. "You are the bravest, stupidest woman I've ever met." His words rose quick and sharp, and slapped against the rafters. "What were you thinking?"

Still in the circle of his arms, she stared up at him with a dazed look in her eyes. Maybe she was in shock. Maybe she wanted a kiss as much as he did.

Maybe I shouldn't keep holding her kissably close.

With effort, Dylan set her aside with tender care. His voice wasn't near as gentle. "You think that colt is a harmless baby? He's not."

A kick to the wall accented his point.

"That colt weighs nearly as much as you do. For Pete's sake, what were you thinking?" She hadn't spoken. Had the colt struck her again? Had he injured her when he manhandled his way to a rescue? "Say something."

"I was... I was..." Kathy shook her head. "No one's yelled at me like that since my grandfather died last summer. Flynn raises his voice, but he never yells at me."

Dylan was overcome with the urge to apologize. "I'm sorry. I'm an insensitive jerk."

"No. I think I needed it. Grandpa Ed was..." She gazed up at him with soft eyes. "He was kind of my hero, but I didn't realize it until too late. So, thank you."

"Excuse me?" She was thanking him for yelling at her? Eileen had hated it when he raised his voice.

"Since rehab, people tiptoe around me as if I'm breakable." Kathy's voice was as soft as a newborn colt's hide.

"You are breakable, Red. Just look at your wrist." Despite his need to be a detached professional, the beginnings of a smile tugged on his lips. Her honesty continued to amaze him.

"I learned my lesson, okay?" An answering smile twitched at the corners of her mouth. "Are you always like this?"

"Suave? Sophisticated?" he deadpanned, professionalism out the barn door, along with the tension of dealing with the colt.

"Bossy. Annoying." Kathy was quick with a comeback, but she softened it with that hint of a smile. "Much as I seem to enjoy talking to you—and I don't understand that at all..."

"I think I'm hurt. Really, really hurt." Dylan admired her spunk and her humor and...

He was becoming too admiring but he couldn't seem to stop himself.

"Why do I not believe you?" Her smile finally blossomed beneath sky blue eyes.

Whereas before her small smiles had made her pretty, her full smile bloomed on her face, stopping him like a field of wildflowers, making him forget his debt, Phantom and his tentative hold on his parental rights. There was only the shelter from the wind, the comforting smell of the stable and her smile.

For a moment, that was enough.

"Dylan is right. You shouldn't go into Chance's stall on your own." Gage wrapped Kathy's wrist in a bandage after Dylan left. "It looks like a bad sprain. Probably didn't help you went about your work today."

"I didn't want to admit I'd made a mistake." She gathered enough courage to ask, "You aren't going to fire me, are you?"

"No, but you need a week off, at least."

"I can't afford a week off." She was saving for the Reedley house. For rent, electricity and groceries.

"A week," Gage reiterated, using his no-arguments-I'm-a-doctor voice.

A dog in the back howled for her attention. At least, she liked to think so. Dylan would probably tell her she was reading too much into things. And she'd probably smile and tell him: *So what?* She'd seen there was hope for Chance today. And maybe, while Dylan had been yelling at her, she'd seen hope for herself, too. "There's a lot I can do with one hand, Gage."

Gage examined his work, then reached for a makeshift sling. "Use your one good hand to operate the remote on the TV at home. Flynn's been boasting about his big screen."

"It's not as big as what's going to go in Slade's mansion." One of Flynn's business partners was building a humongous home. He'd taken them on a tour of the freshly poured foundation last weekend. "I can still clean cages and walk dogs."

"You shouldn't."

"Let the girl do something," Doc rumbled in the doorway, long white strands of hair floating above his head as if he'd been rubbing a balloon on it. He set a fresh ice pack on Kathy's wrist. "Answering phones or singing to that colt."

Gage scowled. "Who's running this place?"

Kathy grinned at Doc, while Gage mumbled about meddlesome old dogs.

There was something on Kathy's mind, something that had been nagging her while she'd watched Dylan work with Chance. She had to ask. "Doc, what did you mean when you said Dylan used to be good?" She could have sworn Dylan had almost kissed her after Chance chased them out of the stall. And as far as she was concerned, she knew far too little about Dylan for him to make her heart pound and her brain think of kisses. She'd like to hear about his faults. She'd like to nip her attraction in the bud.

Okay, maybe she didn't want to nip it in the bud, but she needed to.

The two vets exchanged looks.

"You know Far Turn Farms is our largest client." Gage spoke slowly, as if choosing his words carefully. "They breed and train racehorses. They've always brought their horses for deliveries to the clinics where I work." He put away the wrap and scissors. "Dylan used to work there, too, helping horses achieve optimal performance by being calm on race day."

Kathy could see Dylan walking a racehorse toward the track, humming *Itsy Bitsy Spider*, drawing every woman's eye.

"One day they were collecting semen from their main stud, Phantom, when something went wrong and..." Gage's voice trailed off, and the exam room suddenly felt as bleak as the morgue.

The story was taken up by Doc. "Instead of mounting the padded dummy mare, the stallion reared up and struck the vet tech."

"Awful head wound. Temporary, partial paralysis." Gage's voice was as hushed as if he spoke in a crowded church awaiting the start of the sermon. He'd shared some of his horse-injury stories with her before. Those had been related with equal parts drama and pride. This tale was told grimly. "Lucky for the attending vet, his forehead was only grazed. Dylan was kicked in the knee. Still, he managed to get the stallion under control. Perhaps quicker than some might have done." This last came out slower still, as if Gage was reluctant to give Dylan praise.

The damage the colt had done today was nothing compared to the damage Phantom had wrought. Now Dylan's attitude toward Chance made sense. "A killer," Kathy murmured. "That's what Dylan said when he first saw Chance." And that the colt had a certain look in his eye he didn't like.

Doc made all sorts of disapproving noises.

"I don't believe Chance would do something as severe as what Phantom did." But Gage frowned at her wrist and Kathy was no longer sure.

"Do you think Dylan is...?" She almost said scared, but the word didn't seem to fit. "Do you think Dylan has lost his nerve?" She didn't believe that, either, but...

"Enough of this. Who's to say what's in a man's heart? It's almost three thirty and you promised to help us clip that rottweiler's toenails at five. Takes four of us to hold him down." Doc's white eyebrows waggled. He knew exactly where she was supposed to be at three thirty. "Get out of here."

She'd almost forgotten that temptation needed to be faced.

Kathy swallowed, gathered her courage and hurried off to Mr. Hammacker's house.

When she got there, the door was open and she rushed inside, breathless and on time.

"What's wrong with your arm?" Mr. Hammacker's voice was as sharp as his gaze.

Kathy breathed easier. Maybe she'd imagined the liquor on his breath yesterday. "It's just a sprain." Kathy hurried to clip Dolly's leash on her. "I'll bring her back on time."

Dolly waddled outside, gave a little whine at the end of the walkway and plopped to the ground.

"Oh, man." A voice emanated from within the bushes. A young, familiar voice. Truman's.

Kathy wanted to laugh. Truman was following her. The joyous feeling almost made up for the throbbing in her wrist.

But then she realized how far her son was from home, presumably alone. He'd been out here yesterday, too. She should have been paying more attention to what Truman said every night. It all came back to her. Bea's goats, whom Truman had been visiting, were nearly a mile up the road. Felix and his rescued kittens lived several blocks over. But what could Kathy do? She wasn't going to confront Truman when he was hiding. He'd just run away.

"Come on, girl." Kathy helped the roly-poly dachshund to her feet. They began their walk.

Truman followed. And she might not have known it, except Dolly was a nervous Nellie who kept glancing back and growling as she waddled down the street.

"Should we wait for him at the corner, Dolly?"

Truman was hiding behind the tall hedge on the house formerly owned by the Reedleys.

Dolly grumbled, sounding very similar to Doc.

"I don't want to do it, either, but he needs to know he's not invisible and he shouldn't be over here alone."

They rounded the hedge-trimmed corner onto the town square. Kathy sat on the curb midblock. Dolly flopped next to her with a grunt, staring back the way they'd come.

"I know you're there, Tru," Kathy called when it became apparent Truman wasn't going to show himself. "I'm going home after this, and you'd better be there." Or what? She hadn't parented in so long she didn't know.

Footsteps pounded on pavement, moving away from her.

Kathy doubted she'd be in the running for mother of the year. But at least she'd done some parenting today.

She and Dolly continued around the block. But it took Kathy an extra minute or two once they reached Mr. Hammacker's driveway to work up the nerve to go inside.

Had Dylan felt like this before he'd gone into Chance's stall? Recalling his normally unflustered gray eyes and calm expression, she gathered her courage and marched to the front door.

"We're back."

Dolly managed to make it across the carpet to her master before she collapsed.

Mr. Hammacker held a ten-dollar bill in his hand. "Thank you. I'll see you tomorrow."

She might have imagined his eyes were bloodshot. She might have imagined she smelled alcohol in the room. She certainly imagined lifting a shot glass to her lips. And she definitely could picture Truman's sullen expression when he found out she'd done so.

Kathy approached Mr. Hammacker on shaky legs. A waft of alcohol reached her, tantalizing and terrifying. She snatched the bill and fled, nearly as fast as Truman had. She was still shaking when she reached the clinic.

Chapter Twelve

Wilson needed a drink. Another one.

His schedule was all screwed up. Becca would be here soon.

But it wasn't his schedule that had him tense and craving. It was Kathy. He needed to call Warren and let him know things weren't working out. Except if he did that, wouldn't he or Kathy have to tell the old vet why things weren't good between them?

He scooted out of his chair and stood without toes, real or plastic. He waddled to the kitchen much as he imagined a duck would, on heels, feet splayed. He had his hand on the cabinet door when someone knocked.

"Kathy?" Had she returned to confront him about his drinking? Or to ask him for a drink? He'd give her one in exchange for her silence.

Wilson. Helen's voice. Disapproving.

He waddled back to the living room, Dolly trailing behind him, and opened the door. "Kathy, I..."

Mayor Larry stood on his doorstep, wearing a purple tie-dyed bowling shirt and a pair of khaki cargo shorts. Did the man never recognize the changing of the seasons? It was fifty-five degrees out today. "Wilson, we need a fourth on the bowling team."

Wilson's gaze dropped down to the balls of his feet. "Uh."

Dolly plopped down, resting her head on the arch of his foot.

The mayor must not have had his hearing aids in. He ignored Wilson's hesitation. "I took Takata to lunch today and he moved his walker too quickly.

Sprained his wrist." Mayor Larry was an avid bowler, a competitive bowler. He spent most nights on the lanes in Cloverdale. "We made a bet with the winery team and tonight's match has a lot riding on it."

"Uh." Wilson grabbed a chair and shuffled his feet.

Hello? If you haven't noticed, I have no toes.

He couldn't manage to say the words out loud.

"I thought we were done for. Flynn, Slade, Will, and now Gage? Those young bucks are a challenge." The mayor moved into the foyer and slapped Wilson on the back, hard enough to shake his balance. "And then I remembered how you and Helen won the couples tournament a few years back. You have skills, man. Much-needed skills."

"I, uh..."

Becca came up the walk. "Larry, don't tell me you're so desperate that you're trying to recruit Wilson. I can't get him to stroll around the block, much less bowl." She greeted the hippie mayor with a kiss to his cheek. "You are doomed, sir. Doomed. My husband and his friends will annihilate you on the lanes."

The mayor rubbed his chin. "There's got to be someone in town who can bowl."

Wilson had been a darn good bowler in his day. He'd been good at many things—sports, swinging a hammer, gardening.

"So, I'm worthless now, am I?" Wilson said, anger filling him. His schedule. His secret. His manhood. "Not good for anything? Not even walking the dog?"

"You said it, not me." Becca kissed his cheek as she passed him. "If you can't walk your own dog, you certainly can't bowl. That requires twinkle toes, real or plastic."

"I'm not dead yet," Wilson grumbled.

Mayor Larry finally took a gander at his feet. "Oh, hey. We might want to rethink recruiting you."

Becca laughed as she rummaged for a tester and a test strip. "You've got no one left but Wilson. You'll have to forfeit."

His sound mind. His almost intact body. And these two were treating Wilson as if he was insignificant? He'd been the head engineer at the mill!

Wilson pounded the chair-back. "Where are my toes?"

"Huh?" It was the mayor's turn to be flummoxed.

"My toes. My prosthetics. Where are they?" Wilson jabbed a finger in Becca's direction. "Did you hide them?"

"No. They're probably where you left them last, draped over the magazine stand by your chair." She checked, holding up the plastic slipper toes. "Yep. Cast aside because you don't need them. Ever."

Wilson did the duck walk to his recliner. Dolly trotted ahead of him. "Let's get this blood-sugar testing over with."

She crossed her arms. "Why the rush?"

"Because...because..." Darn if Wilson hadn't backed himself into a corner. He didn't want to bowl. He just wanted to not be considered weak. He was a man, and at his age and state that was getting harder to remember. "Because I can do it. And I'll prove it. Give me those." He snatched the prosthetic toes from Becca's hands and began putting them on.

Bent over, he couldn't see Becca and Mayor Larry exchange satisfied smiles.

Chapter Thirteen

The more Kathy thought about her eight-year-old son running about town unsupervised, the more upset she got.

Truman had the run of the town. Even in somewhere as isolated and sleepy as Harmony Valley, that wasn't right. He shouldn't be allowed this much freedom.

It was time Kathy pulled on her mom jeans and laid down the law.

Truman sat at the kitchen table with a schoolbook open. He didn't look up when Kathy came in. His red hair was tousled and his cheeks were red, the way they got when he was upset.

Abby lapped water in the kitchen, where Becca was making peanut-butter cookies.

"I'm glad you're both here." Kathy collapsed into a kitchen chair, spent after her long and emotional day. Her wrist was throbbing again. And every time she thought about alcohol and Mr. Hammacker, her body stiffened, her movements grew jerky, and she felt as if she might shatter. "We need to have a family meeting."

Truman leaned his forehead onto his hand, covering his eyes. "Uncle Flynn isn't here."

"Your mother's here. And your aunt." Kathy would not be dissuaded.

Becca scooped peanut butter into the bowl and then came to join them at the table. "What's up?" She had a dusting of flour on one side of her nose. On Becca, it looked like the most natural of accents. She scratched her forearm, covered in a long-sleeve T-shirt. Then she noticed Kathy's sling. "Oh, my gosh. What happened to your arm?"

Truman gave Kathy's sling a sideways glance.

"I was kicked by the colt."

For a blink or two, Truman looked impressed.

Yeah, your mom's hardcore.

"Can I do anything? Get you anything? Did you see a doctor?" Becca was always good in a crisis.

"I saw a vet. I'll get an ice pack when we're done talking." Kathy kept her voice even. "Boundaries are on the agenda today. Truman has been unsupervised all over town."

Truman stared at his math book. Although it was a second-grade math book, Kathy was tempted to take a peek to see if there were any sensible word problems inside.

"When he's not with me making calls..." Becca glanced from one to the other. A lightbulb moment must have dawned, for she paused and rephrased. "He knows he can't go beyond the town square on one side of the river and Will's house on this side unless he asks."

"That's too far. He's only eight." Grandpa Ed would have raised his voice like a drill sergeant to get his point across. Kathy chose to channel Agnes's rational tones. "And he goes much farther than the boundaries you've set."

Truman's chin jutted out.

"He acts older than his age," Becca admitted, studying Truman. "We've probably let him have more than his share of independence because he's so responsible."

Kathy knew how responsible her son had been when she'd been drinking, but that didn't mean he could do anything he wanted.

"Everyone around town dotes on him," Becca was saying. "And he has a cell phone in case of emergencies."

Truman thunked his forehead with his palm. He knew Kathy's opinion of cell phones.

"You gave my son—*an eight-year-old*—a cell phone?" Kathy tried so hard to keep the anger from her voice that her words sounded cold and automated. "We need to reevaluate more than Truman's limits here."

"Normally, I'd be right there with you." Becca, always so calm and reasonable. "But he isn't often on his own. Maybe an hour or two a day…" Becca sat back in what might almost have been amazement. "Oh, that doesn't sound good, does it?"

"No." Kathy felt as if a herd of elephants was stomping its way across her chest and out through her wrist. She held out her uninjured hand. "Truman, give me your phone."

Truman didn't look at her. "Aunt Becca?"

"Do not ask her for permission, young man. Hand it over."

Reluctantly, he did. It was an iPhone—an iPhone! Kathy was going to have words with Mr. Technology, aka her brother, Flynn, when he got home.

Kathy powered off the phone and shoved it aside as if it had germs. "When I took the job at the clinic, you and Flynn agreed to watch Truman while I was at work."

Becca nodded. "I'm sorry. It's just things have been getting crazy here, what with Flynn working late on their new app and my growing number of clients. I'm not normally so…irresponsible." She scratched her arm again.

Kathy held up a hand. "As Truman's mom, I insist that he can't go across the river without telling an adult. And he can't go visit people across town by himself. You may think Harmony Valley is a safe place, but not everyone can be trusted."

The urge to drop Mr. Hammacker's name into the conversation was powerful. Did that man drink and drive?

"I don't need your rules." Truman pushed away from the table and ran down the hall, Abby trotting at his heels. "You ruin everything. Everything!" He slammed his door with house-shaking intensity.

"I'm sorry." Becca laid her hand over Kathy's. "Flynn said every kid in town ran around free when he was growing up."

Kathy sighed. "We did have free rein, but as you know, the world is a different place, even here in Harmony Valley." Kathy stood and followed Truman down the hall. She knocked once on her son's door and then pushed it open.

Truman lay face-down on the bed. Abby was curled into a ball at his side. "Go away."

Kathy closed the door and leaned against it. "I'm not going anywhere, Tru. It's time to get used to that fact. I'm back and I plan to stay sober. For good."

"I don't believe you."

Oh, how his words hurt.

"I'm not asking you to, honey. I'm very aware that I have a lot to prove before you can trust me again. But I have a plan as to how we're going to move forward from here." She sighed and slid to the floor, elevating her wrist. Hadn't Dylan mentioned his father was a drinker? Maybe he had some advice for her from a child's perspective, assuming his drunken-parent upbringing had been better than hers. "I'm going to start online college courses after Christmas." Kathy wished she was more excited about bettering herself. "Once I have a degree, we'll be moving to wherever I get a job. For now, we'll stay here with Flynn and Becca, if we can all get along. And when I say 'we,' I mean you and me."

She didn't mention the Reedley house. It would just upset him.

"I like it here." Truman's voice was muffled in the pillow. Abby nudged Truman's arm with her black nose. "I like having a cell phone."

Kathy had turned off her cell phone the day she'd entered rehab. She hadn't turned it back on since. "Do you remember the book about the mouse and the cookie?"

"No." His response was too fast to be believed.

"I loved that book." Kathy could use a dose of the chipper, friendly mouse right about now. "Grandpa Ed used to say if there was mischief to be found that I'd find it. Just like that mouse."

Truman drew a shuddering breath.

"I think you're the same way, Tru. It's why I don't want you running around town alone." That and the fact that if Mr. Hammacker had a drinking problem no one knew about, there was no telling what secrets other residents were hiding.

"I have Abby. She protects me."

"Abby can't tell you what's safe and what isn't. Abby is full of mischief herself." That wasn't exactly true. Abby had been bred to herd animals. She often circled Truman and stopped him from going anywhere she didn't think he should.

He snuffled words into the pillow. It sounded like, "I'm staying here."

"I love you, Tru. I'm your mother. Where I go, you go. Someday I'll prove to you that I'm worthy of your love." She'd get a really good job and be able to provide him with all the things Flynn and Becca did. But not a cell phone. Never a cell phone. And to do all that, she needed to resist the drink at Mr. Hammacker's house. "When you're older, I hope you'll understand. And I hope you'll forgive me."

Chapter Fourteen

Wilson lumbered into his house at eight thirty.

His schedule was blown, but he hadn't cared, not until he walked in the door to the empty house with only the kitchen light on. He'd had fun. The four men had talked about the new winery in town, grandkids, and politics. They'd talked smack with the young men who owned the winery—Will, Flynn and Slade. The young vet, Gage Jamero, had made up the other team's fourth.

Wilson couldn't remember the last time he'd felt like one of the guys.

Yes, he'd thrown some gutter balls. But he'd also got a couple of strikes.

Yes, they'd lost. But he hadn't fallen in the lane. Not so much as a noticeable stumble.

He felt triumphant. The king returning home to his castle. A quiet, empty castle.

Dolly greeted him with a wag of her tail and a sweet little whine. She trotted into the kitchen and showed him her empty dog dish.

"I forgot to feed you. Unforgivable." He bent to pick up her bowl, lost his balance and stumbled forward, hitting his head on the cabinet door. He dropped to all fours.

Dolly rose up on two legs to give him kisses.

His temple throbbed where he'd hit the wood, but there was no blood. He got to his knees and filled Dolly's dish. He got to his feet and wobbled, hanging on to the faux-granite countertops that Helen had installed two years ago, white with brown striations like a road map.

"I'm fine." He shuffled his feet to steady himself. For some reason, he wasn't as solid on his feet as he should be.

Oh, yeah. No toes.

Dolly's vote of confidence came in the form of appearing as if nothing was wrong and crunching her kibble.

But there was something wrong.

Wilson fell backward and hit his head on the opposite wall.

Chapter Fifteen

"That was Mayor Larry." Becca came running down the hall toward the front door, clutching her cell phone. "He checked on Wilson after he dropped Takata off because there were no lights on in the living room and Wilson had said he was going to watch the Stanford football game. Wilson fell and hit his head."

Kathy was willing to bet the old man had been drinking. She stood. "I'll go with you."

Becca was sliding into her jacket. She paused, gaze cutting to Kathy. "Really?"

"Yes, really. I'm sure you've heard. I'm his dog walker. I'm worried." Kathy grabbed her coat. "You stay here with Truman," she said when Flynn started to get up.

Truman had recently gone to bed. She and Flynn had been watching the Stanford football game since he'd returned from bowling.

Becca drove both of them in Flynn's big, black truck. "I feel responsible."

"Becca, the man fell down. He has no toes. How can this possibly be your fault?" Especially if he'd been drinking.

"Mayor Larry and I tricked him into going bowling tonight," Becca admitted. "His leg muscles are weak from all that sitting. He could have had a leg spasm or..."

"He could have just mis-stepped." Because he'd been drinking. Kathy should tell Becca about the booze. Except what if he hadn't been drinking? What if it really was Becca's fault? "You're not perfect."

"Apologies if that's the kind of wife you wanted Flynn to marry." There was hurt in Becca's voice, the kind that called for an apology.

"I wanted him to marry somebody real, which is you," Kathy admitted. "I was afraid he'd fall for one of those plastic women who wear layers of makeup and Spanx even when they're a size zero."

"Thank goodness I forgot to put on makeup today and that my chocolate addiction prevents me from being waif thin." Becca parked in front of Wilson's house, giving Kathy a very real smile. There were several vehicles already there. "Looks like Mayor Larry called in the troops. Agnes. Felix." The latter of which used to be the town's fire chief and had medical experience.

Mr. Hammacker tossed his hands at the sight of them. He wore a purple tie-dyed bowling shirt that was a size too small. The buttons strained across his belly. "Why does everyone want to see a man at his lowest point? Can't I have a little stumble without all the fuss?"

Becca demanded to know what had happened but in that caring way of hers.

While Felix and the mayor briefed her, Kathy knelt next to Mr. Hammacker's recliner, checking out his eyes and trying to sniff as if she was a hound dog searching for the scent of rabbit.

"The answer is no," Wilson grumped, gingerly touching a small bump on his bald head.

No as in he hadn't been drinking? "But earlier..."

"That was much earlier," he whispered. "I was with the boys all night at the bowling alley. Not a drop since you left."

Clear eyes. No alcohol on his breath. No slurred speech. Maybe his fall was Becca's fault.

Kathy laughed nervously.

"What are you two talking about?" Agnes wore bright yellow leggings under a long sweatshirt with a puffy turkey on the front. The gobbler's feathers flopped forward as if he was tired.

Kathy glanced down at her blue jeans and plain white T-shirt. There was just something about living in a town of grandparents that made a person feel better about their fashion choices. She laughed a little again. This time, it came easier.

"I was asking Kathy on a date," Mr. Hammacker deadpanned to Agnes. "She's my dog walker. What do you think we were talking about?" He raised his voice. "It's time for everyone to leave."

There was a chorus of *"I'll stay with you."*

Kathy was surprised that hers was one of the many voices. The booze in the house had silenced its siren call because the old man hadn't been drinking when he'd lost his balance.

"Felix may stay," Mr. Hammacker said with finality. "The rest of you get out."

Felix was a big, wide man with a florid complexion and a layer of what looked like cat hair on the front of his black jacket, reminding Kathy that he rescued cats as well as senior citizens.

"You may go, Kathy," Mr. Hammacker said as gently as a schoolteacher releasing her to recess for good behavior.

"But..." She wasn't sure what she was going to say. *Felix needs to know about your drinking? Everyone needs to know you're a lush?* Neither seemed appropriate.

"Come back Monday to walk Dolly."

Kathy didn't want to. It would ease her mind to be fired.

But she couldn't turn him down—she couldn't turn her back on him and Dolly. She just hoped the booze in the house would continue to leave her alone.

Chapter Sixteen

There was hope yet.

"You like getting exercise, don't you, boy?" Dylan had Phantom on a lunge line, trotting around the paddock. He brought the big black stallion to a halt and led him over to where Barry was waiting for him with brushes and an encouraging word.

Phantom tried to run Dylan over only once before they reached the paddock railing.

"He's coming along," Barry said approvingly. "Why don't you work him a bit longer?"

The fog was thick and floated above them as if it planned to stay all day.

"The blacksmith is due at ten, and Zach is supposed to be here around nine." Dylan tied Phantom to the rail, pushing him back with a firm slap to his withers when he tried to sandwich him into the rails.

"It's already nine thirty," Barry pointed out.

The first hints of unease settled in Dylan's gut. He ignored it. "Maybe there was traffic."

"Maybe." Barry offered the stallion a piece of carrot. "When do you think Phantom will be ready to make a deposit? I had several calls this week wanting his goods."

The unease returned for a different reason. "I'll need to hire someone to help." He began brushing Phantom's ebony withers. With each stroke, he felt the black stallion's muscles relaxing.

"What do you need to hire someone for? You've got me." The affront in the old jockey's voice was palpable. Unfortunately, he chose that moment to shift his feet. He nearly stumbled on a pebble. "Unless you're saying you don't think I can handle him. I'll have you know I rode bigger, nastier horses in my day."

"It's not your balance in the saddle I'm questioning, but your balance on dry land." Dylan brushed his way to Phantom's haunches. "I could ask Gage Jamero to come down."

"The pregnant-mare whisperer?" Barry scoffed. "Stallions are entirely different beasts."

"I tend to agree, but since I don't understand why Phantom attacked last time, I want to bring in some brains with muscle. We need to be more careful this time." He didn't want Barry or anyone else to be hurt.

"A stallion in the throes of passion is like a shark in a pool of guppies. He doesn't discriminate on what he wants to dominate."

"Or where his hooves go." Dylan limped around to the other side, putting a shine on Phantom's coat as hadn't been seen in months. "Emily wore perfume that day."

"Who wears perfume around animals?"

Kathy. Dylan's gut knotted.

"Do you want me to saddle Phantom up after the blacksmith comes? He's probably still got too much pent-up energy. I'd be mad as all get-out, too, after being cooped up for months."

What a recipe for disaster. Dylan shook his head. "You're not getting on him."

"You're as bad as Far Turn Farms. He's not a killer. He's..."

"Misunderstood. Yeah, yeah. I know." The last thing Dylan needed was Phantom taking Barry for a ride. "It's the insurance that kills horses like him. Once a horse has injured somebody, those premiums skyrocket. Don't blame Far Turn for wanting to reduce their overhead."

"Did your premiums go up?"

"I haven't told my insurance company about him yet." Not out of any desire to pull a fast one, but because he'd been torn once Phantom showed up looking like the devil and had spent the next few months reconsidering keeping him.

"Which is why I don't want anyone other than me in harm's way. I'll add him to my policy if we can complete a collection safely." He finished brushing Phantom down. "All right. That should do until the blacksmith comes."

Phantom tugged the tie-down, and when that held, he stepped sideways to squish Dylan against the paddock rails again.

"Easy boy." Dylan gave his haunches a shove. "You liked me thirty seconds ago." He stroked a brush down his long neck.

The stallion stilled.

Barry laughed. "It's like rubbing a puppy's belly."

Dylan's heart was pounding for a variety of reasons. There was adrenaline and excitement and a sense of rightness. He'd been meant to work with challenging horses, not docile ponies like Peaches or worn-out brood mares like Maui. For six months, something had been missing from his life. He'd finally figured out what that was.

This, his heart sang. *This*, his limbs surged with energy. *This*, his brain registered the flick of the stallion's tail, the forward slant of his ears, the rate at which the stallion sucked in air. "We can make this work."

And because he was full of contradictions, Phantom turned his head and bit Dylan's shoulder.

Kathy sat in a plastic chair on the back porch of Grandpa Ed's house on Saturday morning.

She was bundled in her jacket and had her teal leopard-print comforter over her legs. Her coffee was hot, exactly the way she liked it. And the sun was just beginning to slice through the fog toward the river. If only the pain in her wrist hadn't given her a restless night's sleep.

"Want some company?" Flynn pulled up a chair near hers, holding an extra-large coffee mug. "You're looking ragged around the edges."

"It's my wrist. I'm not tempted to drink." She slipped that in to cut off Flynn's daily interrogation.

They each paid homage to their caffeine.

Despite her progress report, Flynn didn't let up on his usual morning inquisition. He just took a new tack. "Penny for your thoughts."

"You're a millionaire. You can afford to pay more than a penny." She liked teasing him. It reminded her of old times in this house.

"More than a penny? Slade would get on my case for spending irresponsibly." Slade was a former Wall Street guru, Flynn's close friend, and one of his business partners.

They sat silently, enjoying the view of the river. Birds sang. Truman's voice drifted to them from the other side of the wall.

Grandpa Ed had loved mornings like this. He'd claimed sitting and drinking his coffee while watching the river was the best way to clear his head. And Kathy was sure ready for her head to be clear of worries and uncertainties.

But who could dwell on their worries when there was a brother in need of teasing. "You want to know what's on my mind? A cell phone? For an eight-year-old?" Kathy rolled her head sideways to give her brother the stink eye.

He shrugged in that unapologetic way most brothers mastered early on in life. "It seemed the right solution at the time. Becca was stressed and it made her less so."

"And you didn't think to tell me. I sense a let's-not-tell-Kathy theme." He hadn't told her Grandpa Ed was dying. He hadn't told her he was eloping. Okay, so maybe she'd been in rehab without a phone and in lockdown both times, but still.

He settled back in his chair, cradling his mug on his chest. "You can't fault my motives."

"I'm your sister. By law, I have to find fault with you." She sipped her coffee. "What else aren't you telling me? Bun in the oven? Another million in the bank? Oh, I know. You bought me a house and started a college fund for Truman."

Her big brother had a tell, a twitch of the cheek beneath his right eye. Said cheek twitched.

"You started a college fund for Tru?" She clutched the comforter instead of wringing his neck. "Or is it worse? Did you prepay his tuition to Stanford?" She wouldn't put anything past him.

"I haven't done any of those things, but if I had, wouldn't you deserve them?" Flynn's voice was equal parts tease and seriousness and affection. "To make up for what she did?"

Kathy looked toward the river. "I don't want to talk about her." Their mother.

"She doesn't deserve more than a passing thought from you, Kath." He ruffled her hair as if she was once more that scared toddler in need of reassurance. "Back then, she barely remembered she had children. As kids, we were more like parents to her than she ever was to us. But I feel as if I need to know she's alive."

Kathy closed her eyes. "I don't want to talk about her. Contrary to what you believe, I don't think about her much." Only the bad parts. And only on bad days. The days when she feared she'd acted too much like her mother when she'd been drunk. She bowed her head. "I was no better than she was."

"You were better." Flynn's hand covered hers. "You didn't lock Truman up. You didn't leave him to go carousing. You didn't let him go hungry. You brought him here."

She wanted to believe him, oh, how she wanted to believe him. "Tru hates me all the same."

"It's just a rough patch." Flynn squeezed her hand tight. "Besides, you have something she never had, Kath."

She opened her eyes and met Flynn's gaze wearily. "What?"

"Heart."

Dylan had been bit, kicked, stepped on, blanked on his son's visitation and had all his afternoon appointments cancel.

He was beat up emotionally and physically. It was time for a change of goals, venue and luck.

"What are you doing here?" Dylan asked when he saw Kathy at the clinic late Saturday afternoon. Though in all honesty, he'd been hoping he'd see her—because he was paid to, of course...or that was what he told himself. But he hadn't *expected* to see her.

Kathy walked a yellow Labrador with a cone on its head through the back gate toward the road. "I needed to get out of the house, and somebody had to sing to Chance today anyway. The town council is at the Home and Garden show in Santa Rosa." The dark circles under her eyes had deepened and made her look like an outfielder on a baseball team.

"Want some company?" Dylan had been about to go into the stable with the colt, but Kathy looked in need of some TLC.

"You may not have noticed, but this is a dog, not a horse." Without waiting to see if he'd follow, she headed toward downtown at a good clip. "I can handle a dog unsupervised."

The fog hung lower in the foothills surrounding Harmony Valley than down on the Double R, tingeing everything gray, including Kathy's complexion.

Despite her protests, Dylan fell into step with her. "How's that wrist?"

"Better." She held it up in its sling. "I can see my wrist bones today. Truman would never admit it, but he thinks the way I got my bruise is awesome. Not to mention it's deep, deep color."

"Boys enjoy the sight of blood." Men knew the danger blood presented. "Maybe I can show him my bruises." He smiled and waggled his eyebrows, upping the cheese factor. He'd discovered that the key to Kathy was engaging her humor.

She slanted a speculative glance his way. "Recent ones?"

"Yep. I've been working with a horse named Phantom. Wanna see?"

She paused, as if needing a moment to put information together, before blinking and smiling. "Do I look like a boy?"

Does she know about Phantom?

He didn't think so. "You don't look like a boy. Not even remotely, Red." Not on her worst day.

Her cheeks bloomed an attractive pink. "Oh, all right." She pulled up short at the corner of Main Street, telling the dog to sit. "Go for the glory and show me."

Dylan held up a hand. The second knuckle on his little finger was black-and-blue. "The blacksmith came today. I got kicked."

"In your pinkie? That barely qualifies as boy gore." She stared him down.

Oh, this is fun.

"It's swollen and nasty-looking." He'd expected a little sympathy. Not this ribbing.

"I have an older brother. You'll have to do better than that if you want to impress me." Along with the color in her cheeks, some of her trademark spunk was back.

"Red, I promise you I can gross you out more than your brother ever did." He sat on the curb, yanked off his right cowboy boot and sock and showed her the hoofprint on the top of his foot. It matched the print on her wrist, only his was bigger. "I know I don't have the prettiest toes in the world, but when you accessorize it with a horse-stomping bruise, my foot looks disgusting."

She yawned. *Yawned!*

The dog bumped Dylan with his cone in a quest to sniff his boot-perfumed feet.

This had gone beyond distraction and trust building. Dylan's pride was at stake. He yanked his footwear back on.

"Nice hole in that sock," she said.

It was small as holes went. "Bachelor Code. Never throw a sock away until your big toe fits through it."

She tried very hard not to smile. She had to bite her lip.

He stood, not done trying to gross her out. He unzipped his vest jacket, unbuttoned his blue flannel shirt, spread the shirttails.

"Whoa, cowboy. I didn't ask for a striptease." She hid her face behind her good arm. But she was definitely smiling.

"It's the pièce de résistance." He tugged the neck of his T-shirt down over his shoulder, revealing teeth-marked bruises on both sides of the joint.

She leaned closer to look, bringing the scent of wildflowers and hay. "Okay, I admit. You're officially tough enough to play professional football."

There was no sympathy, no awe, no gasping disgust. Dylan felt as if he'd just completed the game-winning touchdown pass, only to be told the most valuable player was his offensive lineman. "Yeah, I'm tough. But it'll be hard to sleep tonight when everything starts throbbing." Middle-of-the-night pain flare-up. That always seemed to happen with his bruises. He straightened his clothing. "Did the pain in your wrist keep you up last night?"

She encouraged the dog to its feet. "Tell you what. I won't ask you how my butt looks in these pants if you don't ask me why I look like death warmed over."

"Fair enough." He took the flanking approach. "What's up with your furry, cone-headed friend?"

"Snip-snip." Kathy flexed two of her fingers like scissors. "No more bachelorhood for Cody."

The dog's tail wagged happily upon hearing his name.

"He doesn't seem devastated."

"He's still on his happy meds." She glanced sideways at Dylan. He was getting fond of that mischievous look. "I'm only taking him around the block. He's not going to hurt me."

"Meaning you'd rather not have company." Her silence confirmed it. "Do you like being alone?"

"No. I just want to be left alone." There was a fragility to her voice that convinced him not to budge from her side.

Dylan tried to make light of it. "Ah. Trouble with the overprotective family?"

"Correct, sir." Kathy tapped her nose. "Now would you like to play for a chance at a new car?"

Dylan chuckled.

She stopped and faced him. Up close, she looked like Death in need of a nightcap and a full night's sleep. "Wow. It just hit me."

"What?"

"That's the first time I've made anyone laugh since I was released." She began walking again, fast. Despite her relatively short legs, the dog struggled to keep up. "I used to be the life of the party."

The dog was panting.

Dylan touched Kathy's arm and slowed her down. "Cody needs a break. Were you the life of the party before or after you started drinking?"

Kathy shrugged. "Who can remember?"

"You can."

Kathy wiped at her face with her forearm. An itch or tear? Dylan didn't know.

"I used to be smart, too," Kathy mused. "Without the alcohol. Okay, maybe not at math. But in other subjects."

Atta girl. Remembering the good things associated with sobriety was a positive thing. "I can attest to the fact that you're still smart."

Her hand fisted around the dog's leash. "I've had a couple disagreements with my brother and his wife. I can't believe some of the things that come out of my mouth, especially to Flynn." She blew out a breath, sending her fiery bangs fluttering. "I was voicing my frustrations. I was told that's what addicts are supposed to do. But I was harsh."

This was good. Great even. He nodded encouragingly. "Honesty and clearing the decks of your worries are important, but filtering is good, too. Especially when other people's feelings are involved."

She hit him straight up with an analytical stare, as if the world's balance hung in her next words. "Do you know what addicts should do because your father was one?"

"Yes." The word clung to his suddenly dry mouth. He didn't like lying to her. "Don't all the truths we realize later in life come from our parents? The good and the bad?"

Her expression changed, surprising him. It was thoughtful and honest, sympathetic and commiserate. There was that hint of feminine curiosity and an equal hint of restraint. "I'm sorry we both had less-than-perfect parents."

"Me, too." He was also sorry he couldn't ask her out or hug her just because or kiss her good-night. Some guy was going to be lucky to find her, because once she found out he was being paid to come here, she'd have nothing else to do with him.

Across the street, an old man peered out the barbershop window as they passed, waving to Kathy. He shuffled outside, leaning on the brick veneer for balance. "Walking a dog today instead of a horse?"

"Yes, Phil." Kathy smiled politely, whispering under her breath, "If he offers to cut your hair, don't accept."

"I saw your young man take his clothes off." Phil had a gangly set of limbs that wobbled when he talked. "Everything okay? Want me to call Flynn or the sheriff?"

"Nope. Dylan was just joking around." Kathy traded looks with Dylan. Hers seemed to say: *See all the trouble you made?*

"Oh, okay. I have openings today if either of you needs a haircut." Phil's voice was as shaky as his hands, one of which pointed toward his shop.

"We're kind of busy. But thanks." Kathy tugged Cody along.

"Truman is due for a trim," Phil called after her.

"I'll check with Becca." Kathy frowned and muttered, "I shouldn't have to check with Becca."

"Who's Becca?"

"Sister-in-law."

"Someone you said bad things to."

"Yes. She's kind, kind-of saint-like and... She's just...perfect." Kathy kept setting the bar impossibly high for herself.

"No one's perfect."

"Truman thinks she's perfect." Kathy sighed. "I see cracks in her saintliness, but she's still ninety-five percent perfect as far as I can tell. And I like her even though I'm jealous of the relationship she has with my son."

They rounded a corner at the town square. Cody dropped his head toward a fire hydrant, skittering his plastic cone across the brick pavers. The cone lodged in the lip of the hydrant and prevented his nose from getting close.

Kathy adjusted the cone, holding it so the dog could sniff all the relevant hydrant parts and then water it. "My son looks at me with suspicion. He's only eight." Once Cody was done with his business, Kathy began walking again, staring at the path beneath her feet. "What is it about you? I get motormouth when you're around."

Guilt backhanded Dylan's conscience. He fought against the urge to tell her the truth. That he excelled at making people comfortable and knew the questions to use to encourage his clients to open up. "I've been told I'm easy to talk to."

"Well, that probably gets you a lot of dates with women on the rebound." She pitched her voice high. "Oh, Dylan, I thought I loved him, but he dumped me. And you're such a good listener." She gave him that sly sideways glance of hers as they entered the clinic's parking lot. "Am I close?"

She wasn't.

"Does it matter?" What mattered was the fact that she tried so hard not to smile. She was honest and sweet, with a sense of humor that was engaging. She deserved to smile more. She deserved to enjoy life. She just didn't believe she deserved much of anything right now. Until she accepted herself, faults and all, she wouldn't be happy.

They headed toward the clinic in silence.

Dr. Wentworth poked his white-haired head out the front door when they came into view of the clinic. "Kathy, can you get yourself to Lorene Cornwell's house? She heard about your dog-walking and wants you to take her Chihuahuas around the block."

"Sure." Kathy's response was half-enthused, half-dismayed. She lowered her voice. "Did he say Chihuahuas? As in more than one?"

Dylan bent to pressure and rested his hand on her shoulder. "If you don't want to walk Lorene's dogs, then don't."

She squared her shoulders. "I need the money. I'm just mentally preparing my speech." He must have looked confused, because she added, "My introduction speech? I gave it to you the day we met. The one where I say, 'Hi, I'm Kathy, and I'm an alcoholic.'"

"You don't have to tell everyone that."

"I do. What if someone gives me their house keys so I can walk their dog and they have a fully stocked bar?"

"You wouldn't walk in and pour yourself a drink." He was ninety-nine percent sure of that.

Her face pinched up, making her look like the one percent he doubted. "Alcohol speaks a completely different language to alcoholics. We hear things non-alcoholics don't."

Having heard his father talk to a bottle of bourbon, Dylan could believe that.

They'd reached the back door of the clinic. Cody was panting, but given his doggy smile, the happy meds were still working. His enthusiasm reminded Dylan of Zach, which made him think of car rides and sleeping boys. "How would you like to skip dog-walking for now and go for a drive?" In a sun-warmed truck that put Zach to sleep every time.

Kathy blinked at him. "I don't understand. Where? Why?"

He improvised. "Isabo's halter buckle needs to be replaced. If you're going to work here long-term, you need to familiarize yourself with horse supply stores."

"Really?" Her eyes narrowed.

"Really." Lightning didn't strike him down at the white lie. Maybe he had leeway before it did—two little white lies? Four?

She stared at her boots for so long he thought she was going to refuse him. "If Doc says it's okay... I guess it's okay."

Thirty minutes later, Kathy was asleep in Dylan's passenger seat.

She was beautiful. She was truthful. She was too stubborn for her own good.

Much like Phantom, the horse he couldn't tame.

The realization shocked him.

And that was when Dylan knew that things between them would end badly.

Chapter Seventeen

K athy came out of a deep sleep.

Her eyes were closed and the heater in the house was running. She hadn't realized how loud the unit was before. She couldn't hear anyone in the house. And Grandpa Ed's house was never quiet, except in the wee hours of the morning.

She rolled her head and reached for her blanket. The back of her hand hit something hard. Her eyes flew open, and she sat up only to be jerked back in place.

She wasn't at home. She wasn't in her bed. She was in Dylan's truck, strapped in a seat belt.

"Hey, there." Dylan shot his arm in front of her as if she was in danger of lurching forward and hurting herself. "You don't do anything slow, do you?" He'd taken his jacket vest off and rolled up his brown flannel sleeves. His muscled forearm brushed the skin beneath her neck as he withdrew.

The air became thick and heavy in her lungs. "How long have I been asleep?" They were in slow-moving traffic on what looked like the highway in Santa Rosa.

"About an hour."

Wasn't she the life of the party? "Where is this place you're taking me?"

"About twenty minutes back the other way."

"But...that means... You kept driving just so I could sleep?" She turned in her seat to face him.

He worked his jaw. "Don't take this wrong, but you looked like you could use the rest."

Kathy slumped in her seat. She'd always been a bit vain about her appearance. She'd always been meticulous about the clothes she wore. "Put me in mom jeans and donate my makeup to those less fortunate. All I need to complete this proud moment is for you to tell me I drooled." She touched the shoulder of her jacket. It was wet. Great.

Dylan's look was knowing, but he said, "I didn't *see* you drool."

She groaned. "That means I snored, too."

"It was more like a nose whistle," he deadpanned, exiting the freeway. "Are you hungry? I'm in desperate need of a burger."

Her stomach growled in agreement. "I should get home. Flynn will be worried about me." She didn't want Truman to worry, either.

"Call home."

"I don't have a cell."

"Use mine." He gestured toward the center console.

"And tell them what? I'm out with a man I just met a few days ago?" Everything that had felt loose and relaxed when she'd woken up now felt tense and strained. "That'll go over well."

"Call home."

Kathy's stomach growled a second time. "All right. But I don't have any money on me for dinner."

"My treat. You look like..."

"If you say I look like I need to eat..." Her fingers clenched the loose denim at her thighs. She hadn't realized how baggy her jeans had become.

"Been hearing that a lot lately, have you?"

"You have no idea." She forced her fingers to relax.

Dylan pulled into a run-down burger joint as Kathy finished calling Flynn. "This is the best-kept secret in Sonoma County. They have chili-cheese fries that'll make you want to cry they're so good."

"Please. The next thing you'll be telling me is that they have root-beer floats with real ice cream."

He opened his door and shot her that wicked grin. "They do."

Kathy ate like she did everything else—with unabashed honesty and enthusiasm. She fit right in at Bubb's, which aesthetically wasn't anything to write home about—scuffed beige linoleum, redwood picnic tables and white walls with posters of biker movies from the past five decades.

At Dylan's dare, she'd ordered chili-cheese fries with jalapeños, meat and Velveeta cheese. She'd plowed through her order with a fork. Despite using the utensil, she was currently three napkins down and working on using a fourth. Probably didn't help that she was right-handed and she'd sprained her right wrist.

"You eat like a girl." Kathy gestured toward Dylan's burger patty sans bun.

"I'm watching my carbs. I'm not as young as I used to be." He swiped a gooey fry.

She tilted her head and gave him a teasing once-over. Apparently, food gave Kathy energy and energy made her personality come alive. "Thirty is definitely over the hill."

"How do you know how old I am?" Was he losing hair? Did he have gray hair? Had he grown nose hair?

Kathy popped a jalapeño in her mouth, enjoying her superior smile. "I peeked at your driver's license when you paid."

He rubbed a hand over his hair. Dylan shouldn't have felt as if his manhood had been spared.

"So, explain something to me." Kathy poked a fry with her fork.

"Sure."

"Why are you nice to me?" She spoke without bitterness or suspicion. She spoke with the curiosity of a woman who regularly mapped out the landscape of her life, marking treacherous ground. "I told you the mistakes I've made. You're not recovering from any vice. And you're years older than I am."

"Four years."

She raised a slender, auburn brow.

"Dr. Jamero told me." A lie. It'd been her brother, Flynn. The lie did a slow, sickening roll in his gut along with the others he'd told her, as if he'd eaten too many chili-cheese fries.

"You're avoiding my question. You said you don't want to date me, so what's the deal?" She ate another fry piled with drippy toppings. Her clean hand made a give-it-up gesture.

He liked her like this—loose and playful, challenging. He liked her far too much. But that didn't stop him from playing along. "Maybe I want to be your BFF."

She rolled her big blue eyes and tossed napkin number five at him.

Those baby blues were a definite signal of trouble. They called to him, a call that couldn't be answered. He sucked back a grin and speared the last of his cheeseburger patty with his fork. "I have a kid." Why had he told her that?

She nodded. "How old?"

"Five. He's in kindergarten and a spark plug. The love of my life." *Please don't let me lose him.*

She cast a quick glance at his left hand. "Divorced?"

It was Dylan's turn to nod. "Two years. You?"

"Never married."

It was his turn to raise a brow.

She stared over his shoulder.

Was this part of her problem with addiction? Her ex? Given her sly humor, he decided to use some himself. "Left you at the altar, did he?"

Not so much as an eyebrow twitch.

The hair on his arms stood at attention based on a premonition that soured his throat. He'd ventured onto treacherous ground. But if he let her reaction go now, he might never uncover the truth. "That's tough. Girl gets all dressed up. Special hair. Special makeup. Special bouquet."

"It wasn't like that." And then Kathy went silent again, pushing a fry through the remnants of her chili.

"Not jilted at the altar." It was getting harder to keep his tone light, a frown from his brow, the chill from his spine. Her mother was an alcoholic, and he knew from experience how scarring it was to have a parent who loved alcohol more than their kids. But he was also realizing just now that she was a young mom. Too young. "Okay, I'll go with a close encounter of the third kind. Alien. I haven't seen your kid, but if he has big eyes and blue translucent skin, you can't claim otherwise."

One corner of her mouth tilted up.

Dylan refused to allow his next words to stick in his throat. "He's skinny, right? Those aliens are always skinny. Takes after his dad, I bet."

The hint of a smile vanished. "I wouldn't know." Her voice was as soft as a whisper, as fragile as an autumn leaf.

Dylan couldn't move. Not his arms. Not his legs. Not his lungs.

Kathy rose from the table like a defeated goddess—graceful, weary, defeated, blue eyes glittering with unshed tears.

Around them, people ate their burgers and slurped their shakes, unaware that something important had just occurred.

Kathy had never told anyone—not so much as a hint—that she didn't know who Truman's father was. The bathroom door opened on horror-film-like rusty hinges. She slammed it shut behind her and checked to see that the single stall was empty. She wanted to be alone and thankfully she was. Not to cry, but to have space to pull herself together.

She shivered. The bathroom wasn't insulated. It was as cold as her insides.

What was I thinking to tell him? What will he think of me?

"Don't let life beat you down." Kathy washed her hands in the bathroom sink, repeating her grandfather's words. The porcelain sink was chipped. The drain rusting. The soap couldn't seem to get her hands clean. They felt stained.

"Stay strong. Stay focused." Her reflection in the mirror wasn't clear. The glass was permanently fogged. Black spots grew like mold around the edges.

"You have to want it." Another of Grandpa Ed's platitudes. What did she want? Kathy hardly knew anymore.

Someone knocked on the door. "Kathy?" Not someone. Dylan.

"Just a minute." She'd need an hour to regain her composure. To forget everything again, without the aid of alcohol.

The door opened on creaky hinges, the bottom scraping across the scuffed linoleum. Dylan walked in. "Are you okay?"

"I'm fine." She tried to smile, but that expression seemed permanently on the fritz.

"You're not." He closed the creaking door behind him and leaned against it. "Spill to your new BFF."

Secrets swelled in her throat and pressed at the backs of her eyes. Secrets she'd never told anyone. Not her college girlfriends. Not her brother. Certainly not Grandpa Ed.

Dylan wrapped his big arms around her. He didn't press for answers. He didn't judge her for her many, many mistakes. He took her at face value.

Not that she knew what her value was.

He drew her close, until she could smell the light scent of alfalfa and a woodsy aftershave.

Flynn hugged her every day. His hugs were different. Not as tight. Not as all-encompassing. Dylan's hug was like being wrapped in a warm tortilla, surrounded by hearty fillings and double-wrapped in aluminum foil to preserve the heat. His was a hug that wasn't an obligation, like the one Truman gave her every night. It was accepting. It was endearing. It was safe.

She drew a shuddering breath. "You need to let me go." Before she gave up all her secrets and watched the warmth in his eyes turn into pity.

He didn't release her. Instead, he pressed a light kiss to the top of her head. "You're going to be all right, Red."

His words slid through her head like a melted chocolate milk shake up a bendy straw. She could listen to his deep voice rumble over her all night. When he set her away, she almost didn't let him go.

He opened the door. It creaked and groaned. "Bus leaves in five minutes." He didn't look back.

Kathy stared at herself in the mirror. Sculpted cheekbones. Huge, black-rimmed eyes. Bright red scraggly hair. If she looked deeper inside, she'd see where she was fragile and broken, holding herself together with masking tape and willpower.

Humpty Dumpty had one glorious fall. She'd had many.

She was a wreck. Had been for years.

So why did Dylan make her feel as if she could put herself back together again?

It was her kid.

Or rather, her pregnancy. That was what drove Kathy to drink. And the mother. But there was still something he was missing about the mother.

You're going to be all right, Red.

It felt like a vow.

How could she not know who her son's father was? Every answer Dylan came up with was more horrific than the next. They raked at his gut, those answers.

They pierced and poked and bit until Dylan thought he'd have to pull over and be sick.

They'd left the freeway and were traveling on the small ribbon of highway that wound its way up to the hills. Darkness closed in around them as they left the more populated areas and entered the country. Kathy stared out the window.

Say something.

Where was his detachment? Where was his easy banter?

He'd lost it, because she wasn't yet twenty-six and she had an eight-year-old kid. Father unknown. The reasons weren't pretty to dwell upon.

Say something.

His gut twisted. His fingers gripped the wheel as if he was afraid someone would wrench it out of his hands. As if he might wrench it off the steering column and fling it away.

Kathy's hands were locked away in the weave of her arms across her chest.

Say something.

"Are you working tomorrow?" *Not that.* So mundane. He needed a joke. Something like: *Why did the chicken cross the road? To escape his horse therapist.*

Don't say another word.

But when he didn't speak, the unthinkable went through his mind. Lots of unthinkables. Every one of them made him want to punch something. Or someone. Kathy needed justice. She deserved justice. He could almost see himself standing over that fallen someone who'd received his knuckle-banging retribution. A cape attached to Dylan's shoulders, fluttering in the wind. A big S on his chest.

S standing for Stupid. As in stupid way to throw your life away.

Justice wasn't what he did. Dylan excelled at helping people find peace. It was just that he couldn't seem to find any for himself at the moment, much less Kathy.

"Might rain tomorrow." He was a listener by trade. Not a talker. It showed.

Kathy's forehead was pressed against the window. Her breath had fogged a small circle on the glass. She always made herself so very small, as if she thought she was insignificant. He wanted to see her bloom, like she had at the hamburger joint, as she had the day before in the stable.

Dylan was more determined than ever to unlock Kathy's secrets, to set her free so that she could believe in herself, so she wouldn't doubt her sobriety.

He made the turn toward Harmony Valley, following the winding road by the river, turning down the street that led to her house. He pulled up in front of the army-green ranch home and shut off the engine.

Kathy turned to face him for the first time since she'd sat across from him in the restaurant. "How did you know where I live?"

There was something wrong. Terribly, terribly wrong.

Dylan.

Kathy opened the truck door and started running.

Flynn came down the steps to meet her. She ran into his arms, but his embrace wasn't the same as Dylan's.

Wrong. Everything was wrong. And Flynn couldn't fix it for her this time.

Footsteps behind her. A slight limping cadence. "Kathy, I..."

"How did you know where I live?" She made a slow shuffle-turn out of Flynn's protective embrace, lifting her chin.

Instead of meeting her gaze, Dylan looked behind her. To Flynn.

A crushing weight pressed on Kathy's shoulders, wrapping around her throat until she thought she wouldn't be able to breathe. The most important thing in the world to Kathy was the truth. It took her a moment to work up enough saliva to speak. "Gage didn't hire you." The clinic had nothing to do with Dylan. He hadn't known about Chance when he arrived.

Finally, Dylan met her gaze squarely and shook his head. "Gage didn't hire me."

The world tilted. She'd been tricked, played, manipulated. It was her mother all over again, making her feel weak and stupid. *No one, nothing, invisible.*

Her brother's hand settled on her shoulder. "Now, Kathy…"

"Stop it, Flynn." She shrugged off his hand. "You hired Dylan. Why?"

The two men said nothing. The screen door behind her opened and closed gently. Had to be Becca.

"This is how it starts." Kathy's voice was hurt-roughened and battle-scarred. "People lie and others get hurt."

Dylan's eyebrows assumed the shocked position. This was new. His features had been alternating between thunderous anger and heartbreaking pity the entire ride home.

Her chest felt as if a case of liquor sat on top of it. Dylan and his direct gray eyes, his wicked smile—the one that made her feel as though she was somebody—and that sense of humor, so like hers. It was all a lie. He was a lie.

Don't let life beat you down. Grandpa Ed's voice. As clear as if he was sitting in his recliner in the living room.

You didn't tell me how heavy life's blows would get, Grandpa.

The sling around her neck was choking her. Her jaw felt tense enough to snap off. "Somebody better tell me why Dylan was hired or I'm leaving right now. And I'm taking Truman with me." Presumably, she still owned the condo Flynn had bought for her in Santa Rosa. She knew where Flynn kept the keys to her shiny red sports car. She'd take what was hers and leave.

"Don't go," Flynn said, his voice as hoarse as sandpaper on old wood. "Don't be like Mom."

She whirled on her brother. "In what way? In the way she earned rent money by sleeping with guys? In the way she couldn't live without drugs and alcohol? In the way she abandoned us here?"

"Yes! In all those ways. You don't want to do to Truman what she did to us, do you?"

"Too late," Kathy said flatly, telling Flynn what he wanted to hear instead of the truth. She couldn't tell him that when he'd cut off the purse strings to their mother nearly two years ago, she'd found a way to dip in his pocket anyway. By blackmailing Kathy. By driving her to drink.

What would it take to send Kathy back to the bottle? Being invisible?

Instead of following through on her threat to move out, Kathy walked away from the house. Away from everyone.

Into the darkness. Into uncertainty.

Chapter Eighteen

D ylan felt as if he'd been hog-tied with barbed wire.

So much for integrity and his vow that Kathy would be all right. There was more here than what anyone had told him, than anyone knew. He had to make this right. And he couldn't use training flags or children's songs.

"Kathy, come back. Please." The woman on the porch called to Flynn's sister, but she must have known she'd be ignored. Her shoulders had fallen, and her words were flat.

Kathy's slight form was swallowed by darkness at the end of the gravel driveway.

The woman on the porch came down the steps and wrapped her arms around Flynn. She had a long, dark braid, and she seemed to have the kind of quiet strength a man could lean on. "She'll come back."

Flynn didn't look so sure. He stood rigidly, not accepting her embrace. "I've ruined everything by hiring you."

"Maybe," Dylan allowed, blaming his knee for not being able to run after her. But in truth, he knew she'd need time to process his betrayal.

"What were you thinking taking her for a drive?" Flynn's voice punched with anger, jabbed with hurt. "Taking her to dinner? Driving her to our front door as if you were on a date? You know that's what she thinks." He broke free of the woman's embrace and took a belligerent stance.

"Flynn..." the woman pleaded, capturing his hand. Hers glittered with a diamond ring. She was the sister-in-law Kathy had regrets about hurting with harsh words. The woman who Kathy considered flawless.

"It wasn't a date." But whatever Dylan said, Flynn was in no mood to listen. Not that Dylan understood what had gone down tonight. He'd been watching out for Kathy's well-being, not thinking about appearances or keeping his professional distance. She'd obviously been too hurt physically and emotionally to sleep well for the past few days. He'd wanted to offer comfort, to lend her strength.

Would she accept any of that from him now?

"Flynn, let's hear Dylan out. Kathy's been doing better under his care."

Under my care?

Under his care Dylan would always be limited in how he could treat her. She was like a lone tree in the wilderness when she should be in a forest of friendly pines. He couldn't truly help her if he was lying to her. He should have realized that sooner.

"I quit." Those words lifted the weight Dylan had been carrying. There was still debt and worry about his future, but none of the guilt over lying to Kathy. "I'll send you a refund." Maybe not tomorrow...

"What?" Flynn's gaze, so like Kathy's, sparked to him.

"You heard me." Dylan moved forward and extended his hand to the woman. "I don't think we've met. I'm Dylan."

"Becca, Flynn's wife." She introduced herself almost apologetically, hitting just the right balance between hurt and sympathy. Truly, she was perfect, just not the kind of perfect Dylan appreciated.

"This—Kathy's situation, her pain—has nothing to do with you," Dylan said to her.

"Doesn't it?" She sounded sad.

"Not near as much as you might think," Dylan added kindly.

"You can't quit because..." Flynn's voice died like a cold car on a colder day. He swallowed and tried again. "We need you more now than ever."

"She doesn't need a sober companion." Dylan searched the darkness for Kathy's silhouette without success. "She's carrying secrets about how she became pregnant...and about your mother. She hurt Kathy somehow. Those are the stressors that caused her to drink. And if not addressed, those are the things that will make her drink again."

"I've got someone looking for our mom. When I told Kathy, she didn't like the idea..." Flynn frowned, his brow wrinkled with more than worry. There was doubt in his expression, too. "But what if you're wrong? How do you know this?"

"Because I listen to her." Dylan returned to his truck. "If I can get her to talk..."

"If?" Flynn followed him. "There's no if about it. After this, Kathy's not going to talk to you. I'm her brother. She'll talk to me."

"She hasn't confided in you before. Why would she do so now? No. Somehow, this has something to do with you, too. Otherwise, she'd tell you what's haunting her." Dylan wasn't sure how he knew this, but he felt it in his gut.

He drove away, leaving Flynn and his wife behind.

Kathy sat at the bar at El Rosal, staring into the bottom of an untouched whiskey glass.

A college-football game played silently on the television above the bar. Spanish pop music filled the colorful restaurant—the primary blue, green, red and yellow nearly overwhelming in their optimism. She used to be happy in bars. In them, the ugliness of the past and the dangers of the future would always fade away after a few drinks.

Her attention was at the bottom of the full glass. That was where answers were supposed to be, although she'd never found any by drinking before, so why would she now?

"You going to drink that?" Dylan slid onto the barstool next to her.

Kathy hadn't touched the tumbler up to that point. She gripped it now with her left hand, cradling her injured wrist in her lap. "Who are you? A therapist? Private security?" She glared at him. "One of my brother's flunkies, for sure."

"I'm just a guy who helps people and horses cope with stress." A non-answer. *He lied. He lied. He lied.*

She hated Dylan. She wanted to push him off the barstool and shout at him to leave her alone. She wanted to herd him out the door with cruel, cruel words. She wanted him to go someplace where she'd never see him again.

His words sank in: *I help people and horses.*

And there was that nugget of hope—that he could help rid her of uncertainty and the stress of being an alcoholic. After all, Flynn only ever hired the best. He could afford to.

Kathy moved the glass slowly with her uninjured hand, back and forth across the smooth bar. What was it Dylan said he did? "Stress relief. You must be a masseuse." She pointed at her shoulders. "I have a kink between my shoulder blades. I bet you could work that out."

He leaned away from the bar and stared at her back. "Looks like a knife to me." He pretended to remove it.

She might have laughed if the knife wound didn't hurt so much. "I don't like you." Her statement wasn't as dark and menacing as she'd have liked. The fact was that she had liked him. And she was incredibly disappointed that he'd entered her life under false pretenses.

Incredibly disappointed? No, she was pissed off. Or, at least, she had been when she'd left the house. Now she was just hurt. She hated feeling hurt, because it made her feel weak.

"I should be happy you didn't say you hated me," Dylan said.

"There's a difference?" Why wasn't she tossing her drink in his face and telling him to leave town? "And what about Chance? Was that just a lie, too? Are you or aren't you the horse miracle worker?"

"Horse trainer." She almost didn't catch his softly spoken words.

After hearing the story about Phantom and seeing his limp, Kathy understood his reluctance to accept the grand title. But she would not feel sorry for him. She would not! He'd been lying to her for days!

"Back when I was a kid, my mother used to be strict." Something in his deep voice drew her—an off-note, like the discordant warble of a bird who'd accidentally flown into a plate-glass window and wobbled to find its way. "Not as strict as my dad, but she was a stickler for the rules, and she wanted my brother and me to be safe, even though the home situation we were in... Well, we were never safe. When I was a kid, I used to tell her that I hated her."

Kathy became very still, hanging on to his every word. Because his childhood sounded eerily similar to hers. His words of hate echoed the words flung by a too-young girl stuck in the wrong part of town with a woman who was supposed to protect her.

"Mom never lashed back." Dylan's voice dropped beneath the music until she had to lean toward him to hear. "She'd turn away and say that she'd always love me, through the good times, through the bad and past the hate. So, yes, there is a difference between dislike and hate. I disliked my mother sometimes, but she was right. I still loved her."

Past tense. Kathy's fingers clenched the glass once more. "My mother was never that understanding."

"Neither was my dad." Dylan gave her a careful look. A look that asked the question: *What about your dad?*

"I don't know who my dad is," Kathy admitted. "Flynn's dad raised me for a while...until I came to live here with my grandfather."

"So it's a cycle," he murmured.

Unbelievable. She almost did fling her drink at him then. "There is no Zen to my situation. No karma making a full circle." She sure hadn't set out to pass on the stigma to her child.

"Your mom dealt with her stress with drugs and alcohol. And you didn't know who your father was." He summarized two of the darkest tangibles in her life as easily as if he was ordering fast food from a drive-thru window. "So now here you sit, trying to break the cycle of substance abuse and wondering if it's worth it. You told me the other day that I didn't understand what you were going through because I wasn't an alcoholic. You don't have to share the exact same past to understand someone. I grew up in a family with an abusive alcoholic. I understand you more than you think."

She pulled the drink closer. For two years, alcohol had been her security blanket. If Flynn had been sitting next to her, he would have taken the drink away by now. Maybe that was why she felt so vulnerable. Dylan didn't seem at all concerned that she'd take a drink.

Suddenly, she felt guilty for her judgment of Mr. Hammacker.

Dylan stared directly into her eyes. "You think you deserve all this drama."

The truth to his words slammed into her, nearly knocking Kathy off the barstool. Only the anchor of her hand on the drink kept her stationary. But she wouldn't acknowledge that he'd struck home. "I'd have chosen a stronger word than drama."

Despite everything that had happened tonight, the look in his gray eyes was warm. "Do you want to know one of the differences between those who successfully beat addiction and those who don't?"

Kathy made the I-give-up sign with her hand. "You're just gonna tell me anyway."

"Those who beat it don't blame the world at large for their troubles."

"They blame themselves." She'd heard this before.

"Who do you blame for the bad things in your life? Your immaculate conception of your son? Your fall into addiction? Is it synchronicity? Fate? Your mother?" His gaze probed for the truth. "Or are you to blame?"

Her mother would always blame an outside influence—everyone was drinking; I needed a drink to get through it; if only you were nicer, then he would've stayed.

Kathy was no better. She'd blamed her mother's scare tactics for her addiction. Grandpa Ed would be muttering loudly and shaking his head at her in disapproval if he was here right now.

She pushed the drink away. Even though she'd been asked much the same question by counselors in rehab and by leaders in support groups, she hadn't been ready to accept the blame as much as she was at this moment.

"I'm to blame." She'd been taken advantage of, but she'd been weak. And there were always people ready to prey on the weak. She wouldn't be weak again.

Relief washed through her, but it wasn't enough. It wasn't enough to make her forgive Dylan. "That doesn't mean we're going to be friends. Why are you here? To complete some job Flynn hired you for and make sure you get paid? Or to apologize? Because I don't think I care to hear your apology." Even as she said the words, she knew they weren't true.

Dylan signaled to the bartender to remove her drink. "I care about you." He looked away and it sounded as if he mumbled, "I care too much."

His words resonated inside her, building and filling her like the tolling of a church bell, until she could no longer deny whatever the unnamable something was between them—the connection that caused her to tell him things she told no one else. It was something that could be deep and personal if allowed to grow. But that warm as-yet-unnamed emotion left her feeling vulnerable. And hadn't she just realized that vulnerability was something people preyed upon? She drew herself up and forced herself to look him in the eye. "You lied to me."

A flash of guilt clouded his gray eyes. "I hurt you. I'm sorry. I told Flynn that I like to go about this differently. Honestly."

"So, you're a doctor?" She appraised him. Cowboy boots, faded blue jeans, a flannel shirt beneath a vested jacket. He didn't look like any doctor she'd ever known.

Dylan shook his head. "I've been supporting myself since I was sixteen by working at racing stables. I've studied with the best horse trainers." He cleared his throat. "Some people call them horse whisperers."

"You're not a shrink or a therapist?" She longed for the prop of the drink. Something to anchor her as she looked down her nose at him. "What qualifies you to ease people's stress?"

He passed a hand over his knee. "I'm a good listener. I show people respect, despite their age or the severity of their challenges. I call the situation the way I see it, without roundabout questions." He shrugged. "You want to see me in action? Come out to my place tomorrow. Wear clothes you don't mind getting dirty."

"Flynn has taken away my car keys." She squirmed, embarrassed to admit it. "He had every right. He bought me that car."

"The shiny red thing in the carport? Nice ride. Totally impractical in the country."

"I used to live in Santa Rosa. I'm a city girl. Or I used to be." He confused her. "What are we doing here? Didn't Flynn fire you?" If not, she was going to.

"No. I quit." He chewed on the inside of his lip. "I may have been here under false pretenses, but just know that everything we said to each other was honest."

"Except who you were and why you were being nice to me."

"I'm nice to you because I like you. I respect your honesty and your courage. I have from the moment we met." There was a hint of a smile behind that solemn expression, wry though it might be. "Don't forget it wasn't all smooth sailing. I yelled at you for the risks you took with the colt." He stood. "I'll text you the address of where to show up tomorrow. As a friend, not the guy who's paid to listen to your troubles."

"I don't have a cell phone." For the first time in months, she regretted it.

Dylan chuckled, signaling the waiter for a pen. He wrote an address on a cocktail napkin and slid it to her. "I know. Biggest cliché in the book. Call me if you get lost."

"But... I'm still mad at you." She wasn't. She was hurt, even though he'd apologized. But she was undeniably curious about what he did for people and what he could do for her. Not just curious—hopeful. She was hopeful he was the answer she was looking for. "Does this mean that you won't work with Chance anymore? I won't come by if that's the case."

"You show up tomorrow and I'll work with Chance. Be careful walking home."

He wasn't going to hang around and talk? She was annoyed that he didn't.

He was already halfway to the door when he turned. "By the way, you didn't have your purse. How did you pay for that drink you didn't touch?"

"I put it on Flynn's tab."

He nodded and left.

She should thank him. Everyone in Harmony Valley would know she'd ordered a drink, but just as importantly, they'd know she hadn't taken a sip.

Flynn answered Dylan's call on the first ring.

Dylan pulled onto the highway out of town. "Kathy's going to come out to my ranch tomorrow. Let her bring her boy."

The silence on the other end wasn't encouraging. Finally, Flynn said, "You're asking me to put my nephew at risk."

"I'm not sure I like the implication of what you're saying." That Kathy wasn't responsible enough to take her son on an outing. "In fact, I'm sure I don't like it. Kathy has every right to take her son whenever and wherever she wants."

"I know," Flynn said quietly. "It's just hard to trust her when my nephew's safety is at stake."

No wonder Kathy lacked self-confidence. "I'm officially labeling you part of the problem." Dylan allowed anger to sharpen his words. "Kathy isn't a teenager who has trouble making it in by curfew. She's an adult who wants to get past her mistakes. You not trusting her is only feeding her sense of defeat."

"You'd trust her to drive Truman? You don't think she'll make any side stops?"

"I'm not answering either of those questions. Tomorrow, you need to be relaxed and confident in your sister. You need to show her son that you have that kind of trust in her. Or you might just as well let her go now."

Chapter Nineteen

The next morning, Kathy's mood matched the sky overhead. Dark clouds rumbled around Parish Hill indecisively.

Kathy wasn't sure she wanted to see Dylan today. She didn't know what she'd say to him once she got there. Part of her wanted to cling to the hurt his betrayal had caused her. Part of her trembled with excitement at the idea that he held the magical answer to all her problems. She knew there were no easy fixes to the defect she'd discovered in herself—her weakness for alcohol. And yet if Dylan told her he had the cure, she'd believe him.

She printed directions to Dylan's place off her computer, put her wrist in its sling, grabbed her jacket and her courage.

Flynn waited for her on the porch. "Here are your car keys. I started it up earlier to make sure the battery wasn't dead."

"Thanks." The keys in her hand almost made her feel like her old self—the independent woman who decided what was for dinner and how to spend a Saturday afternoon. She hurried down the steps, eager to get behind the wheel.

"Wait." Truman came outside, letting the screen door bang behind him, looking as if he wanted to be anywhere but there. "I'm going with you."

Kathy's heart did a little hitch-kick. She'd been hoping for a breakthrough with Truman. An olive branch. Even the tiniest of signs that he could forgive her. But this was unexpected. An unsmiling, gaze-avoiding event.

She glanced at Flynn, who nodded. "Dylan insisted."

That took the hitch out of her get-up. And now she knew she'd been spending too much time with horses—Western clichés weren't usually her thing.

But the fact remained: Truman didn't want to go with her. He hadn't even spoken one word to her since she'd taken away his cell phone.

"You don't have to, Tru." She came back up the stairs and ruffled his ginger hair.

Abby sat at Truman's feet, gazing up at her with adoring eyes. Of course, the dog knew she had kibble in her jacket pocket. Kathy gave her a treat.

Truman scuffed his sneakers on the porch. "Becca says I have to."

Kathy's lips cemented into a hard line. Her gaze cut to her brother, who shrugged. There was a battle to be won here, but Grandpa Ed would have said fighting a battle head-on wasn't always the way to win the war. Kathy managed to make her lips move. "Well, if Becca says you have to, that means you have to. Come on."

He followed her across the grass to the carport. The enthusiasm she felt over driving somewhere drained. She should be happy to have her son by her side, but she would rather he not have to be ordered to come. Kathy wanted him to want to be with her.

As they drove away, it began to drizzle. The big drops made polka-dot smudges on the car, which had been parked since Kathy had entered rehab a second time. She hadn't worked up the courage to ask Flynn for the keys before.

Once they were on their way, she tried to tell herself it was just like old times—she and Truman driving down the highway after a visit to Harmony Valley. But it wasn't the same. They weren't rehashing the fun they'd had with Flynn and Grandpa Ed. Instead, Truman was sullen. And she was silently nervous about whatever they'd find at Dylan's. The only sounds in the car were the engine and the flip of the windshield wipers.

"Wake me up when we get there," Truman said, turning away from her.

She suspected he'd said that to establish boundaries, but by the time ten minutes had passed, Truman was snoring in the passenger seat.

Chapter Twenty

"Y ou're awfully quiet this morning," Becca said to Wilson. "You okay?"

He gave her a thumbs-up sign. He didn't feel like talking. He hadn't been alone for more than an hour since Friday night. He was tired. So tired. Company wore him out.

Becca had medical gloves on and was preparing to give his finger a poke. "Your readings last night were great. Let's see how you are this morning. Hopefully, you didn't sneak any snack cakes during the night."

He shook his head. His numbers would be fine. He'd only had a nip of rum when he let Dolly out at...sometime. He couldn't remember when. He was so anxious to be alone that he was beginning to tremble with it. He held out his hand for Becca, suddenly suspecting they were the only two people in the house. "Felix?"

"He left when I came, remember?" Becca took hold of his hand. "You're shaking. Are you cold?"

He was freezing. When had that happened? He tried to speak, but his brain felt fuzzy, and his lips felt as if they'd been shot with Novocain.

She poked him, took his reading and then ran into the kitchen. "Your blood sugar is too low." She returned with a can of juice and handed it to him. "What did you eat this morning?"

Wilson didn't answer. He could only remember the rum. The juice ran down his throat and seemed to spread into his belly like water into a dry sponge.

She handed him an energy bar. "Eat."

He blinked up at her after a few bites.

"Your color is much better now. Good." She studied him. "I feel as if I'm missing something here. I wonder if your insulin dosage is right. I'm calling your doctor."

Wilson sank back into his recliner and watched Becca move around the room. Her words ran together until he couldn't understand what she was saying. And then he felt another poke.

Chapter Twenty-One

The rain had stopped, but the sky remained an indecisive gray.

Dylan's ranch was as contradictory as the man himself.

Kathy parked in front of the historic two-story home. The outer walls were white and streaked with dirt. There were rust stains near the rain gutters. But there was something about the look of the house that was charming. The Reedley place was small, staid and comfortable. This home practically begged to be filled with children, energy and laughter.

On the other side of a stand-alone garage stood the stables. They were neatly painted and well kept. It was obvious where Dylan's priorities lay.

"Tru, we're here." She was reluctant to get out. What if she was disappointed? What if Dylan gave her that grin and she had the urge to kiss him?

There will be no kisses. Ever. He lied.

Truman stretched, peeking over the dashboard to take in their destination, much as Kathy had. "Your new doctor lives here?"

"He's not a doctor. He's a horse trainer."

He rubbed his eyes. "We don't have a horse."

"I know. Weird, right?" She peered at the big white house. "That's a huge house for one guy."

Truman refrained from commenting. They got out and went in search of Dylan.

They found him talking to a young man who looked as if he'd yet to graduate high school. He wore a camouflage pullover hoodie and blue jeans, all new and expensive looking. Introductions were made. The teen, Carter, nodded in acknowledgment and then continued his conversation with Dylan.

Meanwhile, Truman grabbed a porch post and began circling it. He hummed a tune Kathy couldn't identify, other than to know it wasn't *Itsy Bitsy Spider*.

"Sammy's mom thinks it's okay if we drink at her house as long as we don't drive," Carter was saying.

"Oh." Kathy felt like an intruder at a therapy session. "Excuse me." She began to back away.

Carter gave her a once-over. "You're a client of Dylan's, right? You can listen."

Kathy forgot to breathe. She looked down at her arm in the sling, her new jeans and cowboy boots. She wasn't wearing a sash that said Alcoholic. What about her made it look as though she was one of Dylan's clients?

Unaware of, or ignoring, Kathy's distress, Dylan broke things down for the teen. "You and your friends aren't old enough to vote or fight for your country, but someone thinks you're mature enough to know your own limits when it comes to alcohol?" He shook his head. "Don't trust every adult to be smart. Or to know what's best for you."

"My mom and my friends don't believe I have a drinking problem. To them being drunk is fun." Carter seemed torn. "I'm the class president. I used to be the coolest kid in school."

Truman stopped humming to look at Carter.

Dylan broke away from the teen to address Kathy's son. "Truman, why don't you go down and say hello to Peaches? She's a golden pony in the stall one from the end. You'll see her name on the door." He waited until Truman moved off to continue his lecture. "Carter, you used to drink vodka between classes, cheat on your homework, and kiss any girl who let you near her. Are you putting any of that on your college résumé?"

If the subtext hadn't been so serious, Kathy might have smiled.

"There are more parties at college than in high school," Carter pointed out.

"If you're going to be tempted," Dylan said, "maybe you should choose a school that doesn't allow drinking."

"You're serious?" Carter frowned. "Next thing you'll be saying is choose a college where there aren't any girls."

Dylan laughed. "The best girls steer clear of drunks. I bet that girl you like—what was her name? Lisa?—isn't invited to Sammy's party."

"She's not." Carter deflated. "She couldn't go even if she was invited. Besides the alcohol, her parents hate me."

"I won't even ask whose fault that is." And with that, Dylan led the way to a stall with a one-eyed brown horse with a white star on its forehead. "Let's put Popeye on a lunge line today."

"What about Big and Bad?" Carter pointed to the stall at the end, which had a large sign on it that said *Stay Back*.

"You have a long way to go before you take on Phantom."

"But I can take him on one day, right?"

Kathy trailed after them. She spotted Truman standing on a chair outside a stall close to the end of the row, his face pressed against the bars.

"You must be that Harmony Valley lady." A short, wiry man with shoulder-length white hair stepped out of a room filled with bridles, ropes and saddles. "I'm Barry. I keep things running smooth at the Double R." He had the kind of gaze that pinned you and delved until he'd taken your measure. He took his time looking at her, then said, "Wasn't told you had a broken wing. That'll complicate things," he said cryptically as he left her, heading toward the arena, where a woman with graying brown hair rode a white horse.

Dylan was talking to Truman now. It looked as if they were feeding carrots to Peaches.

Meanwhile, Carter took the one-eyed horse into a large corral. And in what seemed like no time, the teen had the horse going through its paces in a large circle.

Kathy was reluctant to disturb Dylan and Truman. She waited near the equipment room for Dylan to return.

On his way back to her, Dylan bent to pet a white cat, which wound its way through his legs.

Did everything love this man? Kathy reminded herself he had a hole in his sock and a bump in his nose. Not to be mean, but just to acknowledge he was human.

"What do you think of him?" Dylan paused at the door to the horse equipment room.

"He's sweet."

"It's tough being Carter's age," Dylan said. "Girls. Cars. Independence."

Kathy pretended to have misunderstood him. "I was talking about the horse. Carter is fine." She lowered her voice so Truman wouldn't hear. "When are you going to address my problems? I was staring into the bottom of a drink last night."

He grinned, the wicked slant of the lips that invited her to grin, too. "You only did that to make a statement."

True. How did he know her so well? He made her forget things. Important things. Like the need to be vigilant against the urge to drink. Although being around him never made her crave alcohol. Being around him made her feel like her old, normal self. "Carter is too young to have the kind of demons I carry around on my shoulders."

"You can kick those freeloading problems to the curb anytime." He was so certain. She longed for his confidence. "Tell me about your mother."

Her shoulders snapped back. "Why?"

"Because I think she put a knife in your back. Want to tell me about it?"

"No."

"You don't have to tell me everything. Just one thing." He stood there. Waiting.

And she stood still, sweating in the cold. He seemed to be good at what he did. And if he was that good, she should probably tell him something...one thing. "I... She...she loves drugs and alcohol more than she ever loved me."

He didn't deny her claim. He didn't make a pitying face. All he said was "My dad was the same way."

She took a step closer, unable to raise her voice above a whisper. "Did he take everything away from you?"

Dylan worked his mouth as if it was too dry to form one simple word. "Yes."

The hurt in his gray eyes nearly undid her. Kathy wanted to hug him, to close the short distance between them and offer him comfort. But there was her son, and Dylan's deception, to consider. The only person she should trust was herself. She shifted her feet, planting them more firmly in the dirt.

"How'd it go last night with your brother?"

"Flynn hugged me when I got home." She set her back to a post. "He apologized." And said she didn't have to come here today.

"Good man, that brother of yours."

"He shouldn't have hired you." She felt it needed to be said. "And you shouldn't have accepted."

"I know. I had regrets about taking the job, but I can't change the past. I can only apologize." He stepped inside the small room, then thought better of it and turned back. "For what it's worth, I'm not sorry that taking the job meant getting to know you."

What was she supposed to make of that? Shades of wicked grins and what it meant to be a woman entered her conscious. She fought back a smile.

Dylan glanced over to Truman. "I'm gonna have Truman help me saddle Peaches."

"He's going to ride?" She was simultaneously excited and worried. Truman had never been on a horse. "Can he handle it?"

"Of course, he can. He's your son. Plus, he'll be riding the gentlest pony on the planet." Dylan pointed to a three-level, narrow set of wooden bleachers in front of the arena. "And you're going to sit over there in the stands while he does."

"Before we ride, we make sure our horse is ready," Dylan said to Truman as he showed the boy how to saddle a horse.

"I'm not a cowboy. I don't even have boots." Truman glanced from his mud-splattered sneakers to the set of tiered benches near the arena where Kathy was sitting. He spoke in the down-to-earth way of the disappointed, reminding Dylan of his little brother, Billy, now an officer in the navy.

"That's okay. Peaches knows what she's doing. As long as you have feet, you'll be fine."

"She likes me," Truman said with a bit of pride. "And I like her. She must be the best horse here."

Thanks for the opening, kid. "Let's not make her head swell. No one is perfect. Peaches has her moments. She doesn't like to circle the track more times than is necessary. And she'll just stop at the gate when she's tired."

The boy's open smile. His ginger hair and freckles. Dylan's heart melted.

"Your mom isn't perfect, either," Dylan said casually. "But she's nice."

Truman's smile disappeared. He seemed to draw into himself and age about twenty years.

Dylan checked the cinch before saying anything else. "Do you know that everyone who comes here to the Double R has made mistakes like your mom?"

"Even Carter?" His eyes grew round, childhood innocence showing through once more.

"Even Carter. And everyone here is trying to do better. That's the most important part—*trying*." He led Peaches out of the stall, directing Truman to walk by his side. "It's hard to try, isn't it? After you've made a mistake? I bet after what you've been through with your mom, it's hard to trust her."

"I suppose." Truman dragged his feet through the dirt.

"Has she said she's sorry?"

He nodded. "But..." He tugged on Dylan's sleeve until he stopped, and then he whispered, "I don't want to live with her alone. She can't take care of herself. And I'm just a kid."

That sounded like adult-fed lines. Some of which Dylan had been fed as a teen when a neighbor finally realized his wasn't a safe household for a boy. But it seemed unfair when Kathy was doing so well.

Truman tugged his sleeve again. "Maybe you could take care of Mama. She likes your house. She looked at it a long time."

Dylan's breath caught in his throat. "Your mom will be fine. You'll both be fine."

Truman didn't look so sure.

Dylan led the pony into the arena, helped the boy up, adjusted the stirrups and gave the pony a gentle slap on the rump.

Peaches plodded forward with her usual steadfastness.

"Place your bets, ladies and gentlemen." Dylan followed at a safe distance behind them. "The Cloverdale Derby is about to begin." He grinned at Kathy. "Peaches and her jockey, Truman Harris, are the odds-on favorite tonight. And...they're off. It's Peaches in the lead."

"You're embarrassing me," Truman said, but he was grinning, and Kathy was smiling, so Dylan kept going.

Since the rain had stopped, the temperature had dropped.

Kathy was cold on the outside, but her heart was bursting with warmth watching Truman ride the golden pony around the arena. She'd taken her wrist out of its sling and tucked her hands in her jacket pockets. The cold air nipped at her nose. But she wouldn't have sought a warmer place, because Truman was smiling. When he rode past, he grinned and waved at her. And it was because of Dylan.

Dylan, the man she'd accused of never being able to understand her, knew her better than her own brother. She forgave him for lying to her, because she had her son back.

The woman rider led her horse out of the arena and back to the stables. Barry stood next to Dylan, watching Kathy's son ride around.

After Truman completed a few laps, Dylan came to sit next to her, leaving Barry with Tru. "Your son is a great kid."

"Thanks." She shivered.

"You're cold." Dylan glanced back toward the stables. "I could get you a horse blanket. But I'm warning you, it's covered in horse hair and it won't smell as nice as your flowery perfume."

He'd noticed her perfume? Her cheeks heated. "No, thanks. I'll be fine."

He scooted closer until he was nearly touching her, the nearly part making her pulse kick up. "I'd send you into the tack room with the heater, but I know you don't want to miss Truman running his race."

Although they sat close together, she didn't look at him. Kathy didn't want him to know how much she was growing to like him. She wasn't even sure why she liked him. Was it the carrot of sobriety? Or his straightforward personality? She suspected the latter. "Thank you for making this time special for him." And for her.

He rested his elbows on his knees. "Are you feeling less stressed?"

"Yes."

"That's all we ask for at the Double R." His businesslike tone reminded her that befriending alcoholics was what he did for a living. That heart-melting grin. Her pulse quickening when he was near. She was reading too much into things, but she couldn't seem to close that book.

They waved at Truman as he passed on his way to another lap. Barry occasionally offered the boy advice on how to hold the reins or sit tall in the saddle. Otherwise, the only sounds were Peaches' hooves plodding in the dirt. The woman who'd been riding bid them farewell, and Dylan seemed to relax.

He patted Kathy's knee, kick-starting her pulse like her brother's old dirt bike. His hand was so large it could have encompassed both her knees. "I'd still like to hear about that knife your mom put in your back."

Oh, she was so not telling him. "What makes you think it was a knife?"

"You're going to make me guess? Is this a game? Mr. Popsicle did it in the stables with a horse pick?" Without looking at him, she could tell he was smiling. Humor buoyed his words.

And then she did look. That smile passed between them on a gentle breath of air until she was smiling, too.

It felt as if they were conducting a verbal dance in the gray zone between keeping things professional and exploring this curious, compelling attraction between them. It couldn't be one-sided. And if she wanted to keep up boundaries, she needed to keep the conversation going. "No games, Dylan. It's just my way of letting you know I'm not telling you. Some things should stay in the past."

"But they don't, do they?" He rubbed a hand over his face, looking worn out. "The past rises up and turns our stomachs. It steals our laughter." His gaze skimmed across her face, as if he knew she hadn't laughed good and long in what seemed like a lifetime. "I see my past sometimes when I look out at those eucalyptus bordering the ranch. When I was a kid, we had lots of those trees on our property. We used to cut them down for firewood to heat the house in winter."

"That sounds snug and cozy." She glanced at her boots and her cold toes.

"It wasn't either of those things." His tone dropped to freezing—icy and crackling. "Not even close."

Her gaze darted to his closed-off features. "Do you want to tell me about it?"

"No." The temperature dropped.

She shrugged deeper into her jacket. "It cuts both ways, doesn't it? The need to know someone's secrets when sharing your own hurts."

He didn't answer. And once more, she felt cold.

Chapter Twenty-Two

"Dad!" Zach hopped on the first step of the bleachers and hugged Dylan's knees. He looked like a cowboy from a magazine ad—hair perfectly slicked back, creases in his jeans and a new bright red jacket. He was a sight most welcome after Dylan's overshare with Kathy. "Can I ride Peaches?"

"Of course. She's already saddled," Dylan said, ruffling his son's perfectly styled hair. "But first, let me introduce you to Kathy." The woman who made him smile and caused his breath to catch.

"Very nice to meet you, Zach," Kathy said, smiling.

"Is she one of your patients?" Zach studied Kathy with the blatant curiosity of a five-year-old.

"She's a friend." He'd known her only a short while, yet the term felt limiting. Dylan glanced back toward the path leading from the driveway. "Where's your mom?"

"She's on the phone with Daddy Bob."

Dylan had never heard the term before. It knotted his stomach. He excused himself from Kathy and went to find Eileen, calling to Carter to put Popeye up. His ex-wife was sitting in her car with the motor running. She rolled down the window as he approached.

"Missed you guys yesterday. Why didn't you answer the phone? We could have talked this through, not taken it to court."

"It was already in the works when I got your check." Eileen didn't look at him but was gripping and regripping her steering wheel.

He waited for an apology or a retraction. When none came, he had to struggle to keep his composure.

"Do we really need to go back to court?"

"Dylan... I'm caught in the middle of this." She finally gave him a pained look, voice wavering. "I'm sorry but..."

Dylan had a bad feeling in his chest, like a lasso accurately thrown and in need of a good tug to trap a horse. Eileen had never been strong-willed and Bob... "Caught in the middle of what, Eileen?"

Eileen bit her lip. "Bob wants to adopt Zach."

"I'm the Zach's father!" Dylan said through gritted teeth.

Her gaze returned to the steering wheel. "Bob thinks Zach deserves better."

"Bob thought you deserved better," Dylan ground out. Bob was the reason they'd divorced.

Careful. Hold your temper. Look at the signs she's giving off.

Watery eyes. Nervous movements. A voice that shook.

Eileen was afraid. Of Bob.

Fear for his son and his ex-wife's safety laid a chilly hand on the back of Dylan's neck.

Dylan had to swallow twice before he could speak. And then the words tumbled out almost on top of one another. "I can protect you, Eileen. You can come live here."

"He's not drinking." Eileen's voice was shaky and unconvincing. "He doesn't lay a hand on us."

"There are other forms of abuse, Eileen," Dylan said in a cold voice. "And if Bob takes me to court, I'll be vocal about that." The fact that Bob was not what he appeared.

"I don't want trouble." But she still wouldn't look at him.

"We can leave things the way they are." But Dylan wouldn't. Not now that he knew what kind of man Bob was.

A commotion in the stables drew his attention. A horse whinnied, as high-pitched as a scream. And then he heard Zach's panicked shout.

After Dylan left to talk to his ex-wife, Zach jumped down to the dirt from the bottom step of the bleachers. "Have you been here before?"

"Nope. It's my first time." And Kathy couldn't wait to come back. It was like taking a trip into the land of her dreams, a place where Truman loved her again.

"Then you have to see Phantom and Peaches." Zach clapped his hands, so full of joyous energy that it seemed to radiate off him and onto her.

Kathy smiled. "I've seen Peaches. She's adorable." And so was Zach.

"Girls." Zach scoffed. "She's not a stuffed animal you nap with. She's a racehorse, just like Phantom."

"Of course, she is," Kathy said straight-faced. "Just look at her."

The pony came to a stop at the gate with Truman.

Zach ran over and stuck his upper body between the rails. He reached for Peaches, rubbing her withers as he talked to Truman. "Was she fast? Did she win? Don't you love her?"

"She's great," Truman agreed, smiling widely as if he, too, was soaked in Zach's happy energy.

Zach tumbled through the rail into the dirt. He giggled and leaped to his feet. Peaches didn't move a muscle. "I bet she liked you, too. Can we trade places? You're tall. How old are you? I'm five."

Truman grinned. "You don't talk much, do you?"

Zach blinked. "I talk all the time." Zach ran around Peaches, jumping up and down until Truman slid off. "Boost me, like this."

He laced his fingers together to show Truman what to do, then put his boot in Truman's hands and squealed when Truman lifted him, faster than Kathy could say, "Careful."

"The stirrups are too long. Dad!" Zach looked for Dylan, but he hadn't returned.

"Slow down, boy." Barry came over and shortened the stirrups for him. "Take it easy on the old gal. She's already raced once today."

Zach's frown was deep but fleeting. "Then I want to walk to the race with my head groom. What's your name, groom?" He looked down at Truman, who introduced himself. "Okay. We're getting ready to race. Here's what's important. The attitude of your horse, the weather and... I forget the rest. You need to take the reins and walk me, groom."

Truman did as he was bid. His face-splitting grin made Kathy wonder if he was lonely in Harmony Valley. Slade's twin girls had spent the summer but were back in New York now.

Behind Kathy, a horse whinnied. It was a shrill challenge, not an excited greeting. A chorus of upset horse noises followed, filling the air.

Barry ran out of the arena. Kathy followed him to the barn. The boys followed at Peaches' pace.

Carter was trying to lead Popeye through the breezeway past the stall that said *Stay Back*. Carter's horse tried to run past, but the teen was holding his position in front of the forbidden stall door. He held the lead rope taut, the exact opposite of how Dylan had taught Kathy to walk a horse.

"Get away from Phantom," Zach shouted as he rode Peaches into the barn behind her. "He's mean. Dad! Dad!"

Barry ran toward Carter. "Move him. Move him, boy."

But Carter was trapped between the stall and Popeye. And Barry's fastest pace wasn't fast at all.

Hooves struck the stall door. Frantic whinnies erupted up and down the stable aisle. Without thinking, Kathy ran toward the pair, slowing a few feet away from the prancing, head-tossing, one-eyed horse.

"Easy," she said, holding up her hands, raising her voice to be heard above the upset horses, yet still keeping her voice gentle, as Dylan had taught her. "Loosen up the tension, Carter. You're holding Popeye too tight."

Carter's handsome young face was pale. He seemed frozen, cringing each time a hoof struck the interior stall door behind him.

"Come on, Carter," she intoned softly. She took a few slow steps toward the next stall down. "Give Popeye a businesslike push in the shoulder. That's it," Kathy said when the teen responded to her. "Now walk this way."

But Carter hadn't walked far enough. A black nose extended through the bars, teeth bared. They opened and closed around Carter's shoulder. Carter cried out and bolted forward, freeing himself and taking a grateful Popeye with him.

Kathy stepped out of the way.

The stall strikes continued, along with a bone-chilling whinny.

Phantom. She recognized the name on the placard. The horse that nearly paralyzed the vet tech. The horse that gave Dylan so many bruises yesterday. The sun wasn't bright enough to break through the clouds and illuminate the interior of the stall. It was dark and shadowy. But something moved inside. Something large and black. The cold Kathy had been feeling deepened into her bones.

Barry helped Carter put Popeye away. "You wanted to work with that horse, boy, but you just wouldn't listen about how dangerous he is."

Carter's face was still white. "He...he bit me." He tugged aside his hoodie, revealing a red mark.

"Well, he didn't draw blood. You were lucky as usual," Barry chastised, his calm demeanor settling Kathy's nerves. "You'll have a nice bruise for all the girls at school to coo over."

This could be Chance in a year or two.

Now Kathy understood Dylan's reluctance to help the colt at first. Horses were big and powerful. They could do damage, serious damage. Unless Dylan was able to work a miracle.

She began to hum, stepping closer to Phantom's stall. Not close enough for him to reach through the bars and bite her, but close enough that the stallion could hear her. Close enough to try to offer him what little solace she could.

Dylan ran around the corner of the stable, limping. "What happened?"

"I looked him in the eye." Carter had removed his sweatshirt and pulled the neck of his T-shirt down so Barry could have a more thorough inspection. "It's my fault. I brought Popeye too close, and Phantom freaked out."

Dylan checked Carter's shoulder, then came to stand in front of Phantom's stall. "Easy, fella. You're okay."

The horse blew a breath. That black nose appeared at the bars, but the teeth were covered in whiskery lips. Heartened, Kathy began another verse of *Itsy Bitsy Spider.*

"Phantom?" A woman in fashionable boots and leggings appeared at the end of the stable aisle. She ran closer, one hand to the fur trim of her jacket. "He's dangerous. How could you bring him here, Dylan?"

"I'm fine, thanks," Carter said, regaining some of his teenage irreverence. "No blood spilled by Big and Bad."

The woman ignored the teen, fear in her eyes as she stared at the younger boys and Peaches. "Zach? Zach! Come here. Now. We're leaving."

"No, Eileen." Dylan's voice hitched from commanding to placating. "Phantom can't get out. There's no danger, just a few anxious horses. You know this."

"*Za-ach.*" Eileen's voice cracked and it looked as though that crack was just the beginning of her breakdown.

Kathy wanted to comfort her. But Dylan wasn't rushing to her side and that told her to be wary, that like the high strung horses he worked with, Eileen had to be handled with care. She continued to do what she could to calm Phantom. Humming. Such a small thing. But she dared not stop.

Zach and Truman were in the middle of the breezeway with Peaches. Zach was still in the saddle, staring at his mother as if he didn't recognize her.

"Get off that horse, Zach." Eileen was pale. She looked about to fall over. "This isn't good. Bob will..."

"I'm entitled to my court-appointed visits," Dylan said firmly, somehow managing to also sound approachable. "Phantom is never out when Zach is around. He's safe."

"It won't matter." Eileen barely managed to lift a protesting Zach from Peaches' saddle.

Kathy stopped humming and moved to Dylan's side. "I work with horses every day. What Dylan says is true. Zach will be fine as long as he respects the boundaries of a stall door."

Dylan's ex-wife rounded on her, tossing her hands in exasperation. She was a woman at her limit. "And who would you be? Another alcoholic?"

Kathy would have shrunk back if Dylan hadn't taken her arm. "She's a friend."

"Consider how this looks, Dylan," Eileen said, pleading. "Bob says you can't save alcoholics. They're a lost cause, just like your father. You know this. He says... Bob says they'll end up just like your dad, wrapped around a tree. Dead."

"That's harsh," Carter said, shoving his hands in his pockets, hanging his head, and hunching his shoulders.

Kathy couldn't fill her lungs with air. Beside her, Dylan seemed to be holding his breath.

Truman's gaze found Kathy's. His eyes soft with concern.

Only the old jockey seemed able to say more.

"You've changed since you married that lawyer." Barry spit in the dirt. "And it's not a good change."

Eileen walked out of the barn, taking Zach with her. It sounded like she was crying.

Chapter Twenty-Three

Z ach was gone.

Dylan ached with the sense of loss, trembled with the threat of permanent dispossession, became cold at the thought of a lifetime spent saying to anyone who'd listen, *"But he's mine!"*

This was Bob's doing. Men like Bob... Men like Dylan's father... They shouldn't be around Zach or Eileen.

"You should call your lawyer." Barry had unsaddled Peaches. He led the pony back to her stall. "She can't just take Zach like that."

"Well, she did. And I can't call my lawyer until Monday." Dylan felt as if someone had punched through his stomach wall and removed his guts without benefit of anesthesia. On autopilot, he went into the tack room, grabbed a training flag and Phantom's halter and strode back the way he'd come. "Don't put Peaches back yet. Lead her to the paddock."

"What are you doing?" Even as Barry fell into step next to Dylan, he argued. "You're not going in with him now. Not after all this."

"Dylan." Kathy's voice. Worried. She watched him approach.

"I can't sit and do nothing." Dylan wouldn't go into his empty house after Kathy left and listen to the silence and wonder how to thwart Bob without giving up his dreams of helping people and horses.

The deck felt stacked against him. But he couldn't believe Bob would be able to adopt Zach and take away Dylan's parental rights.

But there was always a doubt.

"I'm sorry." Carter tagged along at Dylan's heels, almost like Zach did. "I wasn't thinking. And then... I panicked."

"And that's why you aren't ready for a horse like Phantom." That was a heavy load of bitterness the teen didn't deserve to have thrust on his back. Dylan laid a hand on Carter's shoulder and looked him in the eyes. "Don't worry about it. It'll be okay." If not for Dylan, perhaps for Carter.

Kathy stood a safe distance from Phantom's stall door, watching Truman with her heart in her eyes. The notes of *Itsy Bitsy Spider* drifted to him. How could she remain so calm after Eileen's drama?

Truman sat on a chair a few feet away from her, eyes wide, gaze darting from Dylan to Phantom's stall.

"I'm sorry for what Eileen said. She doesn't know what she's talking about."

Dylan glanced at Carter and then Kathy. "I'd trust you—either of you—with Zach."

Kathy nodded and kept on with her musical performance.

Phantom had settled down, but Dylan's insides still felt riotous.

"Is that horse going to eat Peaches?" Truman whispered. "He tried to eat Carter."

"No." Dylan crouched in front of the boy. "Phantom gets scared sometimes. And then he gets annoyed that he's scared, and so he misbehaves. Do you ever feel so scared or mad that you say or do things you don't mean?"

Kathy's tune paused.

Truman nodded solemnly.

"Everyone take a breath. I'm just going to let him run a little," Dylan said loud enough for everyone to hear.

"Run at you, you mean," Barry mumbled. "Carter, stand back. Darn fool."

"I assume you mean Dylan is the fool, and not me." The smile was back on Carter's face, cracking the tension in the air.

"Thank you," Kathy murmured as Dylan came past her to climb through the paddock rails.

"For what?"

She gestured meekly toward Truman and then in the direction Eileen had disappeared. "No one has defended me in so long that I think I forgot what it felt like."

Dylan smoothed a strand of hair from her face. "Red, you deserve to be defended."

She smiled faintly. "I tried to defend you."

A hint of premonition that something more could be wrong, like the tinge of sulfur in the air after someone lit a match, made him pause and look at Kathy, really look at her, deep into eyes so blue he almost felt she was part of the sky. There could never be danger in those eyes.

When he didn't look away, her smile improved, easing but not completely erasing the tension in his gut or the premonition of impending disaster.

"Are you gonna get out there in his paddock or not?" Barry demanded in a curmudgeonly tone of voice. "If so, git!" He pointed toward the rear set of barn doors.

Everyone but Barry dutifully trudged outside. Dylan hopped the paddock fence and rolled his shoulders back.

"Be careful," Kathy murmured, hands on Truman's shoulders.

"Yeah," Carter said, almost seriously. "Don't break another leg."

"Hardy-har." Dylan rolled his eyes.

"You ready?" Barry called but he was already moving the lever that opened Phantom's stall door to the paddock.

Out of the corner of his eye, Dylan saw Truman reach up to clutch Kathy's hands. That fragile bond. It made Dylan happy and sad at the same time. And then there was nothing but Phantom, charging, rearing and making his usual ruckus.

After Phantom settled down, after he'd spent thirty minutes on the lunge line, after Carter had proclaimed he could wait a few more years to handle him, Dylan put the horse away. The sense of impending doom about his custody agreement was still tangled inside him, but it wasn't as overwhelming as before. Exhaustion tended to do that to a man.

Dylan sought Kathy's gaze, her soft, understanding gaze. "I think we could all use some chili-cheese fries."

Carter whooped. "If you're buying, I'm there."

"Maybe we'll just head home." Kathy's gentle expression spoke of the need not to intrude. "It looks like it might rain again."

Truman turned from beneath his mother's arm. "Mama, please." He pointed to the teen and whispered, "He's going."

Kathy couldn't refuse her son.

They drove to Bubb's Burgers in three separate vehicles. Dylan paid. Once more he sat across from Kathy. This time double baskets of chili-cheese fries sat in the middle of the picnic table.

"And that's when I came in second at the Belmont to the Triple Crown winner." Barry picked up a fry. "It's the only time in my life that I was happy to be beat."

Truman and Carter looked suitably impressed.

Kathy was eating and smiling and looking as if every wish she'd made for Christmas had been granted. Dylan wanted to make a few wishes of his own. One of them involved filling the space next to him with Zach's warm, talkative body. The other flitted about his head as if afraid to take form, but it involved Kathy. Of that, he was certain.

"You can really put food away, Red." Dylan finished the last bite of his bunless burger.

"Naw. My mom never eats." Truman paused and stared at the dent Kathy was making in the basket of fries in front of her. "Wow. She must not have had breakfast."

Kathy shrugged. Her eyes glowed with happiness. Dylan was pleased to see that, especially after what Eileen had said to her earlier.

But Dylan didn't want to think about Eileen. Because then he'd have to think of Bob. Take away Zach? He'd fight that to his dying day.

Barry belched, tucking his long white locks behind his ears. "Looks like we'll be making those deadlines you were worried about, Dylan. Phantom is really coming along." He nudged Truman's shoulder. "By this time next year, there'll be lots of little Phantoms running around."

"He's not ready," Dylan blurted. All eyes turned to him. He knew everyone except Truman was thinking about the woman Phantom had critically injured.

"He is." Barry shook his soda cup. The ice clinked. "It's you who isn't."

"I could help," Carter said, smiling. He was always up for a challenge.

Dylan resisted the power of that smile. "Your parents would kill me."

"The two of us can assist." Barry clinked his soda cup against Carter's.

"He's never been well behaved." Dylan stared at his hands. He hadn't been strong enough to contain Phantom the last time—wasn't sure if he ever would be.

"I could help. I'm good at humming. And I think he likes me." Kathy was serious.

This was quickly getting out of hand. A fly missed a good opportunity to dive-bomb into Dylan's open mouth. His gaze landed on Kathy's bandaged wrist. She moved it to her lap.

"When you've got a wounded wing, you can't be a wingman," Barry said gently.

"That leaves me," Truman piped up with the same optimistic attitude Zach had. "I can be brave."

Everyone quickly put the kibosh on that idea. To soften the blow, Kathy ruffled his hair and Carter promised to take him horseback riding later in the week. "Out in the pasture," Carter said. "Not in the arena."

"Are we gonna race?" Truman asked, wide-eyed.

Carter and Barry were winding themselves up to say, *"Yes."* Dylan could see it in the way they leaned forward, and how their smiles grew bigger.

"We only race at a track," Dylan said firmly. The last thing he needed was a horse to snap a leg in a gopher hole in the pasture and someone to pitch to the ground and break their neck. Bob would pounce all over that and call him an irresponsible dad.

"We can take a few horses to the practice track when we deliver some of Phantom's gold," Barry promised.

Carter and Truman high-fived.

"Today was awesome." Truman thanked Dylan without Kathy having to ask him to. He gave Kathy a half smile and then skipped toward the car, saying his goodbyes to Barry and Carter, who both had their heads bent together.

Kathy stood outside Bubb's, trying not to show that she was on Cloud Nine. Truman still loved her.

Dylan brushed Kathy's cheek with the backs of his fingers. "Didn't I say you'd be all right?"

He had. She was. Hope swelled inside her normally empty chest. She raised to her tiptoes and kissed Dylan, diverting just in time to plant her lips on the corner of his mouth, not the bow of his lips, because she wanted to thank him, not make a pass.

Dylan didn't smile or make light of it. He didn't reach for her or set her away. He stood very still, as if overly processing what she'd impulsively done.

"Oh, shoot." Kathy backpedaled, bumping into a bicycle rack. She offered her hand to shake his. "That was inappropriate. How about we shake?" That didn't seem right either.

Dylan ignored her hand and touched his jaw, just short of his mouth. "This time with Truman was important for you." He spoke in the space-creating, gentle tone of a therapist. It was more effective than him pushing her away.

Kathy turned and retreated to her car, but not before he called to her, inviting her and Truman to return to Redemption Ranch on Wednesday night, when he expected Zach to be visiting. Again the neutral, nonjudgmental tone, as if he was reminding her of her next appointment.

She'd been friend-zoned. Or...professional-relationship-zoned.

Kathy swallowed her disappointment and focused on the best thing to come out of the day – Truman smiling at her, reaching for her.

Truman shifted in his seat next to her. He deserved every wish upon every star, to dream of a big future, to believe he could take any branch the road of life offered him. And she'd do her best to make sure every wish he made came true.

They passed a sign that said Harmony Valley was ten miles away.

"Maybe we should get you a pony, Tru." They could keep it at the clinic, at least until the spring, when more pregnant mares began to arrive. She could walk alongside Truman as he rode the streets of Harmony Valley.

"Don't ruin it, Mama." Those few words were devastating. His detached tone. The way he turned away to look out the window.

What had she done wrong? What had happened between Bubb's and now?

They didn't speak to each other the rest of the way home. When she pulled into the carport, Truman leaped out and ran inside, met by an excited Abby.

Kathy followed more slowly, listening to Truman tell Becca what a great time he'd had with Peaches and his new friends.

Chapter Twenty-Four

"The good news is that Bob can't just adopt Zach." Matt Houston, Dylan's lawyer, gave it to him straight up on the phone Monday morning, after what had been a sleepless night for Dylan.

"Thank you." Dylan exhaled a breath and resumed pacing the length of the breezeway. The sun had yet to burn away the fog layer.

"The bad news is that the judge can punish you for your track record. In the past six months, you've been behind on your child-support payments more than you've been on time. You bring Zach for visits to a ranch with substance abusers and dangerous animals, and you return him to his mother's late on school nights. It makes sense that the judge wants you to come in and provide reassurance that this was only a blip."

"I can handle going in and talking." Dylan would limp in, visual evidence that his injury six months ago had been a challenge he was working to overcome. "If Bob can't achieve adoption, what can he possibly hope to get out of bringing me back to court?"

"Given the services you offer on the ranch, he might move that you see Zach less..."

"I only see him twice a week as it is!" Dylan protested, steps faltering. He reached over a stall door to stroke Peaches. "If I lose Wednesdays, then let's push for Zach to spend the night on the weekends again." After the accident, they'd dropped back to days only since Dylan hadn't felt up to having Zach overnight when he was on crutches.

Matt cleared his throat. "Or Bob might ask to put conditions on your visitation, like you aren't allowed to have Zach at the ranch."

"But it's my home!" Dylan had a shaky feeling that his life was derailing. "What about getting Eileen to testify against Bob? He seems to be manipulating her. She was more afraid of him than of the horses yesterday."

"Bob has a stellar reputation with the courts," Matt said, in his lawyerly voice, the one that was decidedly neutral. "Whereas that horse of yours has a dangerous past."

"Phantom's got one injury on his record." Dylan rolled the shoulder the horse had bitten only days ago, thinking about Carter's similar wound. "He's high strung but not a killer."

"Let's just see how it goes. If Bob tries anything out of the ordinary, I'll ask for a continuance and…"

Dylan tuned Matt out as he walked toward Phantom, whose black nose was pressed between the bars over his stall. More of the stallion became visible as he approached. His regal head. The proud arch of his neck. The forward tilt to his ears. Instinctively, Dylan reached through the bars to touch him.

But Dylan was seeing a different horse. A raw-boned, black stallion that his father couldn't break, at least not mentally. The horse had been tied to a post in their barbed-wire corral, shaking from the beating he'd taken with a thick eucalyptus branch. His father was cussing and spent, an empty whiskey bottle on the ground next to him.

His father's eyes had a look wilder than he'd ever seen in Phantom's.

Dylan had hesitated. He'd only come outside because the horse had grown silent. He'd thought his father had passed out or given up and driven to the bar. If so, he'd give the stallion food and water and tend to its wounds if the horse allowed him. But no. Dad was lying on the ground, clutching his leg.

"Damn horse kicked me. He can't be broke." Dad's laughter was drawn out and twisted, as if he might have regrets—if he hadn't been the devil. "Broke both our legs. Get my gun!"

Phantom nudged Dylan's shoulder, stopping the horrific replay of the past.

"Just do me a favor, Dylan," Matt was saying. "Make sure that stallion doesn't hurt anybody else. And don't start dating someone with an abuse problem. That would be the kiss of death." His lawyer hung up.

The dooming premonition Dylan had felt yesterday returned sharper than the morning chill. Kathy's gentle way with animals. Her humor. The way she tried to make herself invisible when her blossoming smile lit up Dylan's day. He liked her. He could more than like her. He could see a future with her. But Dylan also knew that nothing about love was certain. To pursue these early feelings toward Kathy right now would risk his chances with Zach. Their paths had crossed at a bad time. He'd move on with his life. She'd go on with hers. No hearts broken.

Phantom butted Dylan again, more urgently this time, a warning of an escalation coming.

"Whatever happens in court, nobody's going to hurt you," Dylan said, jerking his shoulder out of the way of Phantom's suddenly bared teeth. He stroked the horse's neck, which was what the stallion had wanted in the first place. "Nobody's going to hurt you."

"How do you know when I'm going to sit at my computer?" Kathy asked Abby, who'd hopped into her lap for a cuddle and a little begging for kibble almost as soon as she'd sat down at the desk in her bedroom. "Where were you when I needed a hug last night?"

Kathy pulled up the online university's website again. What was so hard about filling out an application? She'd looked up the codes to send her high school transcripts electronically. All she had to do was create an account and select Business as her major.

And yet, her fingers hovered over the keys without striking any. Outside her window, the birds were singing. They'd probably sing louder if she signed up for school.

"It's the color of the website," she whispered to Abby. "Tomato red." She'd never been able to wear the shade, not even as lipstick.

"Abby?" Truman cracked open the door and peeked inside. "What are you doing in here again?"

The dog leaned into Kathy, resting her head on Kathy's shoulder as she looked at her favorite boy. Kathy imagined she had the same love-struck look in her eyes.

"Drama queen," Truman muttered. Instead of leaving, he sat on Kathy's bed, flopping back to stare at the ceiling. "Do you think Carter is bad?"

"No."

He plucked at one of the leopard spots on her teal comforter. "Dylan said he's an alcoholic, like you."

Kathy nodded. There was something demoralizing about her son being so familiar with the term *alcoholic* that he could correctly apply it to others. She stroked Abby's silky fur.

"But I like him." He kicked out his feet, covered in white sports socks. "I don't want him to be a drinker."

"You can't make people say or do what you want them to, Tru." She thought of Mr. Hammacker sneaking drinks.

Truman made a sour face, thrusting his lips out, duck-like. He wanted to be in control of his life. He was too young to realize that no one had such control, not even Becca, his beloved aunt, who was currently banging pans in the kitchen as she made breakfast.

Kathy tried again. "You love Abby, don't you?"

"Yes."

"She doesn't always behave, does she?"

"No. She's always in here," he said sullenly, as if that was a punishable mistake on Abby's part. He plucked at the comforter again.

Kathy rubbed her chest. She knew her feelings shouldn't be hurt, but she was still thin-skinned where Truman was concerned. "But you forgive her after she's done something bad."

His gaze must have covered every inch of the ceiling before he nodded.

"And you love her even when she's done something wrong."

He nodded.

"It's like that with people, too." Kathy patted Abby, then gave her an encouraging push from her lap. "They make mistakes, and you try to forgive them. If you love them enough, forgiveness comes."

Abby sat on the floor in front of Truman, waiting for attention.

"But what if you know people can be bad? Like Carter or... Chance? Chance kicked you."

Kathy pulled her shirtsleeve up from her wrist, revealing the pea-green bruises. "Even though Chance did this to me, I know he didn't do it on purpose. I scared him. It was an accident. He's not mean-spirited."

"So, you're still Chance's friend?"

"Chance needs a lot of friends right now. He needs people who want to protect him. So does Carter." *And so do I.* But she was a mom. She wasn't supposed to admit a weakness to her child. "You heard some of what Carter said at Dylan's ranch. His friends at school don't realize when they invite him to do things together that they aren't protecting him. Those people are thinking only of themselves. They're part of the reason Carter drinks and part of the reason he needs Dylan to build up his defenses."

Truman sat up. Abby extended a paw for him to shake. For what seemed like a long time, he said nothing. Then he looked Kathy square in the eye and said, "Mama, who made you drink?"

She opened her mouth, but nothing came out. Not her mother's name. And not self-blame.

Becca announced breakfast was ready.

"You really need Dylan." Truman popped off the bed and ran out, Abby at his heels. "He can save you."

Kathy stared at the door, then at the tomato-red website. She wanted to agree with Truman. But the only person who could save Kathy from her demons was Kathy.

"If you came out to say I told you so, Gage…" Dylan tossed up his hands in surrender. "I may have to remind you that you benefited from this charade Flynn talked me into."

Gage leaned on the tailgate of Dylan's truck in the clinic's parking lot. It was the first time they'd seen each other since Kathy had discovered Dylan's true purpose for being in Harmony Valley. "Why would I say anything bad about what happened? The truth is finally out, and you showed up to take your lumps from me." He grinned.

"Lumps?" Dylan shook his head and got his training flag out of the back seat, gaze caught for a moment on the Zach's seat.

"I'm not doling out lumps or I told you sos." There was a smile lurking behind Gage's words. "You showed up to make things right. That's what matters." Gage turned serious. "Besides, the horses benefit from being worked, and between my patients and the improvements I'm making inside the clinic, I don't have time to do it myself."

Dylan nodded.

"Gage!" The older vet poked his head out the clinic's front door. "You have clients waiting."

"Off to trim doggy toenails," Gage muttered.

"Good luck with that." Dylan went around to the back, intending to work Chance. He didn't plan to treat Kathy any differently than he had before. But he did plan to keep his emotions firmly in hand. The tightrope walk that had become his life made him tense. There was more at stake than his son. There was his property. The horses in his care. Even Barry's future.

Dylan heard Kathy as soon as he entered the stable.

"Girlfriend," she said to Trixie from inside the gray mare's stall. "I'm going to tell Gage about your digestive issues. That gas is noxious."

The gray blew out a breath.

"I know you're expecting, but, girl...not another one."

Dylan's chuckle gave him away.

Kathy turned, cheeks blooming pink. "What? You don't talk to the animals, Dr. Dolittle?"

"I do." He crossed the stable floor until only a stall wall separated them. He didn't care that he'd left the warmth of the sun, since Kathy made him warm with her presence. "I just don't talk to animals as much as you do."

"I'm not going to stop." That stubborn streak. How he loved it.

"Why would I ask you to?" Dylan placed a hand on a stall bar, as if reminding himself that his attraction to her had to be locked away. "How's that wrist?"

"Stiff. But good enough to shovel manure." She studied his face a moment before exiting the stall. And then her arms were around him, holding him tight.

He hadn't asked for a hug. He hadn't expected one. Certainly, Flynn wouldn't like seeing his sister hugging Dylan. Bob would crow with satisfaction that he was fraternizing with an alcoholic, while his lawyer would sigh in defeat, but Dylan didn't care. He hadn't known he needed Kathy's embrace like he needed his next breath. He enfolded her in his arms and drew her close, until he smelled the soft, flowery scent of her perfume mingled with the smell of horse and alfalfa.

"I told myself I shouldn't do that." Kathy drew back, still within the circle of his arms. "But you looked like you could use a hug."

She always looked in need of one. But knowing she'd take offense to that remark, he merely smiled.

"Have you noticed anything?" Kathy tilted her head to look at him; her red hair brushed the sleeve of his navy flannel shirt.

He shook his head. He should release her. He didn't.

She smiled. "Chance hasn't kicked once since you arrived. The senior bowling team brought cinnamon rolls and coffee earlier. They talked for an hour. Chance is fascinated by people. Isn't it wonderful?" She sighed, snuggling closer and leaning her head on his shoulder. "I'm just so relieved."

Dylan was of two minds. One whispered in his ear: *kiss her.* The other urged a safer recourse: *let her go.* His life was a mess. Her life was a mess. It was no time for love.

Thinking about the L-word snapped at the careful balance he needed in his life right now.

Before he had time to think on it more, she drew him to the bench in front of Chance's stall. Her small hand warm, comforting around his. "Here. Sit."

Such a simple command. He should have ignored it. With her hand around his, he couldn't. There was the upcoming court date and Phantom's life and Zach's custody battle. There was the colt's future and Kathy's sobriety. There were conversation starters about her triggers scrolling through the back of his mind that would put distance between them.

But Kathy held his hand.

He decided to sit only ten seconds more before re-establishing a boundary between them.

Thirty.

Forty-five.

"Your son is adorable." Kathy hooked the fingers of her injured wrist into her jacket collar, elevating the bruise.

"Yours, too." Whose voice was that? It sounded whiskey roughened and nearly broken.

"I can remember holding Truman when he was a baby. He'd have a full tummy and those eyes would drift closed as he smiled at me. He was content to be held in my arms." She stroked a thumb over the back of Dylan's hand, perhaps without realizing it. "Yesterday, while you worked Phantom, I relived those moments. He sought shelter from me." She sighed and then released him. "It didn't last much longer than those chili-cheese fries, though."

Dylan's hand lay on the cold bench between them. He needed to get up and work Chance. He needed to ask Kathy questions about the things that had caused her to drink—her mother, her pregnancy, Flynn. "Eileen wants her new husband to adopt Zach."

Kathy's eyes widened, but instead of shouting out her shock, she kept her voice soft, for Chance's sake, most likely. "That's wrong. You can't let it happen. But...wait... You don't want it to happen, do you?"

Words of rejection scrambled through his head. He could have spouted hundreds of angry phrases, of bitter recriminations and scathing denial. But he knew once he started, he wouldn't be able to stop. He simply shook his head.

"I didn't want to assume. Some men don't want anything to do with the life they've created."

Here was the opening. Here was the key to unlocking Kathy's secrets. Dylan knew it like he knew the length and color of Phantom's teeth.

And still, he hesitated. Because here was also a change in course, from them interacting as a couple, to him being the sounding board she needed to keep on her sober track.

He was afraid his heart was about to derail.

Chapter Twenty-Five

"There's responsibility in giving life and providing a home for something or someone." Dylan's words seemed as fragile as blades of straw. "Whether it's a child you help create or a stray kitten you find in your yard."

Kathy nodded, weighing his words as carefully as he'd ever seemed to weigh hers.

What was he trying to say?

She couldn't look at him for fear he'd see the truth in her eyes, the one she'd been fighting for days but could deny no longer, not after seeing the defeated expression on his face this morning, an expression that shattered the best of her intentions. She loved Dylan. She loved his steady demeanor and his frank questions. She loved the bump in his nose and his wicked grin. She loved the way he stood strong in the face of chaos, like a panicking Chance, an upset Phantom, or a fearful ex-wife.

Dylan hadn't asked for her affection. In fact, he'd tried to step away from their budding relationship, as should she, but...

I love Dylan.

How did Kathy know it was love? Because she felt both calm and discombobulated when he was near. Because he made her feel normal and special all at the same time.

Her body began to tremble, and her mind to race.

I love Dylan.

But here was the test—the truth about her past. She'd tell him the worst of what had happened, and his reaction would either nip love in the bud or encourage it to blossom. And if it was meant to blossom, she'd wait. She'd force herself to keep love locked away, in the same place where she kept the truth about her past from Flynn.

"Kids can be a joy or a handful, sometimes both at the same time," Dylan was saying. "But no matter what, you need to stick by each other."

"Being back here makes me remember that I was a handful." Kathy traced the support beam to the ceiling with her gaze. "I was always looking for a shortcut. I guess it was inevitable that I'd find one and that it'd be my downfall, just as Grandpa Ed predicted."

The bench creaked beneath Dylan's shifting weight. "What was it?" At her inquisitive look, he added, "The shortcut that led to your downfall?"

She stared at the toes of her cowboy boots. The stable was filled with the soft noise of relaxed horses. Inside, Kathy was anything but relaxed. A tight ball of tension had formed in her chest. She'd kept the truth hidden for so long that it was tangled in that ball, ends unable to unravel.

But Dylan waited in that patient way of his, as if all his life he'd had to sit and wait.

"It was just like any other night," Kathy began softly, letting the ball unravel. "I went to a party."

Dylan nodded.

"I was young and stupid, desperate to have a boyfriend. To be loved. I'd just moved away to college and all I could think of was having someone of my own." She pressed the heels of her hands into her eyes. If only she could erase those weeks from her memories. "Back then I defined myself by the clothes I wore. But I also wanted to define myself by the man at my side." She scoffed, dropping her hands to her knees. "A man? The guys I met were mere boys who'd achieved legal adulthood, but not manhood. At the time, it didn't matter to me who he was or what his future held, as long as I could call someone mine."

Dylan made no sound. In fact, he kept very still.

The ball of tension in her chest expanded, loosened, letting the truth continue to slip free. "It was a college party. And I was thrilled to be invited. I was an invisible freshman." She stared at Dylan levelly, wanting to see his reaction to how immature she'd been. "I dressed like I was easy, because I wanted to be. I craved affection and I planned to give my body to whoever said anything close to the right words."

He still said nothing. No comfort. No judgment.

Was that a bad thing? She didn't know. But Kathy couldn't stop now. "I went alone. My roommate was studying. I thought she was dumb. Miss a college party? As if." Her voice strained with building tension. But the truth wouldn't change her past. Kathy was who she was because of her mistakes and misjudgments.

Dylan took her hand. She gripped it as if she'd just attended that party last night, instead of more than eight years ago.

"The guy who invited me to the party gave me a drink as soon as I got there. I don't remember much after that. I woke up later in a bedroom that smelled...dirty." Her fingers convulsed around his. "I knew something was wrong. I knew something had happened. I just wanted it to go away."

Keeping her hand sheltered in his, Dylan stroked his other hand over her hair. "None of that was your fault."

She shook her head, casting off his touch from her hair. She didn't want his pity. "I put myself in that situation. I put myself at risk. A few weeks later, things got worse. I...I tried to get an abortion. But I wasn't yet eighteen. I needed my guardian's permission. So, I came home, devastated. I didn't tell my family how it happened. And...maybe that's why Grandpa Ed and Flynn talked me into keeping Truman. I quit school and moved back home. I didn't regret it. Truman was the most beautiful thing I'd ever seen, created by something so loathsome that I couldn't speak of it. So, when you say you'll fight for your son...fight to protect Phantom..." Her breath caught in her throat. "Truman will never have a father do that for him. He'll never have a dad take him to Little League or teach him the ins and outs of football. He'll never have a father who loves him no matter what, simply because they share the same flesh and blood."

Dylan drew Kathy into his lap, pressing a kiss to her forehead that reverberated to her toes. "Do you know how strong you are? Or how special?"

"No," she said in a tiny voice. She turned her face to his. She couldn't look into his eyes, afraid of what she might see. Her gaze only made it as far as his lips.

As if magnetized, their mouths drew together. Dylan's lips were soft, bringing warmth and something she couldn't find for herself—forgiveness. It seemed natural to deepen the kiss, to sink against him, to breathe him in. To let love blossom further.

A horse stomped.

Kathy stiffened in his arms. "Oh, no. I'm sorry." She pushed against his shoulders. "I didn't mean for that to happen. You aren't looking for a relationship."

Dylan's arms were wrapped around Kathy.

A smarter man would have left the building, knowing what she said was true. He wasn't looking for a relationship. His life was a mess.

Her lips were still damp from his kiss. Her bright red hair mussed from his touch. For just a moment, Dylan allowed himself to wallow in male satisfaction. He'd put that dazed look in her eyes. His kiss had her trembling.

But he knew what was coming. He knew regret was a breath away.

That was why he didn't breathe.

Her hands rested on his shoulders. His around her waist.

"I should get up now, Dylan." Even Kathy knew what was right. Her hands slid to his chest. She gave a halfhearted, gentle shove.

His arms remained looped around her. "About that kiss..."

She unlinked his hands from her waist and stood. "I know. I'm sorry. It's just you're such a good listener and I'm..." She seemed to freeze, awaiting his reaction.

"You're my friend," he said softly, using the tone required for spooked horses.

Kathy jerked back to life, still agitated. She smoothed her hair, as if aware that she looked thoroughly kissed. "I shouldn't have sat so close to you."

Or held my hand. Or let me pull you into my lap.

"Hang on." Was she taking all the blame? "Are you saying *you* kissed *me*?"

"Yep. Remember me? Honest Abe? I'll take responsibility for that step out of bounds." Her hands fluttered about like lost butterflies. She caught him watching them, knotted her fingers in front of her, then moved them to her waist. "I'm sure you have women make passes at you all the time."

"Not hardly." He drew back and nearly toppled the bench over.

Kathy caught his arm until he steadied, then released him. "I just need to know that we're good."

"Good?" he echoed. Good was Kathy in his arms. Good was Zach on Saturdays and Wednesdays. Good was Phantom alive and kicking air instead of people. Heck, good was Eileen in a safe and loving relationship, Bob just a bad memory.

Kathy sat on the very tiniest corner of the bench as far away from him as she could get. "It's important to me that Truman and I can come to the Double R. You invited us to come Wednesday, remember? I don't want to make you uncomfortable. Forget what just happened. Please."

"Let's get a couple of things straight." Dylan shifted toward her. "*I* kissed *you*. I should be apologizing."

She noticed he didn't, raising her eyebrows.

The truth was...Dylan wasn't ever apologizing for that kiss. It was the best thing to happen to him in a long time. "You're always welcome at the Double R. You and Truman."

"You don't think that I'm..." The last word came out on a wisp of air. "Tarnished goods?"

"What kind of man would I be if I thought that?"

Don't look at her lips. Don't look. Don't...

Massive fail.

He yanked his gaze upward, but not quick enough to miss her smile.

Her smile was there in her tone, too. "Agnes was right."

"Meaning..." He tried to sneak a glance at her.

"That I should watch myself around you." Kathy turned her back on him, fiddling with Chance's halter and lead rope.

"Meaning..."

"There can't be anything more than friendship between us. Not while you're helping me. Maybe not ever. I heard what your ex-wife said. I shouldn't have kissed you, but I..." Kathy heaved a sigh. "Well, I shouldn't have done it. That's all."

She was saying everything Dylan needed to hear, everything that would make his lawyer happy. So why did he feel the urge to argue with her?

Because she understands me. Perhaps too well.

She knew that a woman like her was baggage to a man in his position. He couldn't risk more than that one kiss. "Kathy, I..."

"Kathy, I'm glad I found you." Gage strode into the stable, looking serious.

Dylan moved to Kathy's side and took her hand, ready to offer her strength if she needed it.

The vet raised his eyebrows, but otherwise ignored Dylan. "Trixie looks like she'll deliver in the next twelve to twenty-four hours."

That explained Trixie's tummy troubles. The mare lifted her head over the stall door, stretching toward Gage.

The vet moved closer, scratching under the mare's chin. "Kathy, have you ever thought about becoming a vet or a vet tech?"

"Me?" Kathy seemed incredulous. She looked everywhere but at Gage, as if seeking the source of such a ludicrous idea.

Dylan thought it was brilliant and said so.

Her cheeks bloomed a soft pink. "I don't know if I could or if I'd even like it."

"No one knows until they try." Gage opened Trixie's stall and stepped inside, snapping on gloves. "Doc and I have noticed the way you work with animals. You're compassionate, yet firm. And you're not squeamish around blood."

"I've noticed that, too," Dylan added softly. "She's good in a crisis."

Kathy's cheeks deepened to red. "I don't know what to say."

"How about that you'll think about it." Gage disappeared into the stall, presumably to examine Trixie. His voice drifted out to them. "In the meantime, I'd like you to assist in the delivery."

"Me?" she squeaked, squeezing Dylan's hand.

"Yes. You have a way with horses. They respond to you."

"No." Dylan gingerly lifted Kathy's hand, the one with the wrapped sprained wrist. "It's too dangerous right now. Maybe when she has more training. For now, use her to help deliver puppies or something."

"You're starting to sound like my wife, Dylan." Gage laughed. "Although I like it when she worries about me." He spared Kathy a smile.

Dylan wasn't amused. He didn't want Kathy at risk of injury. "Your wife seems like the more sensible person given the number of times you've been kicked."

"I've never had to have surgery from a horse strike, like some people I could name," Gage countered, good-naturedly.

"But the sheer *amount* of injuries you've had…" Dylan countered.

"Should I leave you two alone to compare scars and broken bones?" Kathy grinned. When the two men huffed, she touched Dylan's arm. "I'll be fine. Trixie is a gentle horse."

Dylan managed not to roll his eyes, but he did gaze heavenward. "Horses lash out when they're in pain or frustrated."

"I know." Kathy moved to Trixie's stall. "Gage, if I'm not here, call the house when it's time."

"It's settled." Gage removed his gloves and came out of the stall, giving Dylan a superior smile. "I'll call when she's ready. Most likely it'll be the middle of the night, though."

"Call me, too." Dylan stepped forward.

"Why?" Gage looked surprised.

"Because we both know how procedures with horses can go wrong without properly trained staff." Although it pained him, Dylan added softly, "*Please.*"

Chance nickered.

Gage glanced from the colt's stall to Dylan. "Maybe I can return the favor someday."

Dylan nodded, making a mental note to talk to Gage about helping him with Phantom.

When Gage left, Kathy shook Chance's halter at Dylan. "One kiss. One kiss and you think that gives you the right to protect me?"

There was a fight to her words that made Dylan want to smile. If only she wasn't putting her life in danger by playing horse midwife. "This has nothing to do with that kiss and everything to do with the hundreds of things you don't know about horses."

She thrust her nose in the air. "I'll be fine."

He came to stand before her, placing his hands on her shoulders. "I'm sure by now someone has told you about Phantom. But unless they were there that day, they couldn't have told you everything..." He circled her shoulders with his palms. "About the mistakes that were made."

Kathy's breath hitched. He felt it through his hands.

"They say there are five things that have to go wrong for an accident of magnitude to happen." Dylan gave her a gentle shake. "It doesn't matter if it's a plane crash, a busted water pipe or a horse who suddenly rampages. The one thing each accident has in common of the five mistakes is human error."

"Who made the mistake?" Kathy whispered. "That day. With Phantom. Who made the mistake?"

"I want to say the vet tech." Certainly, she'd made mistakes—her musky perfume, her dropping the collection tube and kneeling to grab it. "But ultimately, Phantom's behavior was my responsibility."

She reached up and touched his cheek, trying to reassure him. "I won't make any mistakes with Trixie."

Dylan closed his eyes. She had no idea what she was getting herself into. "Are you sure you want to help with this? You're starting to look more rested. The last thing you need is to miss a night's sleep."

She stepped away from him. "You're just as bad as Flynn. I don't need to go through life with layers of protection."

"But what if you went through life with someone who'd always have your back?" Someone like Dylan, whether that meant he had a right to kiss her ever again or not.

That could be me.

She didn't answer.

And since she didn't, he let the conversation drop.

Chapter Twenty-Six

How could Kathy work after that kiss and the realization that she loved Dylan? Or the invitation by Gage to help deliver Trixie's foal? She was soaring with happiness.

Or she would have been. If not for the *if onlys* getting to her.

If only pursuing her feelings for Dylan wouldn't cost him time with his son.

If only she didn't let Gage down during Trixie's delivery.

If only she didn't get injured while she was assisting him.

If only Dylan loved me back.

Kathy knew better than to dream. Hers was a life tied to manure. And the pile just kept growing.

Right now, she was cleaning out the paddock of manure so that Dylan could put Sugar on a lunge line. He was inside talking with Gage, probably trying again to talk the vet out of using Kathy as support for Trixie's delivery. Sugar trailed after Kathy like a loyal puppy, mouthing at whatever piece of clothing she could close her lips around. And then they heard singing. Sugar stopped trying to nibble the waistband of Kathy's jacket and raised her head.

The trio of councilwomen pulled up at the back entrance of the clinic in Agnes' Buick, finishing the final lines of Disney's *Let It Go*. Becca had told Kathy that the ladies had "discovered" the Disney movie over the weekend while attending one of their grandchildren's birthday parties. She almost expected the troupe to be in costume, but sadly that wasn't the case. They wore jeans and colorfully decorated sweaters beneath their jackets.

"Hello, Kathy. We're warmed up and ready to sing." Agnes was the first out of the car. She retrieved Mildred's walker from the trunk.

"I turned on the heaters for you ladies." Kathy was excited to see them. If Chance continued to progress, Dylan had promised to take the colt on excursions outside the stall.

"I've got the sheet music." Rose exited the car with a flourish. "*Annie Get Your Gun.*"

"I brought a cushion." Mildred waved a lime-green paisley pillow. "Those Broadway shows are long and tough on a woman's backside."

Rose harrumphed. "Time flies once you get going."

"I brought insect repellent, too," Mildred muttered.

Kathy helped the women get settled, pleased to see Chance's nose on the edge of the stall door in friendly curiosity. But she had no time to stay and watch. She hurried about her clinic chores. Her last indoor duty was really an outdoor activity—walking whatever dogs were cleared for exercise. They were boarding Olly Bingmire's Yorkie, and Kathy was more than happy to take the bouncy bundle of flowing locks out for a walk.

"For a little dog, you have a lot of pull, Jazzy." The small dog either didn't know or didn't want to know the heel command. She wanted to lead, and she wanted to do the minesweeper walk—back and forth from one side of the sidewalk to the other. "Trust me. Not many dogs have been by this way. The smells can't be that interesting."

But Jazzy thought they were. They rounded the corner onto Main Street at a good clip. Phil barely had time to come out of his barbershop to wave hello before they passed. The baby blue Caddy drove its circuit around the town square with a friendly toot of the horn. On the far corner of the square, Becca waved at Kathy before entering Old Man Takata's house. And the green gable of the Reedley house rose above the bare winter tree line.

There was a predictable rhythm to Harmony Valley that Kathy had never appreciated before. Years ago, even months ago, she couldn't have seen herself living here. When she'd left for college, she'd craved excitement, new people and new experiences. She hadn't appreciated the sense of peace that came from walking to work, neighbors who knew you, and the predictability of small-town life.

Upon returning to the clinic, she put a slightly less energetic Jazzy back in her kennel and made a mental note to walk her again after she walked Dolly.

Dylan poked his head around the separating wall. "Hey, Kathy, why don't we try to take the colt into Sugar's paddock?"

"Now?" If Chance pitched one of his fits, the choir would be in danger.

"Why not? I checked on him a few minutes ago and he was as calm as could be. If the ladies continue to sing, maybe he'll be calm enough to explore his surroundings."

It didn't take long to shift the ladies into the safety of an empty stall.

"We should start from the beginning," Rose announced, smoothing her snow-white chignon.

"Oh, please," Mildred muttered, flipping the seat down on her walker. "We'll miss lunch."

"I think we should just sing a few of the choruses. It's our turn to work at Mae's Pretty Things later." Agnes began singing lines about there being no business like show business.

Rose raised her thin, reedy voice. Mildred settled into her seat and joined in.

"Does this feel like a three-ring circus to you?" Dylan whispered.

Kathy grinned. "Chance loves it. Maybe we should have the ladies sing to Phantom while you get that collection procedure done."

"Being around Phantom is not for the faint of heart." His hand hesitated over the latch.

"It's okay, Dylan. Both these horses are going to be okay. Because you care for them."

He gave her a funny look.

"You may not think of yourself as a miracle worker, but you have the skill and the attitude to make a difference. Even small differences can be miracles to people like me or Carter. You're right where you should be, doing exactly what you should be doing. In a way, I envy that strong sense of purpose." She certainly didn't know what the future had in store for herself.

Vet tech, her mind whispered.

Dylan pressed a gentle kiss to her forehead.

More than anything, she wanted to lean into Dylan, wrap her arms around him and never let go. "What was that for?"

The ladies stopped singing and twittered.

"I needed to hear that," he whispered. "Especially today."

"I can't hear what they're saying," Rose complained.

"He kissed her," Agnes said. "You don't need to hear what he's saying. Use your imagination."

The elderly choir chuckled.

Dylan grinned. It was a full-on wicked smile, the kind that invited Kathy to share in a laugh, a joyful kiss, a squeeze of the hand.

Kathy couldn't catch her breath. She had to remind herself why she couldn't do any of those things with him—her love was one-sided and had to remain so, for Zach's sake. "Go on and smile, Dylan. You don't have to live here. News of that kiss is going to be all over town by dinnertime."

"Ladies," he said in that steady, confident voice that carried. "Could you sing something slow and romantic?"

There was a chorus of gasps.

"He's going to propose," Agnes said. "Quick, quick. What should we sing?"

Kathy didn't dare turn around and look at them, afraid she'd laugh and break the spell—the many spells. The one between her and Dylan. The tense truce between the colt and the world.

"You so rarely laugh," Dylan said, as if reading her mind. "Give them a look. Laugh some more. Everyone deserves to laugh."

"Rose?" Mildred asked in a desperate voice, as if their political futures rested on them choosing the right song. "Rose? What should we sing?"

A laugh, so often missing in her day, rose in her throat. Kathy put her hand over her mouth.

"Go on, Red," Dylan urged. "You could use laughter in your life. You have a lot to laugh about."

She didn't. Or at least, she hadn't for a long time. But...

Kathy glanced over her shoulder. The trio of councilwomen were adorably silly in their sincerity to set a romantic mood.

"Rose!" both Agnes and Mildred said, each poking one of Rose's shoulders because she sat between them.

The laughter began low in Kathy's throat, soft and sputtery and as rusty as a faucet that hadn't been turned on in months.

The colt jumped back, then came forward, stretching his nose toward Kathy.

"Don't poke me." Rose swatted gently at their hands. "I'm thinking."

"Think faster," Agnes urged. "Or the romantic mood will be lost."

They had no idea that Kathy had stopped thinking of Dylan's embrace long ago. But a different mood was overtaking her. Dylan's grin. Chance's friendly curiosity. The ladies' good-natured sparring.

Kathy couldn't hold it back anymore. She let the laughter go, and along with it some of her preconceived notions about the life of a recovering alcoholic.

Chapter Twenty-Seven

"Ow." Wilson cradled his hand. "That hurt."

Becca pressed a medical strip to the drop of blood on his finger. "Millions of people poke themselves several times a day, every day. What's up with you?" She handed him a tissue and inserted the strip into the reader.

He stanched the remaining blood with the tissue. "I'm sensitive."

"You've been sneaking Halloween candy. This says two hundred and ten." Becca glanced around the living room and into the kitchen. There was color in her cheeks as if he'd finally snapped her last strand of patience. "How can a man who doesn't walk or drive have Halloween candy? Where is it?"

Wilson wasn't going to tell Becca it wasn't candy causing his blood-sugar level to spike. Or that the cause of his blood-sugar spike was hidden in his circular spice rack in the kitchen. And he certainly wasn't going to tell her that he had a standing order with a liquor store in Cloverdale that delivered.

The front door opened, and Kathy came in with Dolly, a gust of cold air following them. His little companion waddled over next to his chair and collapsed, panting.

Kathy surveyed the two of them. "Problem?"

"I'm trying to help Wilson manage his diabetes better." There was a near-snapping quality in Becca's voice that Wilson had never heard before. "He's sneaking candy. Is it dark chocolate?" She shook her head. "What am I saying? I'm supposed to deliver someone's groceries next, and after that swing by Takata's to move his laundry. And I haven't even started prepping for my to-do list for tomorrow. I just...I just..." She turned to face him, features drawn in frustration. "Wilson, who's giving you candy?"

"No one." Wilson tried not to look at Kathy, but he couldn't help it. She could ruin everything. She caught him looking. He smiled at her, the I'm-just-an-innocent kind of smile.

Kathy hadn't moved from the foyer. She returned Wilson's stare. She glanced at her sister-in-law, not smiling, not so much as a twitch of a lip.

Come on, Kathy. Don't rat a guy out.

Wilson smiled harder. He smiled so hard his cheeks ached.

Becca had given up staring him down and was busy putting the test kit away. She didn't notice the pair's tense exchange. "Well, something keeps putting his blood sugar up high in the afternoon. He'll be losing his fingers next."

"Really." Kathy hung up Dolly's leash on the coatrack by the door. "Come on, girl. You need water before you nap." She picked up Dolly and carried her to the kitchen.

"While you're in there, you should grab something to eat," Wilson said to Kathy, trying to butter her up. "You probably eat less than Dolly."

Cupboard doors opened and closed. Wilson sank into his chair. Of course, Kathy wouldn't expose him. Kathy understood he knew how to handle his liquor.

"One last time... Where's the candy, Wilson?" Becca demanded in that way of hers that was simultaneously sweet and bossy. Well, maybe more on the bossy side today. She began poking around the living room, opening his old cigar box, Mary's empty candy jar, and even looking in the back of the mantel clock. "You'd tell me if I was getting warmer, wouldn't you?"

"Nope." He extended the recliner. All the late afternoon movies were about to begin. "My sugar number is up only because I had fruit with lunch."

Becca shook a finger at him. "If it was fruit pie, maybe that would explain it."

"Is this what you're looking for?" Kathy came around the corner from the kitchen with a flask of whiskey, a flask of rum and a flask of vodka. "Adult candy?"

"Where did you find that?" Wilson demanded. Oh, the betrayal cut deep. Helen would never have sent him downriver.

"I know all about hiding things you don't want other people to find." She handed Wilson's stash to Becca and headed toward the door.

"Thank you." Becca looked almost as surprised as Wilson felt, but not nearly as mad.

"That was low," Wilson fumed. "You, of all people, should understand that I know what I'm doing."

Kathy's hand gripped the doorknob. "You have no clue what you're doing." She turned, still gripping that knob. "You think you have it under control. You think you're smart because no one suspects a thing. But it's the alcohol that controls you—not the other way around—and I feel sorry for Helen. You were married for twenty years. She admitted she had a problem, yet you never did. How high and mighty." Kathy left, slamming the door behind her. She'd gone without even getting paid.

Wilson hunched in his chair, arms across his chest.

"She knew?" Becca's shoulders sank.

"I asked her to keep it a secret?"

"How could you do that to her?" Becca demanded, stuffing the flasks into her bag. "If she knew, every minute she was in here, she would have been thinking about this. About drinking this. Do you know what kind of willpower that takes?" Becca drew a deep breath, looking as if she might cry.

"Helen did it for twenty years. It can't be that hard." Wilson knit his arms tighter around his chest, trying to prevent guilt from sneaking in. "Those are my bottles. And I don't have a problem. I have a drink now and then. Everybody does."

Her hand went to her throat. "I'm sorry. I'm having a bad day. But...you...
.your wife..." She spied the ten dollars meant for Kathy on the coffee table. "I can't make the past right, but I'm making sure the future is taken care of." Becca snatched the bill and left.

Wilson put down his footrest and began rocking and counting and trying very hard not to shout his displeasure at the world.

Chapter Twenty-Eight

"Kathy, wait," Becca called from behind her.

Kathy had been hoping she'd get around the corner before Becca finished with Wilson. No such luck.

What a day. First, she'd realized she loved Dylan, and now this. She faced her sister-in-law, wondering if she'd accuse Kathy of stealing a drink from Wilson's stash.

"Wilson forgot to pay you." Becca handed Kathy ten dollars. They both knew Wilson hadn't forgotten.

Kathy was probably fired as his dog walker, this time for sure.

"Thank you for finding the liquor." Becca didn't accuse Kathy of falling off the wagon. She looked...genuinely grateful. "I just can't seem to make Wilson understand the importance of taking proper care of himself."

"He earns points for realizing Dolly needed help." Kathy pushed the bill into a pocket with the ever-present kibbles. "But that was because Doc bullied him into it."

"How did you know he was drinking?" Becca glanced back at Wilson's house.

"I smelled it on him. And then the other night when he fell, he admitted as much." Kathy scuffed her boot on the sidewalk. "I gave him up to you. It feels like I broke some unwritten code."

"I'm glad you did. He'll live longer for it." Becca rummaged in her purse, presumably for her car keys. Bottles clanked against one another. "I'm sorry.

I was losing my professional cool in there. I don't know how you managed, knowing he had alcohol inside and not being tempted."

"It bothered me a lot at first," Kathy admitted, hoping that Becca wouldn't think she needed to return to rehab. "But then I realized that I'd lose Truman forever if I drank again."

"I'll find someone else to walk Dolly." Becca continued her purse search. "Agnes or Rose or somebody. You don't have to worry about it."

"That might be for the best."

"I feel so stressed-out all the time. I'm juggling a new marriage, a new business, trying to homeschool Truman and be a good sister-in-law. I can't do it all. Something's gotta give." Even when she was admitting she was wrong, Becca was perfect. She knew exactly what to say, and even while she said it, not a hair was out of place, despite the breeze. "I was wondering if you'd have time..." She rummaged some more in her purse.

If she asked Kathy to help out with some of her clients, the answer would have to be no. Kathy preferred animals to people.

"...to take over homeschooling Truman."

For a moment, Kathy felt a kind of happy elation. But that moment passed, and reality returned. "Truman won't like it."

"Not at first, but it's time, don't you think?" Becca finally found what she'd been looking for and held out her hand to Kathy. "You should have this, too." She dropped a double-heart necklace into Kathy's palm.

Kathy glanced at the jewelry. "This was my grandmother's. I recognize it from her wedding picture." It was a silver pendant on a delicate silver chain. Two hearts were intertwined and could be taken apart. "My grandmother gave it to my grandfather before they were married, as he was leaving for the war. She told him if he fell out of love overseas that she'd understand, that he should mail his half of the heart back to her. Where did you get this?"

"Flynn gave me half when I lost faith in the feelings between us. He was willing to let me go until I realized we were made for each other." Becca closed Kathy's fingers around the necklace. "I thought if you had it, you'd realize that I have faith in you." She released Kathy and backed away. "We all have faith in you. Even Truman. And maybe there's someone new in your life, someone who isn't quite ready to commit, who'd understand what half of this heart means."

Dylan. That kiss. A love she could never have. Kathy's cheeks heated. "How did you...?"

"Truman thinks Dylan likes you." Becca's grin was infectious. "And Agnes saw Dylan kiss you in the stable."

"On the forehead," Kathy felt compelled to qualify. No one needed to know about the full-blown, heart-melting, earlier kiss.

Becca stopped. "Do you want me to take the heart back?"

"No." Kathy rushed forward and hugged Becca. It was the second time that day Kathy had hugged someone impulsively. "It's not the right time for love, but I appreciate the sentiment." That she could find a happily-ever-after with someone. Someday.

If she gave half the heart to Dylan, would he accept it? Or just reiterate that they were only friends who'd happened to share an emotional moment sealed with a kiss?

"You'd be surprised how right something can be at the wrong time." Becca checked her cell phone. "I've really got to run. Thanks again for what you did with Wilson. It was brave. Truman would be proud."

After she left, Kathy stood on the corner for a long time, looking at the necklace, hoping what Becca said was true.

Chapter Twenty-Nine

T he knock startled Kathy into a sitting position from a sound sleep. "Yeah."

Flynn opened her door, spilling light into the bedroom. "Gage needs you at the clinic."

"Thanks." She swung her feet to the floor.

When she didn't move, Flynn said, "You want me to make coffee?"

"Pretty please and thank you." He didn't leave. "What is it?"

Flynn grinned. "I'm just waiting to make sure you don't fall back into bed."

"I'm moving. I'm just moving slow." Kathy pushed herself to her feet. "I'm up."

Flynn flipped on her overhead light, causing her to squint. She heard him chuckling all the way down the hall.

"He was put on this earth to torture me," she muttered.

A few minutes later, Kathy was slurping hot coffee in the kitchen, willing the caffeine to work at hyper-speed. She rummaged in a drawer for a lid to the travel mug, fighting her body's desire to return to a horizontal position.

"I'll drive you over." Flynn hit some buttons on his remote. His truck roared to life in the driveway. "Hop to it. I'd like to get back to bed."

"Oh, sure. Go ahead. Rub it in." Kathy tugged on her jacket and hurried after him, touching her grandmother's heart necklace beneath her sweatshirt.

The night was wrapped in fog that breathed a piercing cold. The porch bulb barely penetrated the gloom fifteen feet from the house. They hurried across the dewy lawn toward the rumbling truck and its welcoming warmth.

When she was settled in the passenger seat, cradling the cup of coffee in her hands, she said, "I love your seat heaters. If I had any money, I'd buy a truck with seat heaters."

"You have money." Oh, how her brother's derogatory tone grated on her sleep-deprived nerves.

"Your money," Kathy scoffed. "My paycheck is more like your petty cash."

"No. Grandpa Ed left you half the house and half the money in his savings." He gunned the big truck down the gravel driveway. "I told you."

"Seriously?" Kathy felt wide awake. "How did I not know this?"

"I told you... Okay, maybe I didn't tell you at a good time. I was driving you back to rehab after Grandpa Ed died." He scrubbed at the scruff of dark whiskers on his chin, slowing to make the tighter turns in town. "I guess you don't remember me saying I was going to buy you out of your half of the house, either."

"Nope." She thought about the Reedley house on the other side of the town square and Dylan's shell of a house in need of some love. "I'd like a place of my own."

"I, uh... Do you think you're ready to take that step?" Flynn posed the question in a way that said he wanted to be supportive, but he still wasn't sure she was ready.

"Not yet, but soon." Kathy liked her answer. It felt decisive and confident. "When I'm ready, you'll be the first to know."

"I'm proud of you." Flynn spared her a glance, his face shadowy in the dashboard light. "You know that, right?"

She made a sound of assent. "You have to say that. We're family."

"Dylan seems to think that one of the reasons you started drinking had to do with Mom."

Kathy slurped coffee instead of answering.

Flynn didn't let the conversation drop. "I realized over the past few days that we talk about a lot of things, but not that."

"I can't tell you everything." She'd told Dylan, though. It used to be Flynn she shared her secrets with. How things had changed.

"I just want to help." He was an endearing, big lug, her brother.

"It's not like I'm riding a bike. You can't run behind me ready to catch me before I fall." She slugged his shoulder gently. "There comes a time when you have to let the birdie fly out of the nest."

"Can't blame a guy for trying." Flynn pulled up behind the clinic. The lights were on in the stable. "Can we talk later?"

"We'll see." Ha. Every person alive knew that meant no.

"I can take it," Flynn said in a quiet voice. "The truth. About you and Mom. And Truman."

Kathy pressed a quick kiss to his cheek. "Someday. Soon. I love you, you dork."

"I know. Call me if you need a ride home."

"I will." Kathy hopped out of the truck and made her way uphill, hugging herself against the damp, nippy air. She was excited about the opportunity to help with a delivery, thrilled that Gage had such faith in her and worried that she might do something wrong.

Sugar plodded sleepily along the fence next to her until she reached the stable.

Gage's wife, Shelby, greeted Kathy at the stable door. Her short blond hair was rumpled, bed-head style, and her jacket had what looked like red wine stains on the front. That was a distinct possibility given she was the winery's cellar manager.

Shelby grabbed Kathy's hand and dragged her toward Trixie's stall. "I'm so glad you're here. Gage won't let me in."

"Why not?"

There was grunting and heavy breathing coming from inside the stall.

"Because horses sense my fear." Shelby kept her voice a whisper, church-service level. "Because horses have hurt Gage before. I mean, you've seen pregnant women, right? They get a little nuts when they go into labor. It's not as if this mare is just going to throw ice chips in Gage's face—she could plant her hoof in his midsection again."

Kathy had mostly disregarded Dylan's concerns, but somehow hearing Shelby's made her hesitate. And in her hesitation, fear threaded its way through her insides.

"Take a breath, babe. You're scaring Kathy." Gage's voice held a quality to it that Kathy had never heard before—utmost tenderness. "Besides, you're carrying a little bundle of our own. I don't want Trixie to jostle our baby."

"Congratulations." This was news to Kathy. "Don't worry, Shelby. Trixie wouldn't hurt me."

"Kathy," Gage whispered. "Come inside."

The stall had a heater running above it, making it warm and cozy. Kathy handed her jacket to Shelby and entered quietly. Trixie walked in a tight circle, panting as if she'd run a race and needed to cool down. She paused as she circled past Kathy and reached out to nudge her shoulder with her nose. And then it was back around the stall.

"Give her room." Gage had on clear plastic gloves that ended at his elbows. He guided Kathy back against a wall. "She's about to roll."

Before Kathy could ask how Gage knew this, Trixie lowered her bulk to the thick layer of straw and rolled like a dog who'd found something smelly. Back and forth. Side to side.

"What's she doing?"

"Trying to find relief from the contractions."

"I guess they don't teach Lamaze to horses, do they?" Kathy said nervously. "Do you want me to teach her a little hee-hoo?"

Gage held out a hand, not smiling. "Nope. Just stay back."

Her previous hesitation, laced with fear, returned.

Kathy clutched her injured wrist to her chest.

Trixie rolled up to her feet and resumed her pacing. The pattern went on for another thirty minutes. Pacing, rolling, pacing, rolling. And then, finally, she didn't get back to her feet.

"It's go time." Gage came around behind Trixie, pushing hay away from the mare's hindquarters with his foot. "Stay by her head and start talking. I'm going to make sure everything's all right."

"Be careful," Shelby whispered over the stall wall.

"I'm always careful," Gage murmured as he knelt at Trixie's tail.

Kathy got on her knees in front of Trixie.

"Stand up," Gage said. "You don't know if she'll strike out with a hoof."

Kathy stayed where she was. "But you're on the ground."

"He's been kicked before," Shelby said. "Now you know what I go through, Kathy." She added in a mutter, "And I've got two of them to worry about."

"Are you comfy, girl?" Kathy pitched her voice the way Trixie liked. "I've been through this. Trust me, it's worth the effort."

"Two hooves." Gage tugged on something that looked as if it was wrapped in bluish-white plastic from beneath Trixie's tail.

The mare panted in a deep, raspy rhythm.

"I wish I would have been able to walk right up to the time of Truman's birth," Kathy sing-songed, feeling the tension in her body ease. "Instead, I spent a good deal of time complaining in a hospital bed."

"Oh, jeez. Thanks for that tidbit," Shelby said.

Trixie strained and wheezed.

Kathy was concerned. "Is she supposed to sound like this?"

"She's supposed to sound uncomfortable," Gage said.

"Then she's supposed to sound like this," Kathy confirmed.

Someone was whispering outside the stall. A man's baritone. Perhaps Doc had arrived.

Gage tugged a few more inches of foal free, which seemed to be primarily long legs. He poked a hole in the birth sac. "That's right, girl. Keep pushing."

"She's the superstar of pushing," Kathy said. "Hee-hoo, Trixie."

Gage kept tugging and tearing goo away. The foal was a dark gray, like its mother. Its chest heaved, just like its mother's. This was different than when Kathy had given birth. She'd been young and frightened. This was nature in all its power and glory. And she was part of the event.

"So close," Kathy encouraged. "Push a little more."

The foal slid the rest of the way into the straw. Gage removed the birth sac completely, leaving the umbilical cord intact. "It's a girl." He was clinical in everything he touched, rubbing the sac between his fingers, testing the thickness of the cord, peering at the afterbirth. "I think we're good here."

Kathy stroked Trixie's sweaty neck. "When will she get up?"

"In a few minutes. Let's retreat to the door and give these two some space to bond."

As soon as Kathy left her side, the mare sat up, extending her front legs as she began to rise.

"Trixie, don't get up," Kathy protested, scuttling back and falling to her knees. "Gage, stop her. She just gave birth."

"Let her go." Gage stood on the other side of the stall. "Mares and their young have to be ready to run from danger almost immediately after birth."

Someone slipped into the stall. Dylan. He helped Kathy to her feet and pulled her out of harm's way. Before she knew what was happening, he had her behind him. All Kathy could see was the black jacket covering his broad back. "Where did you come from?"

"Cloverdale. I had a bit farther to drive than you did." He still held her hand. He gave it a slight squeeze. "Enjoying yourself?"

She peeked around his back. "Immensely."

Trixie turned around in a small space, as if realizing her baby was behind her. She nuzzled the foal, who extended spindly legs forward and tried to get to its feet. It took several more minutes and several more tries, but finally both gray four-legged beauties were standing.

"Are all of you coming out now?" Shelby said in a strained voice. "I'm ready to slide the latch if you are."

"A few more minutes, hon. I just want to make sure everything's good." Gage was in his element.

Kathy felt as if she was, too. Everything was so beautiful. A mother fussing over her child. The delicate movement of the little one. Her hand within Dylan's.

"We can get out of here now." Dylan led her out of the stall.

Kathy didn't want to go, but she didn't want to make a fuss, either. As soon as she was out, she turned and peered back into the stall. "I haven't felt like this since Truman was born." Warm and fuzzy and full of love and...a feeling that everything was right in the world, even herself.

A few minutes later, Gage joined them. He pulled off his gloves so that the gooey parts were on the inside and then tossed them in the trash. Shelby immediately embraced him.

"Piece of cake, hon." He wrapped his arms around her and gazed at Kathy. "Well, what did you think?"

"I think this is the most wonderful thing I've experienced in a long, long time." Dylan hadn't moved from her side, although she'd released his hand. Her shoulder rubbed against his jacket. Some of that love and satisfaction inside of her was just itching to get out, all caution forgotten.

"I think it's wonderful, too." Gage grinned at Kathy over the top of Shelby's blond head. "Have you thought any more about becoming a vet or a vet tech?"

She hadn't. Not seriously. But the feeling of beauty and love from what she'd just witnessed strengthened and grew with the idea that she could make a career of this, something that gave her life purpose. The joy of it the experience burst out of Kathy in a laugh that echoed throughout the stable.

"That's a yes." Gage didn't stop grinning. In fact, his grin widened. "I'll help you study. You can do this."

"Thank you. Thank you for pointing out what I couldn't see and for showing me this." Kathy gestured toward Trixie and her foal. It was one of those moments where the world seemed to shift into place. The idea felt right. The world felt right. And for once, Kathy felt right with the world. "Shelby, I hope you don't mind, but I need to hug your husband." Kathy didn't wait for Shelby to step out of the way. She hugged her, too.

"Pardon me if I don't participate," Dylan deadpanned.

Kathy held out her hand to him. His calloused palm slid against hers. She reeled Dylan into the group hug.

"You should have taken a picture of Trixie's foal to show Truman," Kathy told Dylan.

Just a few hours after Trixie delivered, Kathy sat next to Dylan at the kitchen table. She was still drifting on the euphoria of the experience and the realization that she wanted to work with animals. No more staring at a tomato-red website and feeling uninspired.

Kathy clasped the heart pendant at her neck and glanced at Dylan. She hadn't worked up the courage to talk to him about it. She might never work up the nerve. "Trixie's foal is adorable."

Outside, the sky was beginning to lighten. The birds were singing. It felt like the start of a new day. The kind of day where everything went right. Kathy laughed for no other reason than she was happy.

Flynn was measuring coffee at the counter. He stopped and looked at her, a slow smile building on his features.

"I'd love to see the foal." Becca was making pancakes, wearing those baggy gray sweats of hers, the ones that lessened her perfection and made Kathy like her that much more. "I might be able to swing by in another day or so."

"You're too busy, Becca." Flynn's smile dimmed. "You need an assistant."

"Kathy's going to take over Tru's homeschooling." Becca flipped a pancake with panache. "If I can just get over this hump…"

"Then three more residents will hire you." Flynn was always grumpy when he missed his eight hours of sleep.

Truman stumbled out to the living room, more asleep than awake. He let Abby out, then collapsed into a kitchen chair, laying his head on the table. Kathy smoothed the unruly spikes of ginger hair on his crown. He didn't shy away from her touch. Once more, she felt the joy of a fresh start.

"Why didn't you take a picture with your phone?" Dylan picked up Truman's phone from the middle of the table. "Is this yours?"

"No." Kathy couldn't get the word out fast enough. "I don't have a phone."

Truman yawned. "Mama doesn't like the bad people texting her."

Kathy's feeling of euphoria drained as everyone stared at her. She'd had no idea Truman knew about the texts.

"What bad people?" the three adults asked in a discordant chorus.

And just like that, Kathy was back on treacherous ground, sinking, if the slightly horrified looks on everyone's faces were any indication. The smell of burning pancake filled the air.

"Why do I get the feeling this has something to do with your drinking problem?" Dylan leaned closer, curling his fingers around hers beneath the table.

Kathy checked her coffee cup. Yep, still empty. She couldn't take a drink to delay saying something. "This was an important night for me." The room seemed to shrink. Kathy was aware of everyone's scrutiny, of the heat in her face and the feeling of panic in her throat. "Can we not talk about my problems? Just once?"

"Kath." Flynn gripped the chair-back across from her. "Dylan said you needed to tell all your secrets to stay sober."

Truman raised his head, glancing first to Dylan, then to Kathy.

She was not telling the ugly truth in front of her baby. Kathy's gaze dropped to Dylan's hand on her own. "Is truth a guarantee of sobriety?"

"Kathy..." Dylan sounded weary. "You know as well as I do there is no cure-all. But the wounds of your past are festering. You need to clean them out."

"Rip off the Band-Aid," Flynn added.

"You're confusing your metaphors, hon." Becca flipped a pancake into the trash.

"I'm just saying she should tell me...*us.*" Flynn never took his eyes from Kathy. They'd had stare-downs as kids. Whoever blinked first lost. He'd always won.

Kathy looked away. "Brothers are annoying." Then and now.

"I wouldn't know," Truman murmured, propping his head in his hands.

"Tell us about the texts," Dylan gently urged. She'd grown used to the gruff-honeyed quality of his voice. It comforted and smoothed the path to secrets being spilled.

But not this morning. Kathy laid a hand on Truman's soft hair. She wasn't going to say a word in front of him.

Flynn understood. "Let's go outside, Kathy."

Dylan didn't wait for her to agree. He stood and gently pulled Kathy to her feet. "We'll listen. Both of us. You know I'm not going anywhere."

But for how long? Their friendship was so very new. How much more drama could one man take from a woman? Why had her heart been set on loving a man so quickly? It was sure to break.

The air outside was bracing. Their breaths puffed white clouds. The fog so thick she couldn't see the river. Kathy followed Flynn to the back porch. He leaned against the porch rail. Kathy and Dylan took seats on the white plastic chairs. Dylan still held her hand.

Flynn noticed and frowned at Dylan.

"Down, big brother," Kathy told him. "We're friends."

Disbelieving—because he'd almost certainly have heard about at least one kiss by now—Flynn crossed his arms over his chest and gave her that brotherly look she resented. "The texts? Who sent them?"

Kathy couldn't just tell him who it was without first telling him what they were about. "Flynn, do you remember when you first started making money from your farming app? Real money?" She felt the cold from her toes to her ears. It wasn't just the chill of the morning. It was the bone-deep frigidness that came from exposing her weaknesses, even if it was to those closest to her. "You bought us things. A new television. A laptop and tablet."

Flynn nodded, but his frown didn't waver.

"Do you remember asking me where they'd gone to a few months later?"

Flynn's jaw ticked. He gave the barest of nods.

"I had to sell your gifts. To protect Truman." The icebox that had become her body numbed her lips. She could only speak in fits and starts. "Someone wanted money from me because... They threatened to tell you—and the world—who Truman's father was...unless I gave them money."

Beside her, Dylan stiffened.

"The truth is...the truth is... I don't know who Tru's father is." If Dylan hadn't been holding her hand, she'd have been wringing hers. This was the hardest part of the story. Harder than who'd sent the texts. "I was drugged and raped at college. I don't even know if it was by one man or many."

Flynn swore. He paced.

Dylan's hold on her hand tightened.

Flynn stopped, fists ready to strike an unknown foe. "Whoever did this to you will pay. For the original crime and for the blackmail."

Kathy shook her head. "I don't know who Truman's father is. And the blackmailer didn't know, either."

"I'm confused." Flynn deflated a little. "Explain."

"When did the texts stop?" Dylan asked. The intensity in his eyes clearly asked: *Will they start up again?*

"I turned off my phone the day I went into rehab." Kathy drew a deep breath. "The day after I found out that my mother was the one sending the texts and demanding money."

"Mom?" Flynn nearly howled. "Kathy, why didn't you tell me?"

She rushed on. "I didn't know it was her until the day before I dropped Truman off here. By then, I was more concerned with getting sober."

Flynn took up pacing again, his gaze unfocused. No doubt, the cogs in that genius brain of his were turning fast enough to blow a gasket. "And afterward?"

"Grandpa Ed died. And I went back into rehab." Still without turning on her phone.

"All those times we talked about Mom since you've been home... You should have said something."

Dylan cleared his throat. "I think the important learning from this morning is that now you know, Flynn."

"You don't understand," Flynn said urgently. "I've been looking for our mother. I've sent out messages saying I want to see her." He wiped a hand over his face. "If she's still alive, she could show up here at any time."

"She'll want money." It was Kathy's childhood all over again, doing a double take at the sight of any redhead, listening for the harsh laughter, wondering when her fairy-tale, safe life here would end.

"She'll get nothing from me." Flynn's gaze narrowed on Kathy. "Or you."

He'd get no argument from Kathy on that score.

"I need to make some calls." Flynn left them on the porch.

Dylan brushed hair from her face with a tender touch. "How are you feeling?"

"Like I'm a balloon and someone punctured me." *Like I need a hug to stay aloft.*

Dylan brought Kathy into his lap and drew her close, in a way that gave her heart hope to a future with him, a future they shouldn't pursue until their lives were straightened out. "You're going to be okay, Red."

"You always say that." She'd happily hear him say that to her every day. If only...

"It's true." Dylan leaned his forehead against hers. "What will you do when you see your mother?"

"What you really want to know is will her appearance make me drink?" Kathy didn't have to think twice. "That's a no. But it's the unknown that's scariest." She sighed. "My mother is going to show up here with some new twist, some new demand. And I'm going to worry about it every day until she appears, because I don't want her to hurt Truman."

He rubbed her back. "There's a place you can be safe, if you need it."

"Rehab?" Just the thought made Kathy feel defeated.

"Redemption Ranch."

She pushed back to look at Dylan, heart pounding. "What are you saying?"

He hesitated. Whatever he'd been thinking, he hadn't followed through to the conclusion she'd already made—that he needed to protect his son by keeping her at arms' length. "I..."

"You don't have to say anything." Kathy could hardly get the words out. But they needed to be said. "I get it. I'm a black mark in your custody battle."

"You're not." His jaw jutted out.

She stood. "Zach is your top priority. Keeping your son is more important than exploring what may or may not be between us." The words squeezed her heart.

And if all that amounted from their friendship was a better relationship with Truman, it was enough.

It had to be enough.

Chapter Thirty

"Why can't you teach me anymore?" Truman clung to Becca as if Kathy was going to take him away.

The day of the homeschooling switch had come. Despite Kathy and Truman getting along better, Truman still rebelled on this issue.

His rejection hurt. But Kathy was accepting of the fact that her life would always have challenges to endure along with moments of joy.

With an apologetic glance Kathy's way, Becca extricated Truman's arms from around her waist. "There are too many people in Harmony Valley who need my help. I can't keep up. I need help. And you're it."

"I'll try harder at math," Tru promised.

As mornings went, this one wasn't shaping up very well. It required big-girl panties and mom jeans. Kathy stepped into both. "Tru, grab your backpack and come along. Chance is waiting."

"Huh?" Truman turned, blinking at her.

"Your new classroom is in the stables. You'll be reading aloud to Chance, solving math problems with Isabo, and presenting your science experiments to Trixie and her baby." Kathy used her mom voice as she moved toward the door. "Abby can come as long as she doesn't upset the horses."

"Abby loves horses." Truman scurried around, gathering up his things.

Becca mouthed, "Thank you."

It was Becca who needed to be thanked. Kathy hadn't seen Dylan in days. He'd postponed their Wednesday visit, and she might have been mopey if not for Becca asking her to help out by running errands for residents. She felt needed rather than extraneous. She appreciated anything that occupied her mind so she wouldn't wonder about Dylan and what-ifs and the heartbreak of love unfulfilled.

Kathy finally got her son out the door. He talked the entire walk to the vet clinic. He talked about Peaches and Zach, Phantom and Dylan, his preference for pancakes versus waffles.

If her son went into politics one day, he'd be the choice to conduct a filibuster. Truman could talk about anything.

Kathy listened happily. It'd been too long since he'd been in the mood to babble to her. Once at the clinic, she set her son up with a bench and a small wooden table in the stable.

Truman tapped his pencil on his notebook. "How old is Chance?"

"Two months old, I think." Kathy measured a morning servings of oats for Chance.

The horses nickered, eager for their breakfast treat.

Truman straddled the bench. "Chance's scars are wicked-awesome."

"Where did you learn that term?" Kathy poured oats into Chance's feeder.

"From Faith and Hope." Slade's daughters, who split their time between their mother in New York and their father here in Harmony Valley. "Did they name Trixie's baby yet?"

"I don't think so." Kathy moved on to Isabo's stall next.

"They should call her Princess. Those white spots around her ears look like a crown."

Now Kathy knew why Becca was stressed about Truman getting his schoolwork done. He was easily distracted. "No more questions until you show me your finished math assignment."

Truman sighed heavily. He tapped his pencil again.

Chance pressed his nose to the edge of the stall door and sniffed, causing Truman to giggle.

"I bet Carter is good at math," Truman said.

"Tru..."

"That wasn't a question," he pointed out.

"At this rate, you'll be here all day."

He grinned.

Kathy smiled back.

Why did it seem as if she'd lost a battle but won a war?

"That could have gone better," Matt said to Dylan, who was making the effort to keep his head up as they came down the courtroom steps. "The only thing that went our way was the judge had a bout of stomach flu halfway through the session. You're going to have to put that horse down or risk losing Zach."

"Supervised visitation." Dylan repeated the words as if they were a death sentence. And no visits to the Double R. That was what Bob wanted. "Are you sure there's no scuttlebutt on Bob? Can we call on Eileen to testify? Hire a private investigator?"

Matt shook his head, smoothing the tie that fluttered in the breeze.

Cars drove past, heedless of Dylan's turmoil.

Barry pushed his shorter stride to keep up with them as they headed toward the parking garage. He'd driven into town to support Dylan. "We need a payday from Phantom, something to show he isn't a lost cause. You always say money makes the world go round."

"Not now, Barry," Dylan told him.

"Bob made a strong case," Matt said. "He had pictures of that woman's injuries from the stallion. In color. Might have contributed to the judge's fragile constitution." Matt was young and polished and ruthless—the right opponent for Bob. Or so Dylan used to believe. "Plus, he documented your late payments. He portrayed you as irresponsible, trying to start a business rather than heading back to work."

"Three days. The most I was late was three days." The sun was shining but Dylan didn't feel its warmth.

"Late is late." Matt adjusted his black leather laptop bag on his shoulder. "We'll come back tomorrow to finish presenting our side. Then we've got a few weeks to clean up your act. Sell the horse. Go back to being a full-time paid horse whisperer. You have to give me something positive to work with here, Dylan. Or Bob will come back at you in six months with some other complaint."

"If he's a proven breeder, we can find him a home." Barry tossed his white hair over his shoulder. "Don't give up on him."

"It's too soon." He would hurt someone if they tried it before he was back to respecting his handlers. Dylan couldn't sell Phantom at this point—not with his reputation or his behavior. And putting him down wasn't an option. Nor could he stop helping people like Kathy and Carter. Dylan liked helping animals and people—it was his life. If they took that away from him, who was he?

Dylan mumbled his goodbyes and got behind the wheel, still wrestling with the corner he was being backed into.

He hadn't realized he was driving to Harmony Valley until he pulled up at the vet clinic. In his suit and tie, he wasn't dressed to work with horses. He shed his fancy jacket, turning at the clip-clop sound of hooves on pavement.

Kathy led Chance out onto the street. At first glance, the chestnut colt looked like a stuffed pony who'd lost his stuffing and been stitched up to keep the rest of his parts in. But he moved with the grace and power of a future champion. Chance pranced sideways at the sight of Dylan, but Kathy used the training flag at his flank to right him.

"That's awesome." Dylan smiled for what felt like the first time that day. "Want some company?"

Kathy rolled her big blue eyes. "Even if I said no, you'd still come along." But she was smiling.

I need that smile.

He fell into step next to her, heading toward Main Street to do the usual circuit through town. "Want me to take him?"

"I've got him. Don't I, Chance?"

The colt gazed at his surroundings curiously. She clearly had him under control. There was hope for him yet, maybe not as a racehorse but as something less stressful. And Kathy...

She looked fabulous. Color in her cheeks. Energy in her step. A small, intricate silver heart pendant swung from her neck. And she'd finally mastered the art of walking in cowboy boots. It had been only a few days since he'd seen her last, but the change in her was incredible. "How are you, Red?"

"Good."

"Walked any dogs today?"

"Yep."

Why were her answers suddenly so clipped? "Am I missing something? How are you really?"

"Who's asking?" Kathy kept her eyes on the road. She didn't so much as slip a sly sideways glance his way.

Dylan felt as if he'd been given an ice-cream cone that was melting in the heat before he could enjoy it. What was wrong here? "I've only been gone a few days and you've forgotten me already?"

"No." She adjusted her grip on the lead rope. "Am I talking to the miracle worker? Or my friend Dylan O'Brien? Or is there some other label we should consider?"

On the heels of the disastrous court appearance, Dylan felt as if his tie was choking him. They turned down Main Street. He undid his tie, slid it free and unbuttoned the top button of his shirt. He still didn't breathe any easier. "I'm not sure how to answer. Someday, I might hope to be all three."

They walked in silence.

"Sobriety-wise, I'm okay," she said smiling softly, as if knowing there were challenges to be overcome before someday arrived. "How goes your custody battle?" Typical Kathy. She cut right to the chase.

"If anything, it's worse." He was being backed into a corner. And he should have taken those steps alone. But he needed to be with Kathy. He needed to hear her humorous take on things, see her smile, hear her rare laughter. He needed it in order to face the hard job ahead of him.

"Is that fella of yours going to strip again, Kathy?" It was Phil, the elderly barber, standing in front of the red and white barber pole and swaying like a scarecrow in the breeze. "Do you need me to call Flynn or the sheriff?"

Kathy waved. "Everything is okay, Phil."

"Everything is not okay." Dylan wasn't sure if anything would ever be okay again. He was losing control over his life.

The colt swiveled its ears toward Dylan and his bitter words.

Before Kathy could comment or soothe, a door opened on the right side of the street. Agnes stepped out, waving. The sign above her proclaimed the shop to be Mae's Pretty Things. The front window display was filled with quilts, crocheted afghans, knitted caps and an assortment of purple pot holders. "He looks so handsome today, Kathy."

"You can take that as a compliment, if you'd like," Kathy said to Dylan, waving to Agnes as they passed. "But I'm pretty sure she meant it for Chance."

The baby blue, bubble-fendered Cadillac they almost always saw out and about town entered Main Street from the town square. The driver honked.

Chance freaked, rearing and bucking and prancing at the end of his rope. Kathy was no match for his antics. The training flag fell to the pavement. Dylan took the rope and began murmuring soothing words to the colt. His tail swished in annoyance, and he tried to back away from Dylan, until his hindquarters crossed the yellow line in the center of Main Street.

The Caddy roared past, striking Chance's tail. A burgundy scarf waved out the car's open window as the elderly driver passed. She tooted her horn again at the next corner.

"Did you see that?" Kathy shouted. "What kind of idiot drives past people in the road at that speed?"

Chance was listening, and Kathy's upset only made him more frantic.

"Calm down, Red." Dylan spared Kathy a quick glance. "Calm down."

"Oh, shoot. Sorry." Kathy attempted to hum *Itsy Bitsy Spider* as she picked up the flag.

"Lilac Miller is at it again." Agnes shook her fist at the retreating Caddy. "Always speeding somewhere. I'm going to call her right now and leave a piece of my mind on her answering machine."

It took the colt a few more minutes to settle down.

"I'm glad you were with me when that happened," Kathy said when they were able to proceed down the road again.

"So, you do like my company."

"Don't pout and fish for compliments." Kathy slipped her hand into his. "Why don't we walk Chance around the town square? He might enjoy the grass."

"It's kind of bare for a town square." Dylan was in the mood to pick. "There's just grass, an old tree and a bench."

"Are you kidding me?" Kathy gasped. "This is where everything happens in this town. Every festival. Every parade. Tons of marriage proposals."

"Tons?" Dylan looked at the place with a jaundiced eye. "It's scraggly."

"It's winter. Look there." She pulled him toward the spreading oak tree and the bench beneath it. "I can't tell you how many marriage proposals have been made at this bench. It's one of those small town traditions. I wasn't here for the spring festival, but there was a marriage proposal made in front of the entire town." She stopped in front of the bench and tilted her head to look up at the oak's branches. "And every kid in town has climbed this tree. The fire department had to rescue my friend Tracy once because she climbed so high after a kitten that she got scared and wouldn't climb back down."

"This sounds like a great place to grow up and grow old in."

"It was." She frowned and glanced around. Her gaze landed on a green craftsman-style home on the corner. "It could be again."

"And here I thought you were a city girl."

"I did, too." She released his hand. Moving slowly, she stood in front of the colt and stroked his forehead. "I've changed. Because of you."

"Me?" Dylan's heart beat faster even as his chest swelled with pride.

"I used to think I'd be happy if only Truman loved me. And then I thought I'd be happy if I had a friend like you." Her hand stilled. She met his gaze steadily.

"But I look at you and I want more than friendship. More than walks around the block and holding hands during the tough times." She blushed but held his gaze, her head high. "But I adore Zach and I'd never risk your chances with him." The colt butted against her shoulder, begging for more attention. "So, I guess I'm asking where this is going. You know, after your legal challenges are through. Because if you feel the same, I can wait."

Dylan didn't know what to say. How to answer. What if his life fell apart tomorrow? He'd be no good to anyone, especially her. "My court date didn't go well. I need one of your hugs." There. He'd said it. Stopping himself just short of asking for a kiss.

She gave him a one-armed hug. A friendly hug.

And wasn't that par for today's course? "The judge seems to be siding with Bob. In order to keep my visitation rights, I have to give up everything that's important to me—working with troubled horses, helping people stay sober. Kathy, who am I if I don't do these things? Who am I if they're ripped away from me?"

"I know the right thing to say." The colt moved closer, resting his chin on her shoulder. Kathy snuck a look at him, eyes glowing with happiness. "I can't weigh in on that decision. Some people would judge me for keeping and loving Truman. Some would judge me for not keeping him. But it was my choice." She touched Dylan's cheek with the back of her hand. "You have to be at peace with the choices you make, even if it hurts or disappoints someone you love."

The L-word banged around in Dylan's head, growing stronger and more significant. It banged his chest. It banged his lungs. It banged his heart until it beat faster. Dylan loved Kathy. Holy cow.

I love her!

Dylan hadn't seen that coming. He knew she was special. He knew she was important to him.

But love? It blindsided him and gripped his throat like his dad used to—digging and squeezing until he could hardly breathe—because he couldn't do anything about loving her. Not now. Not yet.

"I need another hug," he said huskily. "A better hug."

She shook her head. "Dylan."

"I don't think I can do what the court wants," he blurted. He hadn't come here with the intent to tell her. He was always the one who prompted conversation and then listened. But just now, he needed a friendly ear, a loving ear. "It's impossible."

"What is...?"

"Putting Phantom down." He almost didn't recognize his own voice. It was rough, stripped and broken. His gaze dropped to her hands, the ones stroking Chance. He wouldn't ask for a hug again, no matter how much he needed her arms around him.

A man had so few things that made him who he was. His pride. His principles. His loves.

"They can't make you do that as a condition of..." Kathy gulped.

"It's a strike against me. There are many strikes against me." Dylan was considering discarded everything good he'd started and putting down a horse just to stay in his son's life, instead of being a good man and a better father than his had been.

Kathy took Chance's lead rope. "Relationship-wise, I'm a strike against you, just like Phantom."

"Don't say that." He shifted his weight off his suddenly aching right knee. "I'm back in court tomorrow. They're going to crucify me." His throat closed up so tight he almost didn't get the last words out. "They want me to choose between my son and everything that's important to me. Strip away enough of a man's values and he's nothing. That's what happened to my father, what led to his drinking." Dylan drew a deep breath. "He was accused of doping a racehorse and banned from the sport after that doped horse caused a multi-horse accident. He always claimed to be innocent. But circumstances crushed him. He only seemed happy when he was nearly black-out drunk and had something – or someone – under his control."

"That won't be you." There was anger in her voice. The breeze lifted her red hair, making her look like a warrior, ready to do battle. For him.

She didn't understand how easily that could be him. Bob's demands would break his spirit and crush his soul. And then he wouldn't be good enough for Kathy or Zach or anyone.

Dylan took a step back.

Kathy fiddled with the heart pendant. "I want you to have this." She freed half of the heart from the necklace and handed it to him. It was as small as a dime. "Consider it my heart." She met his gaze and in hers he saw the reflection of his own feelings—love. "Hold on to it and know that I believe in you. You're one of the most caring men I know. They can't take that away from you."

The silver was warm in his palm.

"If you get through this rough patch and you still want to explore these feelings between us, I'll be waiting right here. In Harmony Valley. But if you decide to choose another path, send my heart back to me." She spoke in a low, urgent voice, tears in her eyes.

Dylan curled his fingers around her precious gift, imprinting her beautiful, courageous face in his memory. Because he was afraid that after tomorrow there'd be nothing left of him she'd want to love.

Chapter Thirty-One

S omeone was knocking on Wilson's door.

No one ever knocked on Wilson's door at midday, not even Becca. If she was coming to check up on him, he wouldn't let her in. He turned off the television and tottered to the door. But when he opened the door, it wasn't Becca.

"Can I come in?" It was Kathy, looking as if she needed a drink.

I'm not wearing my toes.

He felt naked. Wilson shuffled back on his heels, clutching a chair for balance. When he'd invited Kathy to visit him in time of need, he hadn't expected her to come. And after the way she'd turned him in to Becca, he'd never expected to see her again. Nor had he wanted to.

Without taking her pink jacket off, Kathy sat on the couch and lifted Dolly into her lap.

Standing near the door, Wilson felt the first twinges of annoyance. Dolly should be in his lap. "It's too cold outside to walk the dog."

"I was just... I didn't come to... I'll go." She stood, still holding Dolly.

"No. Please stay." Why had he said that? The midday news shows were just beginning. He'd miss a recap of the day's stories before the afternoon movies began. He duckwalked on his heels toward his recliner. "I meant it when I said you're welcome here." And didn't that cost his pride? "Even if you aren't a very loyal friend."

She ignored his dig, stroking Dolly's long back, staring down at his dog as if she'd never seen her before. "How did your wife stay sober for twenty years?"

Wilson sat heavily in his chair, considering what to say. "Helen did everything by the book. Went to meetings. Talked to her sponsor. Was honest about her addiction."

Kathy's gaze game up to meet his. "But she lived with you. A...*drinker*."

The fact that Kathy hadn't called him an alcoholic wasn't lost on Wilson. "I may not have been drinking during that time." He'd been employed for some of it, after all.

Kathy raised an eyebrow.

Wilson squirmed, tucking the empty shot glass into the crack between the cushion and the armrest. "I may not have *drank* as much during that time."

Kathy nodded. "And she stayed sober?"

"Yes." From his seat in the recliner, Wilson could reach Kathy's hand. For some reason, he felt compelled to take it. "It's okay to ask for help."

"I'm not." She drew her hand back. "I'm sober. I'm not tempted."

"Ah, but you are. Every time you announce to someone that you're an alcoholic. What you're really saying is '*I'm broken and don't let me drink.*'"

Her frown was as intense as her fiery red hair. "That's stupid."

"Is it?"

She frowned at the silent television.

He wondered what the lead news story would be—weather, sports, politics, some new deadly virus?

"How does someone fall in love with an alcoholic?" Kathy's voice was small and soft, the voice of someone who'd been hurt and didn't want to be hurt again. "How can you ever trust them not to drink?"

"I loved Helen. The alcohol part didn't come into play. Ever."

"Did she tell you up front that she was...like me?" Kathy's blue eyes were haunted.

Wilson hesitated. Was this why she'd come? To see if there was a chance for love in her future? "I guess I knew from the moment we met that she and I were destined to be together. I don't remember when she told me exactly." It wasn't at first, of that he was certain. "For better or for worse, love is a risky proposition. If you think you're in love with someone, you need to take that bull by the horns and never let go."

"What if your bull shouldn't be taken by the horns?" Kathy slumped against his couch cushions. "What if just being an alcoholic means you hurt the one you love?"

"I don't have the answer to that, Kathy. But you're a smart, caring woman." Wilson glanced at the picture of Helen on the mantel, feeling her loss like a gaping hole in his heart. "Just be true to yourself and follow your heart."

"But I already gave it away," she murmured.

Chapter Thirty-Two

Truman was waiting for Kathy outside Mr. Hammacker's house. Abby sat at his side. He didn't have hold of her leash.

Despite having given away her heart—and who was she kidding? It wasn't coming back because Dylan would choose Zach, as he should—Kathy's burdens lightened at the sight of her son. "Aren't you supposed to be at Mildred's, reading to her with Becca?"

"Mildred didn't feel well. I was just walking by, and I saw you go in."

Kathy wasn't buying that. "Tru."

He shrugged. "I was."

"Okay. Let's get back to the clinic." Kathy looped her arm around his shoulders. They walked toward the town square. Abby was in the lead, her leash dragging behind her. Kathy may have lost the chance for the love of a good man, but she had her son back. For now, that was enough.

"Mildred says Mr. Hammacker is a drunk." Truman very carefully did not look at Kathy.

"That's not very nice."

"Is he?" Truman gazed up at her, expecting the truth. Deserving the truth.

"He's trying to quit." That wasn't quite true. Becca had tracked down the liquor store he was ordering from and canceled his order. "But you shouldn't listen to gossip."

"Phil and I got into a fight over gossip."

"Oh, you shouldn't fight with Phil, either." The barber was old and rickety.

Truman's lip thrust out. "He said mean things about you."

"Really?" The barber was always so nice to her, waving as she walked past his shop.

Abby flicked her ears back, perhaps picking up on the tension in Kathy's tone.

Truman nodded. "He said I should be ready for you to drink again. He said I had to watch you closely and tell an adult if you did anything wrong."

"I'm sure he meant well." *But wow, didn't that suck!*

"He didn't, Mama. He said you'd fall off the bus."

The bus? "The wagon?" Was that why Phil waved to her every day? To see if she was drunk? Kathy frowned.

Lilac turned her bubble-fendered Caddy onto the town square, honking her horn.

Truman continued working himself up. "Phil said it would happen." Truman stopped and stared up at her, waiting for Kathy to say that was a lie.

Most addicts relapsed at least twice. Kathy had already relapsed once. She never wanted to let Truman down. But could she make that promise?

When she didn't immediately answer, Truman made a guttural noise and started running. Abby immediately went to his side, jumping and leaping in excitement, sending her leash curving like a bullwhip in her wake.

The Caddy came around the square's corner. Unaware of the danger, Truman stepped off the curb. Kathy lunged forward, shouting for him to stop. Abby was quicker. Her herding instincts had her leaping in front of him, forcing Truman back to the curb. But her leash swung around and got caught beneath one of the Caddy's tires, yanking her back against the fender when the little dog would have leaped forward to the safety of the curb.

There were yelps and screams and tires squealing.

Kathy made sure Truman was okay, and then picked up Abby and ran.

"Barry? Carter?" Dylan walked through the empty stable yard at the Double R, one hand in his pocket, fingering Kathy's heart.

Both men's vehicles were out front. Neither was around.

And then he heard Phantom's distinctive whinny. It came from the indoor working area next to Maggie Mae's stall, the one where they'd put the mare look-alike and equipment to collect the stallion's breeding samples. Cold fear crackled in Dylan's veins.

He ran as if in slow motion.

He heard Barry and Carter shouting, and everything sped up. He burst into the room.

"We got it. We got it. We got it." Barry slid to the floor, holding the collection tube. He was wearing a white riding helmet. It was cracked above his ear and blood trickled onto his cheek. "I see stars. Dancing stars." His voice sounded distant, and he began listing to one side.

Carter was holding Phantom's lead rope, but the stallion had dragged him to the doorway of Maggie Mae's stall. The teen glanced over his shoulder at Dylan. "Help."

Nostrils flaring, the black stallion pranced in front of Maggie Mae, nearly trampling Carter.

"Easy, boy." Dylan came up to the stallion from the side, not wanting to startle him. "Easy." He took the rope from Carter. There was blood on it and on Carter's palms where the rope had sanded away skin. And on the back of them, too.

Phantom was too preoccupied with looking good for the mare to notice the change in handler.

"Are you okay?" Dylan asked, heart pounding.

"He struck my hand when he mounted the look-alike." Carter pressed at the flesh on top of his hand. "I might need stitches. Oh." He hunched over, suddenly panting. "I shouldn't have looked. I get queasy at the sight of blood."

Dylan hurried out with the stallion, got him safely put away in his stall, and then ran back to help the two idiots who'd risked their lives for a payday.

Carter was on his knees vomiting. Barry was babbling, nearly fallen over, and holding the collection tube like a beer stein he was toasting with.

Dylan righted Barry. "How many fingers am I holding up?"

"Ten," Barry said when Dylan hadn't been holding up any. "Could have used an extra pair of hands. I think I might need to see a doctor." He thrust the collection receptacle into Dylan's chest. "Put it into cold storage before you take me."

"You're more important than this." Dylan's voice rang with anger.

"If there weren't two of you, I might punch you in the nose right now." Barry gestured with his head toward the unit that would gently drop the temperature of the sample and freeze it for delivery. "I didn't go to all this trouble to get nothing out of it. It'll help save him, won't it?"

Dylan didn't know.

Across the room, Carter moaned, pressing one hand over the cut on the back of his other. "If we went through all that for nothing, I might need a drink."

"Don't even joke about that." Dylan relented and handled their revenue stream quickly, but carefully. Then he wrapped Carter's hand in gauze tape, cleaned him up as best he could, and helped both fools into his truck.

"Why are you driving so fast? Why am I still wearing this helmet?" Barry asked from the front seat as Dylan drove toward the closest urgent care clinic. "Are we in a NASCAR race?"

"I'm afraid to take that helmet off in case your brains spill out," Dylan deadpanned, only half joking. "You have so few brain cells anyway. What were you thinking?"

"We wanted to prove that even two harmless people like ourselves could handle Phantom," Carter said in a shaky voice. "Uh-oh. I think I left my phone back at the ranch."

"I'm not turning around for a cell phone."

"Okay, just let me take a picture with your phone, then. That selfie is gonna earn me lots of street cred. More than downing shots ever would."

Dylan was reminded of the photos Eileen had shown the judge. "There won't be any pictures. What's your mother's number?"

Hours later, when Carter had six stitches on the back of his hand and Barry had been checked in to the hospital for observation due to a suspected concussion, after Dylan had tried to explain to Carter's mother how such an irresponsible thing could happen and how coming to the Double R was, in fact, good for her son, Dylan finally arrived back at the ranch just as the house phone was ringing.

"Dad?" Zach whispered in a high-pitched panicky voice.

"Yeah, buddy."

"Pappa Bob says I can't come see Peaches anymore." Zach sniffed. "He says I can't come see you anymore. Or Barry. Or Carter. Or Phantom."

"Nothing's been decided, buddy." But nothing would change, unless Dylan changed everything about his life—and ended an innocent one.

"Pappa Bob took my boots," Zach wailed, as if this had been the last straw.

"Zach?" Eileen's voice in the background. "Where are you, honey?"

Zach hung up.

Dylan walked on numb legs to Phantom's stall. The stallion pressed his nose between the bars, but his nostrils didn't flare, and his teeth weren't bared. Dylan pulled up a chair and sat, placing his elbows on his knees and his head in his hands.

He saw again the rawboned black. Heard the screams and the gunshot. He faced the choice once more.

But there was no choice. He couldn't do this again.

He'd have to let him go.

Kathy had never spent so much time in the clinic's waiting room.

It was painted a sterile white. There were blue plastic chairs with metal legs. They were cold. There were no calming landscapes to look at, not even a calendar of playful kittens on the wall.

But the lobby wasn't empty.

Truman sat in her lap. Kathy touched her heart pendant each time their friends and supporters came in.

Flynn and Becca, who brought coffee.

Mr. Hammacker, who sat next to Kathy and took her hand.

Agnes, Mildred and Rose, who sang show tunes quietly in the corner.

Conspicuously absent, at least to Kathy, was Dylan, not that she'd let him know her son's dog had been hit by a car.

"I could arrange for a medi-flight to the university," Flynn said in between pacing the room. "They have one of the highest-ranking veterinarian schools in the country."

"I have faith in Gage," Kathy said firmly.

"Me, too," Truman echoed, but not with as much conviction.

The sheriff stopped by. "I cited Lilac with reckless driving. I've been giving her warnings for months. She feels bad."

"She should," Agnes said hotly. "First, she nearly runs over a baby horse, and then she almost kills a dog."

"Even I gave up driving," Mildred said mournfully. She'd been a race-car driver in her youth. "Comes a time when you just have to do what's right for the safety of others."

"I wonder if she'd sell me the Caddy," Rose said thoughtfully.

Everyone shushed her.

"But it's a classic," Rose argued, crossing her arms when people shushed her again.

"Is Abby gonna die?" Truman whispered to Kathy, not for the first time.

"Gage has superpowers when it comes to animals." Kathy repeated the same thing she'd been telling him for over an hour. "I'm sure he'll be out soon to tell us the good news." She probably wouldn't have been so calm if she'd been alone.

Alone. Dylan would be alone in court tomorrow.

Kathy glanced up to find Gage in the hallway. The vet's smile was grim, not at all reassuring.

The lobby fell into silence.

Gage's footsteps echoed across the linoleum. He knelt in front of Truman.

In the back, a dog howled.

Oh, no. No-no-no-no.

Preparing for the worst, Kathy's arms tightened around her son.

"Abby is very lucky," Gage said gently. "But she has a long road ahead of her."

Truman gasped. He glanced up at Kathy. "What does that mean? Is she taking the long road to heaven? The...The rainbow bridge?"

Kathy wasn't sure. "Gage...?"

"She's going to be fine. She had internal bleeding, broke two legs, and at least one rib..."

"When I get my hands on that Lilac," Agnes muttered.

Seeing as how she was barely five feet tall and a town councilwoman, the chance of any real violence occurring was slim.

"We had to set one leg with pins," Gage continued explaining to Truman. "She's going to need lots of rest."

Kathy made a mental note to talk to Gage about his bedside manner. He needed an upbeat smile if the news was good.

"Can I see her?" Truman's voice was as shaky as Phil's hands.

"In a little bit. She's still sleeping."

Truman turned and buried his face in Kathy's neck. He hadn't cried yet, but now he let it go.

"Thank you." Kathy reached for Gage's hand. She'd probably be working to pay off his bill for a month. But Abby was worth every penny.

Love was precious. Life was short. It shouldn't be spent alone.

"Flynn, I need you to do something for me." Later that afternoon, Kathy stood in the kitchen, gripping her grandmother's pendant. Truman had fallen asleep on the sofa. "I need you to find out where and when Dylan's family-court date is tomorrow."

Flynn set down his coffee. "Why?"

"Because..." Her voice became very small. "I think he needs me there. It's a hearing for custody of his son. His ex-wife's husband is causing trouble and – "

"I don't know, Kath." Flynn rubbed a hand around the back of his neck. "That might not be a good idea."

"Because of what I am?" she whispered.

"No. Because it can get harsh between a man and his ex. I know I heard enough sharp words from Slade's ex-wife to last me a lifetime." Flynn shivered.

"She's already said nasty things about me to my face," Kathy admitted still talking in a whisper. "She can't hurt me anymore. But she can hurt Dylan. She and that lawyer husband of hers. And I think... I feel that he needs me there."

Flynn took Kathy by the shoulders and bent his knees to look her in the eye. "What if he doesn't want you there? As a friend or as anything else?"

"I gave him half of this." Kathy opened her hand to reveal the pendant. Her brother would know what it meant. "I need to go. He shouldn't be facing something like this alone."

"Okay." He sighed, relenting like the caring brother she knew he was. "I know a guy who seems able to find out just about anything. And quickly."

"The same one you have looking for Mom?"

"Yeah. The man who found you when you disappeared into rehab. Maybe he can help find a leverage point with this lawyer."

"Call him, Flynn. Call him."

Chapter Thirty-Three

D ylan showed up at the appointed court time wearing the same suit he'd had on the day before.

It was late afternoon and he was hoping the judge would be feeling better and more likely to show some compassion.

No such luck. She went straight for the jugular.

"Mr. O'Brien, your ex-wife has raised serious concerns about the environment you bring your son into, concerns I tend to agree with." The judge was as cold and immobile as her graying helmet hairstyle. "What do you have to say on this matter?"

Matt stood. "Your Honor, we're willing to comply with every demand Mrs. Johnson's attorney has raised and..."

The door at the rear of the courtroom creaked open.

For some reason, Dylan felt compelled to look back. Barry entered with a baseball cap that mostly covered his bandaged head. Carter came in with his mother, who was frowning. And just as the door began to swing closed, Kathy entered, holding Truman's hand, followed by Flynn.

The heart pendant in Dylan's pocket seemed to grow cold. She'd given him an open door. And he was going to close it. He didn't want her to witness what he had to do, who he had to be.

"Wait." Dylan stood, despite nearly choking on that one word. "Wait, I... Just wait."

"Oh, man," Matt whispered urgently. "Whatever you're thinking, don't do it."

"Do you want to address the court, Mr. O'Brien?" The judge stared down at him, as she must have stared down hundreds of deadbeat dads in the past. There was a cold impatience behind those round wire lenses of hers.

"Yes," Dylan said.

Matt sank into his chair, muttering, "It's your funeral."

Dylan thought of Zach, his bubbly personality, the way he ran as if he'd been born in cowboy boots. He thought of Kathy's way of approaching life. She took what life dished out and fashioned a life she could find happiness in, taking one step at a time toward her goal. And he thought about Phantom, once a proud racetrack contender, now a confused, high-energy horse in need of guard rails and a path forward to redemption.

"Your Honor, I can't submit to the demands of a man who wants to take away everything from me, including my son and the principles I stand for." Dylan had meant to stop there and let the chips fall as they may. But he was reminded of Kathy telling her truths and how much more compassion he had for her afterward. And so, he went on. "I was a ward of the court. I know when a father is bad, and I am not a bad father."

He thought he heard Barry murmur, "Hear, hear."

"I counsel people who've experienced setbacks. I provide them with the tools and experiences that will help them stay clean. I don't accept junkies or those battling withdrawals onto my property. I only take those who've completed a multi-step program, those who seem genuine about wanting a lifelong recovery. Some of the younger ones are my son's friends, his role models. Not because they've done wrong, but because they're trying to do right."

"Your Honor." Bob stood, despite Eileen tugging the sleeve of his expensive suit jacket. "We're talking about the welfare of a child." He sneered at Dylan and then at the people who'd come to support him, the ones sitting behind him now. "Look at them. Bandaged and bruised. Were they drunk and fell down? Were they in a car accident?"

Dylan pressed his lips together.

Bob's eyes narrowed. "It was him, wasn't it?" He sneered at Dylan across the aisle. "That horse did this to them." At Dylan's nod, Bob spun to face the judge. "How much more evidence do I need?"

The judge sighed. "Mr. O'Brien, how did these people get injured?"

Dylan's hopes sank. "The stallion."

"Tell them why. Tell them you weren't there." Barry stood up too fast, wobbled and grabbed the small half-wall separating the defendant's table from the viewing chairs. "I take full responsibility for what happened."

"Me, too." Carter raised an injured hand.

The judge pounded her gavel. "Gentlemen, sit and be quiet. Or I'll have to charge you with contempt."

Dylan's support group obeyed.

"Your Honor," Dylan began again. "You're asking me to choose between my son and the good things I do in the world. You're asking me to..."

"He puts everyone ahead of his son, just like he used to put everyone ahead of his wife," Bob railed. "That's why I should be Zach's father. Legally. To protect him."

Barry muttered something under his breath that Dylan was grateful he couldn't hear.

"Let me finish," Dylan said, staring at the judge, hoping she'd give him a chance. "*Please.*"

The judge stared at him, taking an inordinate amount of time to answer. And then an abrupt, "Sit down, Mr. Johnson."

Dylan nodded his thanks. "I was raised by alcoholic parents, Your Honor. My mother was recovering, and my father had no interest in ever giving up the drink. He took in horses to train...to break. And one Thanksgiving, he brought home a stallion. It was a war of wills like no other I'd ever witnessed. Finally, in a fit of drunken rage, my father beat the horse with a tree limb. He broke the horse's leg. I came out to see what all the screaming was about, and my father locked me in the stall with a gun and the horse. A proud, beaten animal." Dylan's throat threatened to close. "My father...he said he wasn't letting me out until I put that horse out of its misery. But the horse... He nuzzled my hand, as if..." As if he wasn't done yet. "That horse wasn't dangerous to anyone but the man who was hurting him. That horse needed compassion and the strength of someone else to help him." Dylan swallowed. "And so, I refused my father's command. *I refused*," he said louder.

And then the fight nearly drained out of him. "I refused until my father brought out my little brother and put a gun to his head. I had to either shoot the horse or he'd shoot Billy. I had every reason to believe my father's threats were real. And so, I made a choice." Dylan drew himself up, swallowing thickly. These next few minutes were where he lost everything—Zach, Kathy, his friends. "Killing can break you inside. It almost broke me. Today, my brother Bill is an officer in the navy." Dylan heaved a breath, half-glancing at Barry and Carter. "This horse requires experienced handlers. But he's not a killer. He doesn't lash out without provocation. Since I regained my strength, I've been working with him, and he's shown progress. I can bring in the blacksmith that recently shod him to testify. I can show you video of Phantom taking carrots from my hand. He's difficult, but not a danger like Bob is making him out to be. The point is, Your Honor, that I won't be bullied into pulling the trigger again, not when another horse doesn't deserve to die."

The courtroom was silent.

And then when Dylan thought he had no more words, no more fight, he spoke again. "I was put on this earth to make a difference – with people, with living things that need someone stable in their life." To make amends for that horrible, horrible night, and perhaps even for the horrible things his father had done while walking this earth. "So, if you're going to tell me I have to make a choice between continuing my work to rehabilitate people and animals, and being able to help raise my son, I have to argue the logic behind that choice. And I have to hope that someday...my son will understand the reason I couldn't compromise my values and choose him."

Dylan sank into his seat, slipping a hand into the pocket that held Kathy's heart. She'd come. She'd witnessed one of his darkest hours. Whatever love she felt for him was surely dead. The pendant had to be returned.

A chair creaked at the table across from his. "I can't let you do this, Bob."

"Eileen." Bob sat back in his chair, frowning at her. "Be quiet."

Eileen flinched and said in the smallest of voices, "No."

"Eileen." Bob's face turned a rageful red. His hands fisted.

He may have been a lawyer. He may have hidden his temper from the courtroom. But he was hiding nothing now. Bob's dark side was showing.

"Stop." Dylan's stomach churned with sickening slowness. He glanced at the judge and the bailiff before getting to his feet, ready to defend his ex-wife if need be because they seemed as shocked by the drama as the rest of the courtroom.

"I can't let you take Zach away from Dylan." Eileen's voice was still low, strained. She'd shrank back into a chair.

"*No.*" That one word. It came from a deep, dark place inside Bob.

Eileen flinched. "And I want a divorce."

She might need a restraining order.

"This is still my courtroom," the judge intoned coolly. "Would counsel approach the bench?"

Matt stood, pressing Dylan on the shoulder until he sat back down before obeying the judge, waiting for Bob to stand before approaching the bench side-by-side with the opposition.

The bully.

Eileen came to sit next to Dylan.

He put his arm around her. "You'll be safe now," he whispered.

From the rigid set of her shoulders, he wasn't sure she believed him.

"You can stay with me until things get sorted out," he promised, hoping to reassure her.

Matt was talking low and fast to the judge, who was nodding. Bob stood still and stiff, a raging man on the brink of losing control.

Matt returned to their table. Bob returned to his, glaring at Eileen.

The judge cleared her throat. "I'm appointing an outside source to evaluate the horse in question. We'll reconvene in a month." She pounded her gavel. "Next case."

Eileen scurried out. Dylan stood in Bob's path, in case he decided to go charging after her.

He didn't. But he took his time gathering his things.

"I thought you were hanging yourself there." Matt had been slowly gathering his notes and placing them in his laptop bag, helping delay Bob's departure as long as he could. But he was done. He drew Dylan out of Bob's path. "It looks like you bought yourself a few extra feet of rope. And if Eileen is leaving Bob, I'm hoping we won't need it."

"Me, too." Dylan followed his lawyer into the hallway, where he was greeted by his supporters.

"You're my new hero." Barry hugged him. "I'll never disobey your orders again."

Dylan didn't believe that for a minute.

"What you said in there was wonderful," Carter's mother said. "Of course, Carter will continue at the Double R. And maybe I'll come, too. I get bouts of anxiety and could use some help recentering myself."

"Mom." Carter was momentarily speechless, wrapping his gangly arms around his mother before letting her go and finding that cocky voice of his. "Dylan, you and Big and Bad were meant to be together."

And then it was Kathy and Truman in front of Dylan. Flynn stood over by the exit, checking his phone.

"Thank you for coming." Dylan's fingers curled around her heart pendant in his pocket, but he couldn't bring himself to return it to her.

"I wanted to be sitting up there with you." Kathy drew Truman closer. "We both did. But... I think we should keep to our end of the valley for a while. I have some things to sort out, and you do, too. Important things." Her eyes were bright, but she met his gaze levelly. "You'll know how to reach me no matter what you decide."

He could tell her he'd made a decision, that he loved her, and wanted her to wear both halves of that pendant. But she was right. There was a lot riding on the next few weeks—Eileen and Zach's safety from Bob, his custody of Zach, and Phantom's life. Before he could say anything to Kathy, more people spilled into the hallway.

"Mr. O'Brien." A disheveled man with a reporter's badge crowded Kathy aside. "I was in the courtroom waiting for another case. I think your story would be of interest to our readers."

Dylan didn't want his life distributed for the entertainment of others. "I don't know..."

"If it'll help save Phantom," Matt said with a significant look at Dylan. "My client would love to do an interview."

Dylan held on tight to the pendant in his pocket during the entire exchange. When he finished answering the reporter's questions, Kathy was gone.

Chapter Thirty-Four

A month had passed since Kathy had seen Dylan at court. Thanksgiving had come and gone. Kathy's wrist had healed.

Nothing had changed substantially. Kathy put on her grandmother's heart pendant every morning, hopeful that the new day would bring word from Dylan. And she took it off every night before bed with fading hopes. She'd signed up for her vet-tech certificate and still worked at the clinic and walked the odd assortment of dogs. Sometimes with Truman, sometimes without. Mostly, Truman did his schoolwork sitting with Abby, who was still on restricted exercise. Agnes, however, had persuaded him a few times to join the singing councilwomen at Chance's stall.

The private investigator Flynn had hired discovered that their mother had overdosed while Kathy was in rehab. It was a time of sadness and relief. Kathy was convinced her mother was in a better, more peaceful place, one without temptation and trials. The investigator had also discovered that Eileen was married to a serial abuser. Bob had a record in another state. Flynn had passed on the information to Dylan. Kathy hoped that meant Eileen was going to stick to her decision to divorce Bob, keeping herself and Zach safe.

Mr. Hammacker was doing well in his recovery. He enjoyed being part of the bowling team and had taken to walking Dolly himself. He claimed he no longer needed alcohol to make it through the long, lonely days. Kathy tended to believe him since he wasn't lonely anymore.

"I finally heard back from the Reedleys." Today Agnes had come by the clinic to deliver news to Kathy. "They'll rent you the place." She named a ridiculously low amount.

"Seriously?" Kathy scoffed. "How much was it before Flynn decided to supplement my rent?"

Agnes looked confused. "He didn't offer to supplement anything."

Kathy was taken aback. This was not the brother she knew and loved. He meddled. He worked deals behind the scenes. He tried to make sure that everything was hunky-dory for everyone he cared about. "I don't get it. I couldn't rent an apartment in Santa Rosa for double that amount."

"They're just happy someone will be living in the house." Agnes glanced over Kathy's shoulder. "Well, hello, cowboy." She kissed Kathy's cheek and hurried off.

Cowboy? Kathy turned.

Dylan stood in front of her, looking much the way he had the day they'd met—jeans, boots, vest jacket, baseball cap. A grim face with gray eyes that seemed to see everything. "You look good, Red."

Kathy's heart seemed to stop. And then it started back up, double-time. "You look better than average."

"Thanks again for showing up in court."

She didn't want to waste time on mundane conversations. "Why are you here?" Was he completing her heart or giving it back?

"I thought I'd work with the colt. Maybe take him for a walk." There was only a hint of a grin on his face, as if he was trying to be friendly.

He came for the colt, not me.

Kathy's hopes faded. "You're too late. Chance is gone. They came to get him this morning."

Dylan seemed to freeze. "Is he...? Was he...?"

"He and Sugar went happily into the trailer. Far Turn Farms has high hopes for him." She'd told them that if Chance didn't live up to their expectations, she wanted him. Not that she could keep him at the Reedley place. But if it came to that, she'd figure something out.

Dylan glanced around, frowning slightly, as if at a loss. "Are there any dogs that need walking around the block?"

"Nope." Kathy bit her lip, unable to figure out why Dylan had come if not for her. Her heart felt as if it'd been stuffed in a too-small canning jar and was pounding to get out. "Did Gage call you?"

He shook off her question with a shake of his head. "How about you, Red? Do you want to take a walk around the block to the town square?"

She couldn't handle it anymore. She had to know. "If you came to return my heart and move on, we do not have to complete some karmic cycle." She held out her hand. It trembled. "Please. Just give it to me and go."

"Same old Kathy, cutting right to the chase." Dylan smiled tentatively. "That's not why I'm here today. I came because I can't stop thinking about you, Red."

She stuck her empty hands into her back pockets and quirked an eyebrow at him.

"And when I say I can't stop thinking about you, I'm not just being nice. I spent the past month working with Phantom so that he'd pass his evaluations for the court." He tilted his head to study her. "Didn't Gage tell you? He came down to help me with the collections."

Kathy shook her head. Wait until she saw Gage. She didn't care if he took away her employee discount. He hadn't said a word about seeing Dylan or helping with the stallion.

"I'm solvent. And more importantly, Phantom passed his court-ordered evaluation. He's a handful, not a killer and..."

He won't have to be put down.

"I'm so glad." She was truly happy for Dylan and Phantom, but she'd waited so long for an answer that her legs felt as unsteady as wheat in a breeze. Did he love her? Or were they going to be just friends? She had to know.

"Eileen finally found her own place," Dylan went on. "She and Zach moved out a few days ago. The court granted her a restraining order against Bob, and he agreed to a quick divorce. I called Flynn earlier. That private investigator he used helped a lot."

"Great. I'm so happy for you. For them." For everyone. But she was dying here, waiting. Couldn't Dylan see that.

His soft smile turned unexpectedly wicked. "You used to hug me when you were happy."

The first inkling of hope tickled her veins. But she wasn't jumping into his arms and letting him off the hook that easily. He'd made her wait a month! "Maybe I just got up on the wrong side of the bed."

His smile slipped, his expression turned soft. "I've been getting up on the wrong side of the bed every day, Red. Every day since I let you slip away in that courthouse, wondering if it was you that didn't want me." When next he spoke, his voice was low and husky. It skittered along Kathy's spine. "I love you. I couldn't say it before because I had to make some hard choices. You'd never have chosen a horse over your son. And I thought you'd despise me for that. I had to prove it was the right choice for everyone to save Phantom."

He loves me!

Her heart soared. "I approved of what you did, Dylan. I understood once I heard your story in court." Her throat closed, choking her with emotion. "I told you so many of my secrets and you only hinted at a few of yours. I would have understood long before you stepped into that courtroom if you would have only told me." It was a thought that kept her awake at night. Wouldn't he have told her the truth about his childhood and the choice he faced before that day if he truly loved her?

"You are the strongest woman I know, Red. The strongest person I know. Stronger than I am. I needed your love to unlock my secrets, whereas you seemed to trust me from day one." He got down on one knee, but instead of a ring, he handed her the other half of her grandmother's heart pendant. "I wanted to do this under the oak tree in the town square. But you didn't accept my invitation to take a walk." He smiled tentatively. "Kathy, I needed time to get my life in order, but I'm ready now. I'm ready to say more than just how I feel. I want to tell you how I see things for us. Our future."

She took the heart pendant and pressed it against its match at her neck, locking the two pieces together. She could have sworn she heard Grandpa Ed sigh approvingly.

And then she offered Dylan her hands.

"We're going to help people and horses, you and I. And in addition to Truman and Zach, we're going to raise a few more kids of our own. There'll be bumps in the road. From the kids, from the challenges we both face because of our pasts. But we'll meet them head-on, together, and move forward. Our love will get us through."

He'd acknowledged she might relapse. He'd acknowledged he'd help her rebound. It was everything she'd wanted to hear weeks ago when the time hadn't been right. She loved him, and that love bloomed in her chest and bubbled out of her throat in a joyous laugh.

He grinned up at her. The wicked grin that she loved so much. "I've made hard choices. I've bared my soul. I'm ready for my turn at happiness." He took a deep breath. "Say you're ready, too."

Kathy drew a deep breath and...

"Mama?" Truman led a splinted and limping Abby from the dog kennels.

Kathy held out her hand, inviting him to join them. "Dylan's asking us to marry him."

Truman clasped her hand, a small frown on his face. "Can he do that? Ask us both?"

"He can."

"I asked Zach for permission, too," Dylan said, giving Kathy another reason to love him. "He's excited about having a big brother. But no one told me about Abby. How did that happen?"

"It was so scary." Truman went into story mode. Eyes bright. Volume on high. "There was an old lady and a blue car and squealing tires. But Mama knew exactly what to do."

"That was the moment that I knew nothing was more important than love and people, including animals, who give love back to you many times over. It was the day before we went to see you in court." Kathy stroked Truman's ginger-colored hair. "But let's get back to the offer on the table. So, you're proposing we come live with you on Redemption Ranch?" The Reedley house with its small, charming rooms beckoned, along with the people she'd come to appreciate in Harmony Valley, but nothing was strong enough to outbid love.

Dylan nodded. "Truman can ride the bus to school."

"A real school. With kids?" Truman raised his hands and whooped. Abby wagged her tail. "I love you teaching me, Mama. But I want a real teacher and friends."

"So?" Dylan stared up at Kathy. "What's it going to be? Will you marry me, love?"

"Yes." Kathy helped him to his feet. "It's always been yes."

"I think I've loved you from day one." Dylan framed her face in his large, calloused hands. "I knew you were my better half from the moment I saw you in the paddock with Sugar."

"I love you, Dylan." Kathy tilted her face up to receive his kiss. "I needed you to show me how to live again."

"And I needed you to give me hope once more." And then Dylan kissed her. He kissed her with truth and tenderness and hope. All of which built a solid foundation of love upon which they could build a future.

Truman interrupted that kiss, throwing his arms around their legs. "Can I... Can I call you Dad after the wedding? I never had a dad."

Dylan smiled at her son...*their son*...

He placed a hand on Truman's head and looked upon him with tender affection. "I would be honored to be your father. To be called Dad. And to call you son. To take you to Little League games and talk the ins and outs of football. And to encourage you to grow into a good man your mother can be proud of."

Kathy gasped. And in a burst of clarity, she knew that she'd found the forever man...*the forever family*...that she'd wanted since she'd been a young girl headed off to college.

And this forever family was worth the wait.

Epilogue

There was nothing more exciting to a horse lover than the Kentucky Derby. Kathy stood with Truman in Far Turn Farms' owner's box. They'd been invited for the big day. She clutched her wide-brimmed hat as the breeze threatened to sweep it off her head and scanned the horses coming out onto the track for the last race of the day. The most important race of the day. "Do you see him, Tru?"

They'd taken this trip to celebrate Kathy's completion of her veterinary-assistant certificate. All her dreams were becoming reality.

"There!" Truman pointed to a two-year-old chestnut colt wearing the distinctive purple and yellow of Far Turn Farms. There were still scars across his chest, but they were faint. And the story of his survival made for great PR. He may not have been the odds-on favorite, but he was a crowd favorite. Everyone wanted to root for Sugar's First Chance.

Dylan dodged through the crowd to join them, barely limping anymore. He smelled of hay and horses. He put his arm around Kathy. "You should have seen him down there, prancing around like this is no big deal."

"Have you decided to root for him, then? Instead of Phantom's colt." As if on cue, a colt black as night entered the track. He'd been bred before Dylan rescued Phantom.

Dylan scoffed. "That's like asking which of your kids is your favorite."

"Me." Truman laughed. "Zach had to stay at home."

"You're my favorite older son." Dylan ruffled Tru's ginger hair. "Zach was celebrating his mother's birthday this weekend."

Truman raised his binoculars and watched the horses parade past.

"You didn't visit Phantom's Revenge, did you?" Kathy knew her husband too well. He loved all animals, and he still carried home injured ones and strays in addition to the horses that were regularly brought to them. "Please don't tell me you bet against Chance."

Dylan kissed Kathy until she was breathless. "I know better than to bet against that horse. He's a survivor. Like you."

"It takes one to know one, love." She wrapped her arms around him and didn't let go until Chance crossed the finish line. First.

The End

Want more of Dylan and Kathy? Go to my web site (MelindaCurtis.com), click on the Love in Harmony Valley page, then on the Forever Family in a Small Town page to find a free, special Bonus Epilogue. While you're out there, sign up for my newsletter to receive new release updates.

If reviews are your thing, I'd appreciate one.

Are you ready for the next book in the series? Make sure to get a copy of Book 6: *A Small Town Memory*. Still unsure? Read on for a sample of this book.

A Small Town Memory

Excerpt

Did he love me?

Jessica Aguirre didn't know if he loved her. She didn't know if he knew her. She stood on a gravel drive in the midst of a vineyard in Harmony Valley. Heart pounding. Head pounding.

Did he love me?

The man in the photograph would tell her.

Jess clutched a newspaper photo and stared at the group of men and women in front of a two-story farmhouse with a vintage weathervane. There was a man in the back row on the left. He was the one.

She recognized him right away. Recognized dark hair with a curl at his temple. Recognized a straight, no-nonsense nose. Recognized caramel-colored eyes. Those eyes. If only she could remember...

What if it isn't him? What if this is a dead end? What if...?

Jess drew a steadying breath against the panic rising in her chest and lifted her gaze to the well-looked-after farmhouse. The day the picture had been taken there'd been big fluffy clouds in the sky above the cupola. Today the sky was clear and blue. The late January air was crazy cold, stinging Jessica's toes in her sneakers.

The slender woman who'd greeted Jess on this Monday morning hurried down the front porch steps. "He'll be here in a few minutes. Come inside the tasting room." Christine was the winemaker for the newly opened Harmony

Valley Vineyards, which was headquartered in the farmhouse, the subject of the newspaper article, and where he worked. Christine's carefree smile told Jess the woman had never lost a moment, a day or weeks from her past. "We have all the amenities inside—hot tea, a bathroom and a place to sit down."

"I don't want to be any trouble." Jessica resisted glancing at the clipping again. Would her unannounced appearance be welcome? Or create mayhem?

"It's no trouble. You're no trouble." Christine had the kind of smile that invited you to relax, to open up, to be part of the family. "Come inside. It's cold out here."

It was cold. Jessica's jacket wouldn't zip up anymore. And family...

In no time, Jessica was sitting at a table cradling a cup of hot tea. The tasting room was elegant in a simple way that fit the farmhouse. Dark wood, intimate tables for two, out-of-Jessica's-price-range granite slabs on bar tops. But the room was oddly empty.

"Where's the wine?"

Christine followed the direction of Jessica's curious gaze to the bare shelves behind the bar. "Barrel aging. I'll be blending some for limited release soon. But most of our harvest will age another year."

"Aging wine is all about patiently waiting, isn't it? Even when you don't know how it will turn out." Jessica had become good at biding her time. "Making wine is like waiting for bread dough to rise." Or babies to be born.

"Exactly." With a contented sigh, Christine's gaze lingered on the room as if seeing it filled with bottles of her making.

Outside, the wind whistled past, drawing Jessica to the window in time to see a muddy gray truck pull into the gravel drive.

"There he is." Christine gave Jessica's shoulder a sisterly squeeze, and then headed toward the door. "I'll be upstairs if you need anything."

Did he love me?

A man got out of the truck. Dark hair. Straight nose. Familiar eyes.

It's him.

She leaned forward, peering through the paned glass, her heart sailing toward him, over ever-hopeful waves of roses and rainbows.

Jess didn't usually let herself dream. But now...today...him...

And yet...

He wore a burgundy vest jacket that clashed with a red long-sleeve T-shirt. Worn blue jeans. A black baseball cap.

Instead, she saw him in a fine wool suit. Black, always black. A navy shirt of the softest cotton. A silk tie in a geometric pattern. Shiny Italian loafers...

He took the stairs two at a time, work boots ringing on wood.

Jessica's heart sank as certainly as if someone had drilled holes in the boat carrying her hopeful emotions. Clouds blocked the sun. The rainbow disappeared. Unwilling to sink, Jess clung to joy. To the idea of him.

He entered without a flourish or an energetic greeting. He entered without the smile that teased the corners of her memory. He entered and took stock of the room, the situation, her.

Their eyes met. His were the same color, same shape, so heart-achingly familiar.

It was the cool assessment in them that threw her off. Not a smile, not a brow quirk, not an eye crinkle.

He came forward. "I'm Michael Dufraine, but everyone calls me Duffy."

His name didn't ring true.

Had he lied to me?

She couldn't speak, could barely remember her name.

The wind shook the panes. The house creaked and groaned.

He smiled. A polite smile, a distant smile, an I-don't-know-you smile.

Disappointment overwhelmed her. Jess resisted the urge to dissolve into a pity puddle on the floor.

"And you are...?" He extended his hand.

On autopilot, she reached for him. Their palms touched.

Jessica's vision blurred and she gripped his hand tighter while clips of memory assailed her—his deep laughter, him offering her a bite of chocolate cheesecake, his citrusy cologne as he leaned in to kiss her.

It is him.

Relieved. She was so relieved. Jessica blinked at the man—*Duffy*—who she vaguely recalled and, at the same time, did not.

She'd practiced what to say on the hour-long drive up here from Santa Rosa. Ran through several scenarios. None of them had included him *not* recognizing her.

She should start at the beginning. Best not to scare him with hysterics and panicked accusations, of which she'd had five months to form.

Don't raise your voice. Don't cry. Don't ask why.

And don't lead the conversation with the elephant in the room.

Despite all the cautions and practicing and caveats, she drew a breath, and flung her hopes toward him as if he were her life preserver. "I think I'm your wife."

Grab your copy of *A Small Town Memory* today!

About the Author

USA Today bestselling author Melinda Curtis has written and sold over 70 titles, mostly contemporary romance, but including two writing craft books. Working both traditionally and as an indie, Melinda writes sweet romance, women's fiction, and sweet romantic comedies. One of her romances – *Dandelion Wishes* – was made into a TV movie – *Love in Harmony Valley* – starring Amber Marshall. Melinda is married to her college sweetheart, has three children, and currently lives in Oregon. When she's not writing, Melinda enjoys brief stints of gardening (if it's sunny) or catches up on cleaning and laundry (begrudgingly), all done efficiently so she can get to her to-be-read pile and list of shows to binge.

Check out Melinda's Shopify Store for autographed books, bundles, and sales:
ShopMelindaCurtis.MyShopify.com

Other Sweet Books/Series by Melinda Curtis:
A Cowboy Worth Waiting For, Book 1 in the Cowboy Academy romance series
A Kiss is Just a Kiss, Book 1 in the Summer Kisses (Grandma Dotty) romcom series
Can't Hurry Love, Book 1 in the small town Sunshine Valley romcom series
Kissed by the Country Doc, Book 1 in the small town Mountain Monroe series
Her Alaskan Valentine's Day Matchmaker, Book 1 in the bearded, Alaskan Matchmaker series

A Son for the Mountain Firefighter, Book 1 in the emotional, action-packed Mountain Firefighter series

Christmas, Actually, Book 1 in the long-running Heartwarming Christmas Town series

Christmas at the Sleigh Café, a 1st person romcom from the Christmas Mountain series

Discover more titles and a reading guide at:
https://www.melindacurtis.net

Happy reading!
Melinda Curtis

Made in the USA
Las Vegas, NV
03 March 2025

19025050R00152